INGENIOUS

THE PRAETORIENNE
ONE
INGENIOUS

LISA KARON RICHARDSON

WhiteSpark

This is a work of fiction. All characters and events portrayed in this novel are either fictitious or used fictitiously.

INGENIOUS

WhiteSpark Publishing, a division of WhiteFire Publishing
13607 Bedford Rd NE
Cumberland, MD 21592

ISBNs: 978-1-946531-23-0 (Paperback)
           978-1-946531-25-4 (Hardcover)
           978-1-946531-24-7 (Digital)

For Crystal Strader,
my greatest cheerleader and best friend.
Your unwavering belief in me helps me
to have the courage to do hard things.

Prologue

Barley-on-Rye, England
August 9, 1832

My first mistake was daring to be born a girl. I subsequently disappointed my parents further when I failed to be a pretty child, having a face full of freckles and hair the color of a well-used penny. Nor was I particularly sweet-natured or docile. Instead, curiosity made me inquisitive, and I learned more about the people of the neighborhood than the daughter of a noble family ought to know. My numerous *faux pas* might have led me down a great many paths, but all the trouble I might have created for myself was abruptly rerouted when I was ten years old.

But I should start at the beginning. And for me, life truly began when I met Dame Guinevere Withers, headmistress of Saint Scholastica School for Young Ladies, which, as I was to find out, was the most exclusive female boarding school in all Great Britain.

An inkling that something unusual might be about to happen came as I was cheerfully disobeying my mother by riding one of the kitchen boys' velocipedes. The steam engine chugged away merrily, the wind danced through my hair, and my legs pumped, adding my power to the machine's. Having mastered the tallest hill on our estate, I sat for a moment looking out over the Blithe holdings.

Even from up here, I could not see where they ended. The view on offer included an expanse of green fields broken up by stone fences and the tuft of a copse here and there. The river sectioned off the northwest corner of our property. From afar, it looked like a brown silk ribbon lying across the landscape. Nestled against a far bank of hills, the village looked precisely as one would expect a fairy-tale village to look.

Nearer and just to my right sat our old ramshackle house. It still occupied the site of the original keep built centuries ago. Every generation of Blithes since then had apparently felt it their duty to "modernize," resulting in a weird amalgamation of architectural styles and more rooms than a family three times the size of ours could possibly use. The floors weren't all precisely level, and one would have to step up or down to enter some rooms. It was full of odd nooks and crannies. Out of father's hearing, my mother called it a monstrosity.

I loved it.

I drank in the view, then turned the borrowed contraption and flew back downhill, hands raised as I shouted with joy at the freedom of it.

The velocipede gathered speed, and I hurtled faster and faster. Just as I came near the bottom, a figure stepped through the hedgerow into the narrow lane. My hands dropped to the handlebars, and I jerked to the left. But the momentum was too much, the correction not calculated, and the velocipede hurtled into the hedge on the far side of the road. Perched atop the high wheel, I was launched over the hedge to tumble headfirst onto the soft pastureland that lay on the other side.

The stranger, a tall woman, well-dressed for the country in tweed jacket and wide riding skirt with a crop in her hand, popped her head through a gap in the hedgerow. "Do you often ride in such a fashion?"

Winded, I lay without answering, though my sides wheezed with laughter. She probably thought I was having a fit. At last, I managed to gather myself. "Every chance I get."

Cool gray eyes assessed me, and I had the sensation of being weighed in the balance. "I am Dame Guinevere Withers. When you can collect yourself we will continue."

"Continue what?"

"Your assessment." She turned and pushed through the hedge.

I scrambled to my feet and followed her back to the lane. "Assessment for what?"

She barely spared me a glance over her shoulder. "Admission to Saint Scholastica."

"What is Saint Scholastica?"

That brought her up short, her skirts swishing around booted ankles. "The finest and most exclusive school in England or any of its dominions. Dukes' daughters are regularly refused admittance."

"Never heard of it."

She narrowed her eyes. "Are you trying to be deliberately provocative?"

I didn't know what provocative meant, but I liked the sound of it. I was being deliberate. "Yes."

Rather than rant or stalk away in a huff as mother would have done, she turned to face me fully. "Why?"

I swiped my suddenly damp palms over my torn pinafore, leaving more dirty smears. "I don't know."

She raised an eyebrow.

I kicked the still spinning tire of the velocipede. The silence stretched and stretched, and all the while her inquisitive gaze burned a hole into my forehead. I shrugged. Sighed. "I wanted to make you angry." The words spurted out on their own.

A small smile cracked her glacial expression. "My dear girl, you do not want to see me angry, I promise you."

I believed her.

She stooped and helped me right the velocipede.

I glanced at her sideways. "Why does everyone want to go to this school?"

"Because most of them can't."

I cocked my head.

She continued. "We only allow six students at a time. Never more and never less. We call them a cohort, and almost all of them will serve as a lady-in-waiting."

"So, it's about being important?"

"For some it is."

"If all these other people want to send their daughters to your school, why are you here talking to me?"

"That's a very good question." She pulled out a notebook and scratched something down. "We look for a certain combination of qualities in our students because our curriculum is very…unique."

Had I known then what I know now, I would have pursued that line of questioning further, but as it was, I had another question burning the back of my throat. "Dame Guinevere, are my parents wanting to send me away?" I met her gaze, refusing to look away.

Another pause stretched between us. "Your grandmother nominated you."

"Grandmama Blithe?" My very favorite relative had passed away eight months before. If Grandmama Blithe liked this school, then it was a sure bet that Mother would not. This in itself was a recommendation for the place as far as I was concerned.

"Your grandmother attended Saint Scholastica herself when she was young."

"Did she really?"

"I'm not in the habit of telling falsehoods."

"What makes this school so good?"

She waggled an eyebrow at me. "At the moment, I do." With that she marched away while I pushed the velocipede in pursuit. The front wheel wobbled and shook making it hard to control, but I chased her doggedly. I wasn't sure I liked her, but I was more than a little intrigued.

Chapter 1

London, England
May 5, 1837

The city throbbed with life and possibilities—all the things I had been craving while tucked away at school in the Outer Hebrides. And I do mean the Outer Hebrides. That is not some joke as the groom had thought that morning. Saint Scholastica's curriculum was…different. Space and privacy had been essential. Unfortunately, that meant that we had been somewhat secluded.

But no more.

We had come to the capital, and I meant to make the most of it.

"Lady Portia stop dawdling."

I ripped my attention away from the tempestuous London streets and picked up my pace.

"My dear young lady, you are not a horse. Do not gallop." One of Dame Guinevere's most notable skills was her ability to cut a student down to size.

Eleanor and her minions covered their mouths with gloved fingers but did not bother to smother their titters of laughter.

I slowed to a more decorous gait.

Dame Guinevere seized the opportunity for a teaching

moment. "Remember ladies—glide. It makes our movements graceful and elegant."

I remembered the rest of the lecture as if I'd heard it yesterday, which I had. "*It can also mask remarkably swift movements, so those around you fail to realize how quickly you are moving.*"

I adopted the half-sliding, half-rolling walk we had been taught. It worked. I caught up to the others and did not trip over anything in the process.

"Better." Dame Guinevere favored me with a nod.

I knew better than to smile, so I merely inclined my head and climbed the stairs into the waiting steam carriage and claimed the last window seat, eager to see more of London. In all honesty, it was more of an omnibus than a regular carriage. It had to be in order to accommodate all of us students as well as Dame Guinevere and her second-in-command Lady Pomeroy. But as ladies of gentle birth, we would never admit to riding in an omnibus.

I gaped through the glass of our coach windows at the steam of countless mechanicals swirling in the streets until the vapor was caught by the breeze and whisked away. They ranged from the street cleaner that looked like nothing so much as a great hairy dog snuffling along the curb to the imperious, blue-painted traffic wardens adorned with the official royal seal that stood at every busy intersection. Their shrill whistles would sound, and clockwork arms extend to halt one line of carriages so that cross traffic could go. Then with a tick and a whirr they would swivel and wave through the next set of waiting vehicles.

Overhead the pigeon corps swooped and flapped. Long before I was born, some enterprising soul had decided that the scourge of the city—its pigeons, could be turned to a profit. The birds had been domesticated and trained and now they provided an efficient messenger service. These avian delivery agents would wing their way to a hub, where the message would be routed to a different bird and sent along. Every well-appointed home now boasted its own dovecote. They even held a grand race one year, and a message had made it all the way across the city in just twenty-minutes. Of course, the pigeons worked best for short messages. A really good chatty letter was too heavy for the birds to carry effectively, so the royal mechs in their jaunty red caps and vests still delivered mail twice a day in the metropolis.

We turned the corner, and my wondering gaze fell upon the track for the flying train. The great iron girders that held the modern marvel aloft somehow managed to look lacy against the sky. As I watched, a car came trundling along its track. Suspended some sixty feet in the air, it swung pendulously from side to side.

Beside me, my best friend Colleen was equally enthralled. She kept nudging me and pointing out things, and I did the same to her.

Across from us, Eleanor affected a bored expression as if this was all humdrum. Perhaps it was for her. She was always telling us about her trips to London whenever we returned to school from holidays.

I rolled my eyes. Not even Eleanor could dampen my spirits. Not when such a feast for the senses was all around.

Aside from the technological marvels, the most immediately evident thing about London was the people. People everywhere. And all of them talking at once.

As if the city was on parade, I found first one then another fascination to divert my attention. A burly costermonger with a walrus mustache and a tatty apron cried his wares on the corner, a stick in his hand to teach a valuable lesson to anyone who tried to swipe an apple from his cart. An achingly thin flower

girl carried a basket of blooms in reddened, chapped hands. A man wearing a great sign that shrouded him back and front bawled out news of a play being put on at one of the Drury Lane theatres. A well-to-do lady in an emerald dress with enormous sleeves swept into a milliner's shop, followed by a harassed-looking companion in dowdy brown. A portly businessman puffing on a portly cigar marched along, confident of his own importance in maintaining the nation's prestige. Around them all filtered ragtag children looking for opportunity. In short, it was a gloriously undisciplined riot of color and noise.

I sighed like a prisoner who had finally eaten a full meal after a week's punishment rations.

Dame Guinevere clapped her hands to get our attention. "Ladies, no other cohort of Praetorienne have ever been given the opportunity you will have. Like the Praetorian guards who served the Roman emperors we have a noble calling. Members of our organization have served every queen since Elizabeth first founded our society, but since then, we have not had the honor or privilege of serving a queen ruling in her own right. Until now. Princess Victoria is poised to make history and, therefore, so are we."

A little frisson of excitement skittered through me. The other girls sat a little straighter too.

Dame Guinevere continued, "As queen, she will face challenges and even dangers that few young ladies have had to face. And she will need each of you. Eleanor, she will need your ability to sway opinions and gain trust. Marianne, she will need your ability to build connections." Her gaze slid over me. "Irene, she will need your fierce loyalty. You were each chosen not just for your family names but for the qualities you bring to the court. This will be our finest hour. She will need staunch companions by her side. Allies who are committed to her safety no matter the cost."

Irene, sitting next to Eleanor, held her back straight, her chest puffed out and a faraway look in her eye. Given the slightest encouragement, she would have saluted.

I exchanged a glance with Colleen but bit the inside of my lip to restrain the grin that threatened.

"King William and Queen Adelaide made the arrangements for our meeting with the princess today, but I cannot stress enough that the princess herself has not yet been informed of the existence of the Praetorienne or our function. Her mother and everyone else in her household are similarly ignorant. They must remain so." Dame Guinevere looked at each of us in turn to make sure we all knew how serious she was on this score. "Our existence is a secret. Our purpose today is simply to begin to know the princess and for her to know us. Am I clear?"

"Yes, ma'am," we murmured in chorus.

"I'm sure I need not explain how important first impressions are."

"No, ma'am." Once again, our voices came in unison.

Apparently satisfied that she had drummed the momentousness of the event into us, Dame Guinevere subsided, and I went back to looking out the window.

We'd arrived. The grounds of Kensington Palace and the adjacent Hyde Park created an oasis of green amidst the harshness of stone and cobbles. It was almost possible to forget the teeming city beyond the gates and imagine oneself in the sedate English countryside. Although come to think of it, no pastoral landscape in the real countryside had ever been quite so ruthlessly tended.

Hubris thy name is—someone or other. I couldn't recall the rest of the line.

Eleanor and her cronies maintained their studied air of nonchalance as if a visit to the princess was commonplace. Which, of course, it wasn't. Due to Sir John Conroy's "Kensington System" very few people of the princess's age were allowed to visit her. Very few people at all, in fact. She was secluded from the court and, therefore, rumors were rife.

No one had anything negative to say about the princess, but criticism of her mother, the Duchess of Kent, was a favorite topic. Sir John Conroy, comptroller of the duchess's household since the death of the duke years before, also came in for his share of speculation. Conroy was not well liked, and what many considered his undue influence over the duchess put him in line for a lot of nasty innuendo. Whether or not they had earned it? Well, I was in no position to judge…yet.

Our coachman, in sky blue livery, pulled up smartly in front of the queen's entrance, and the other girls and I began fluffing skirts and pinching cheeks for our presentation.

Dame Guinevere had not overplayed her little speech. This was quite possibly the most important day of our lives. If Princess Victoria liked us, we could expect to be given positions in her household once she was queen. Gossip held that, though the king's health was declining, he stalwartly refused to die before Victoria reached the age of majority. No one wanted a regency that would allow the duchess and Conroy to rule the nation—at least, no one but the duchess and Conroy.

Now, with the king ailing and only a couple weeks before Victoria would be of age to rule in her own right, the usual order of things was being turned on its head. The students of Saint Scholastica were being presented early. We hadn't even officially graduated.

We dismounted from the carriage in order of precedence, using every ounce of grace and charm we had been taught during our years at Saint Scholastica. I as usual, came third. My family is an ancient and honorable line, but we haven't the wealth or the influence remaining to do our title justice.

The Duchess of Kent stood waiting for us, a showy smile firmly in place. The princess stood beside her, looking neither pleased nor displeased. Her form was neat and compact, and she was turned out beautifully. Her hair, a glossy nutmeg brown, was intricately dressed with braids pinned up over her ears into a coronet that resembled a crown. An interesting touch.

I wondered if it had been her choice or her mother's.

As we had been instructed, our line halted, and we approached her individually, for all the world as if we were debutantes being presented at court. Which, in a way, I suppose we were.

As each of my peers stepped forward, I tried to see them dispassionately as if I was the future queen assessing candidates for her court.

Chief amongst us was Lady Eleanor Plum, daughter of the Duke of Ridcully. I found Eleanor odious, but I was clearly in the minority. The other girls bowed to her opinions in almost everything. I wasn't really sure why this was the case or how she worked this magic, except that she was pretty, well connected, and rich. Her belief in her inherent superiority was so strong that others accepted it as a matter of course. Even without Saint Scholastica, she would have been a top contender to be one of the next queen's ladies-in-waiting. It pains me to say it, but she was also exceedingly clever, a good tactician, and a first-rate manipulator. Whether she or I would take top marks for our class was still a toss-up.

Lady Marianne Morley was another duke's daughter. But she didn't possess Eleanor's force of personality. She could often be swayed to one side or the other, by which I mean, mine or

Eleanor's. Marianne found conflict distressing and was forever trying to smooth ruffled feathers. She excelled at field doctoring and at gaining people's confidence but did poorly with tactics. Her greatest love was anything with ruffles, frills, or flowers.

After Marianne came me. Portia Boadicea Beatrix Blithe, at your service. I'd always been the shortest of the cohort, a trait even more annoying than my red hair and freckles. I tended to excel at subjects the others loathed, such as our regular bartitsu lessons.

Dame Guinevere murmured, "Lady Portia Blithe, only child of the Marquess of Bridgely."

On cue, I sank to the ground. I managed to execute my curtsy competently, if not gracefully. My curiosity got the better of me, however, and I glanced up to see how the princess was enjoying the pomp. She met my gaze, and I glimpsed a deep unhappiness. An instant later, the expression was gone, her gaze as politely masked as mine.

I only stumbled a tiny bit on my skirt as I backed away. All in all, a respectable performance.

Following me, came Eleanor's most devoted acolyte, Lady Harriet Kingsley, daughter of the Earl of Longstreth. She even looked a bit like Eleanor with the same blond hair, blue eyes, and straight nose. But where Eleanor looked hard, Harriet looked somehow mushy in comparison. She was most definitely a follower, not a leader. Which is not to say she was stupid. She had an encyclopedic knowledge of all the scandals and gossip among the *ton* in the last thirty years. She was competent in most of our subjects, especially anything requiring grace and agility. She would make an effective guard should she be added to the queen's court.

Next was the Honorable Irene Finch-Norton, daughter of the Baron Grunthorpe. She was definitely a believer in the idea that might makes right and had memorized *Debrett's Peerage*. She was the sort of person who paid attention to every trend of fashion because she wanted to be correct rather than because she liked it for its own sake. Irene was nothing if not precise. She too would be a good, if unimaginative, Praetorienne.

Last to be presented, but foremost among us in my opinion, was Colleen Tinewall, daughter of Sir Martin Tinewall, newly granted Irish honor. Easily the most beautiful girl I've ever seen, with rich auburn curls, a creamy complexion, a straight, narrow nose, and shell-pink lips. Contrary to what one might think, Colleen hated being forced to spend time on her appearance, much preferring to be left alone with noxious chemicals, tools, and a few bits of metal. She was brilliant and despaired that her intellect was ever at the mercy of her beauty.

If Colleen had a flaw, it was a tendency toward clumsiness when nervous.

As she backed away, she stepped on the train of her gown and, not realizing it, took another step backward. The next moment, she was out of extra cloth, and with her third step, she was brought up short and landed on her posterior with a little yelp.

I broke ranks to help Colleen up, while the other girls snickered. Except for Eleanor. Normally, she had no compunction in mocking someone, but her face was red and jaw set as if Colleen had disgraced her personally.

The princess did not smirk. She even started to step forward to help, only to be stopped by her mother's hand on her arm.

Once Colleen regained her feet, she was the least flustered person, her expression as enigmatic as a Renaissance masterpiece.

The duchess made a stiff speech of welcome, which was at

times difficult to understand due to her German accent, then led us all inside for tea.

"Are you all right?" I whispered, once attention had shifted elsewhere.

"Fine," Colleen whispered back. "It was for the best. Now, I can focus on my work."

Had she fallen on purpose? I wouldn't put it past her.

But her expression remained inscrutable, and at the sound of Dame Guinevere's pointedly cleared throat, I turned to face front again.

Our royal tea was disappointingly mediocre, with the duchess glaring at us all as if we were taking the food from her mouth. Begrudging though her hospitality was, she was more animated than the princess who sat quietly and observed the proceedings as if doing so from a royal viewing box, rather than as a participant in the tableau.

The party enlivened slightly when Sir John Conroy joined us and set about trying to find out from Dame Guinevere why this little gathering had been arranged. She parried his every verbal thrust effortlessly. It didn't take much intuition to gather the distinct impression that he was unhappy about our intrusion into the princess's jealously guarded circle. It became clear that the king and queen had given the duchess no choice but to receive us.

Following tea, it seemed we were about to get the brush off when the princess spoke up. "It is a shame you must leave so soon. I usually visit the orangery about this time of the day. Would you like me to show it to you all? It is lovely." She punctuated her invitation with a charming smile.

The duchess protested, her accent thickening. "You are so sweet always, to think of entertaining the guests, but I don't want you to overdo."

"I shan't." The princess's flat reply left little wiggle room for the duchess without appearing to be rude, and as we had among us the daughters of some of the most notable peers in the country, she acquiesced with only a twitch.

Our party strolled toward the orangery. Eleanor and most of the others jostled for position, trying to entertain Victoria with amusing anecdotes and humorous tittle-tattle. Colleen and I hung back. I had long been resigned to the fact that I was not really fit company for a princess. I tend too much to independent thought and action, and I don't possess the requisite gravitas. Not to mention that I haven't the income to keep up with the other girls in matters of fashion. As for Colleen, I think she simply didn't care that much. She would have rather been tucked away in a laboratory.

Another girl from the princess's household joined our group as we emerged into the garden. We gathered around to be introduced to Sir John's daughter, Louisa. She tried to loop her arm through the princess's.

With a withering glare, Victoria pulled free. As it happened, I was just behind them, and when she turned, the princess grasped my arm instead. Again, I glimpsed her unhappiness, and I immediately led her away at a fast clip, not sure if we were headed toward the orangery or not. Neither of us looked back to see whether the others chose to follow.

My tongue positively itched to ask about the little scene, but as I was also conscious that I was with my future queen, I restrained myself. Instead, we walked briskly and in silence.

"There it is." They were the first words Victoria had uttered to me. She made a motion with her chin toward a long, single-storied brick building set with so many wide windows it seemed to be constructed largely of air.

She paused at the steps and glanced around.

The others had fallen quite a distance behind us but were still in sight. She sighed. "Take my hand."

I did so but raised an eyebrow.

"I am not allowed to attempt anything so rigorous as a few stairs on my own." She practically dragged me up the short flight.

I was trying to formulate a response to this revelation when she turned on me. "Why aren't you conversing? Your friends possess a wealth of witty stories to share."

I opened the door for her and held it wide. "I don't excel at witty stories, Your Highness."

"What do you excel at?"

Knife throwing, climbing, archery, tactics, and needlework. "Needlework."

"I have a large collection of dolls, and I used to spend hours with Lezhen, my governess, making clothes for them." She said this almost shamefacedly—an admission.

"Surely, a harmless enough occupation for a young girl?"

"Yes. Harmless." She scowled. "Everything I do is harmless and ineffectual. When I said I used to, I was speaking of last week. I keep at it because I have few other means of occupying my time." As she spoke, a pink flush marked her cheeks and her blue eyes flashed. She looked downright pretty and definitely royal. She passed me into the orangery, and I followed obediently.

She continued. "But now, all you fine ladies arrive, and it seems that I *must* choose at least some of you to attend me when I am queen." Her voice dropped to a conspiratorial level. "Which I rather resent on the one hand, but on the other, my dear mama and her lackey resent it, which rather inclines me to accept it gracefully."

The orangery was airy and full of light. The green of the

trees was punctuated by an abundance of oranges and lemons. The air was heady with a slight citrus tang. But as we walked deeper into the place, a heavier scent swirled around us. It was sweet, almost cloying, and irritating to the back of the throat.

The princess turned to me. "My uncle's mandate would be easier for me to accept if I knew the reason."

A quandary. Dame Guinevere's command rang in my ears. "Ma'am," it seemed strange to address a girl a couple of months older than myself in such a fashion, "I'm afraid I cannot say."

Her cheeks drew in. "I demand you tell me. Or I swear that when I am queen, I will have none of you attend me."

"You can't do that," I blurted.

"I assure you, when I am queen, I will do as I like, and no one will gainsay me." Her jaw was set stubbornly as she glared at me.

Also, that itch at the back of my throat was growing worse, and for some reason I was feeling woozy. I cleared my throat then sighed. If anyone had a right to know it was the woman to whom we would pledge our allegiance. "We have been trained to protect you."

She stared, open-mouthed. "I don't need any protection and certainly not from a bunch of girls no older or more capable than myself." She stormed away then whirled to face me. "I am not going to abide the Kensington System when I am queen. I assure you! Everyone thinks they know what is best for me, and they all disguise it under the assertion that they are 'protecting me.'"

I followed her, unsure what else to do. I was growing more light-headed by the second. "Ma'am, I did not say we are meant to advise you or direct you. That is not where our training lies."

She did not hear or perhaps did not care what I had to say.

I caught up to her and had she been a classmate, I would

have grabbed her arm. We were about the same height which was lucky because most people can simply lengthen their strides and make it hard for me to keep pace. "When I said, protect, I meant it. We are an order—a secret order—of trained guards. All ladies of high birth, so that the world does not know our true purpose. There are places and times where male guards cannot attend their queen. Our graduates have protected every queen since Elizabeth. Her ladies were kept busy indeed protecting her from domestic and foreign threats, I can tell you."

Victoria slowed, then stopped and turned to me. "Official guards? Because I am to be queen, not because I am considered a weakling."

"Not at all because you are thought to be a weakling, Ma'am. As I said we have served—"

"Does Conroy know?"

"No, Ma'am. Neither he nor your mother are aware of our true purpose."

She swayed and blinked, but a small smile touched the corner of her mouth.

I seemed to be swaying as well, and when I studied her closely, her eyes were glassy. This was not right.

"Ma'am, we need to leave now." My words tasted strange and sounded slurred to my own ears, now that they were attuned to the difference. I fumbled with the wide ribbons of my bonnet.

"I don't wish to go."

I wouldn't wish to go if I were her either. The opportunity for a few moments away from her mother's watchful eye must have been refreshing. But I had glimpsed two masked figures slinking toward us.

Clumsily, I wrapped the broad ribbons over my mouth and nose, hoping to filter out whatever was in the air. The princess began to list to one side, and I grabbed for her. At the same time, the men approaching us picked up speed. I lowered Victoria to the floor while endeavoring to make it look like I was slumping too.

One of the men reached for me. His hands closed around my waist, not ungently, but I brought my elbow up in a sharp jab. I would have aimed for his nose, but as it was covered by a mask, I aimed for his Adam's apple instead. My elbow connected, and I felt as much as heard a crunch.

The man staggered backward gurgling and clutching his throat.

The other fellow had bent over Princess Victoria and was lifting her in his arms. He whirled in time to see his comrade's retreat and released his hold on the princess who thudded back to the ground.

I struck out with my heel, smashing the inside of his knee and knocking it outward. As he howled and began to fall forward, I snapped my knee into his chin, smacking his jaws together with tooth-shattering force.

Blood dribbled from his lips, and he limped after his friend.

I lurched after them a few paces. Then I stopped. I shouldn't leave the princess unguarded.

As I turned to stagger back to her side, my gaze fell upon some sort of contraption on the floor. It was of clockwork construction and consisted of fan blades, a belt, and an open vial of something. It must be the device they had used to pollute the air. My impulse was to smash it to bits, but some hazily logical remnant of my brain stopped me. If I smashed the vial, who knew how strong the fumes might be? And I could be destroying a clue. I tore off a bit of my petticoat and stuffed it in the top of the vial. I pawed at the machine until I managed to switch it off.

Head swimming, I left the device and returned to the princess's side. I patted her cheeks, and when she didn't stir, I used perhaps a bit more force than was strictly necessary. She lolled her head away.

"Your Highness?"

She squinted up at me. "You look like a bandit."

Whatever she said next was drowned out by a screech from her mother.

Chapter 2

The duchess rushed to her daughter's side, though Dame Guinevere kept pace with her without appearing to even speed up.

Her Grace shoved me aside.

Caught off guard, I flopped backward in an ignominious heap. I hastily pulled the ribbons from around my face and retied my bow, before the duchess thought to pay me any more notice. Now that the fumes had been stopped, the effects of the drug, whatever it was, were fading.

Dame Guinevere offered me a hand, and I accepted her assistance in standing. Her nose flared as she sniffed the air.

While the duchess alternated between clucking over her daughter and hurling unnecessarily personal comments at me, the princess tried to shoo away the flurry of her mother's words and sit up.

Dame Guinevere raised an eyebrow at me. I turned slightly away from the royal personages. "Two assailants. Dressed as footmen. Fled through the rear. A device behind that screen of topiary was used to drug us."

She motioned with two fingers for Colleen. Her words were as quiet as my own. "Discreetly remove the device behind the trees there and take it to our carriage."

Sir John approached and actually tried to embrace the

princess. She jerked away from his touch as if she had been scalded. He chuckled like she had made some sort of joke, but his eyes held no light.

The duchess decided to deflect attention from the obvious animosity between Victoria and Conroy. She rounded on me. "What were you doing to my daughter?"

I opened my mouth, but before a defense could form, Princess Victoria interrupted. This was a very good thing as I would have been less than diplomatic.

"Mama, Lady Portia did me a service when I came over faint. She kept me from coming to any harm. Do not repay her kindness thus. I think you may have been right that I have overdone things today."

This last brought the duchess up short. I had a feeling that Victoria did not often admit any sort of fault. The duchess then regarded me as if I had transformed from frog to prince before her eyes. "Ah, you were trying to help my precious. I was overwrought. I am sure you understand the mother's distress."

I managed a thin smile, which I plumped up with the added incentive of Dame Guinevere's parasol tip jabbing my side. "Of course, Your Grace. I am pleased that her highness is feeling better now."

"Yes, it has been a lot of excitement for one day, and," the duchess waved a hand in front of her face, "it is close in here. It is no wonder she came over faint."

She led her daughter out, and we all dutifully followed. The royal visit was over.

"Tell me precisely what happened." Dame Guinevere pinned me with her gaze.

Luckily, I had been expecting that as soon as we returned to our temporary headquarters at Cadogan Hall, she would drag me to her inner sanctum and demand a full accounting. I rattled out my report taking care to tell her everything that had occurred.

"They said nothing?"

I shook my head. "Not a word."

"You let them get away."

"My primary concern was to assure the princess's safety." I desired to give her the answer she wanted but sometimes it was hard to know what that was. Her calm stare and pointed questions had the power to paralyze me.

This time, she nodded, and a warm glow spread through me. "In this instance I shall not fault you. You are still learning. However, now the ruffians have gotten away, and we have no clue who sent them or what they wanted."

"I should have left the princess and followed?"

"You should have incapacitated them, so they could not escape. Your attacks were weak."

They hadn't felt weak to me. I had a purpling bruise the size of a grapefruit just above my knee, and my elbow—well, my elbow was fine, but still the criticism rankled. "Ma'am, I do not think this was merely an attack on the princess. I think they meant to kidnap her."

The ghost of a smile touched Dame Guinevere's lips. "Explain."

I struggled to articulate why that had been my impression. Then I had it. "The second man. He was trying to pick her up to carry her away. If he meant to assassinate her, he could have done so while I was occupied with the first fellow." She didn't stop me, so I carried on. "I think the drug was meant to incapacitate her and anyone with her. That would make her docile, so they could carry her off quickly. I assume some sort of getaway vehicle waited nearby."

"Well done. I believe you're correct." She gave me a nod of approval that was akin to a standing ovation from mere mortals. "At least you were able to fend them off. All was not lost. Though we are stuck with no clues."

I perked up. "We have a clue—the device used to spread the gas."

She shook her head. "It seems likely they meant to leave it behind in order to let it continue to drug whomever was with the princess in order to ensure they were not immediately followed. They would have taken care that it could not be traced back to them. Indeed, it looked like a perfume diffuser which can be bought at any number of shops throughout London." She rose from behind the desk. "It will be examined minutely, but you should not take false hope from it. We cannot expect attackers to be incompetent. This is why it is vital to capture them, not merely thwart them."

My lips tightened. She could criticize all she liked, but if I hadn't been there, the princess would have been kidnapped. That knowledge was a bulwark I took refuge behind.

Dame Guinevere stared out her office window and tapped her bottom lip.

I stayed perfectly still since I had not been dismissed. After a while, my mind began to drift. I stifled a yawn.

She turned her scrutiny back to me, and I snapped to attention once more. "They will try again. The plan was well conceived and executed. They somehow knew it was her habit to go to the orangery, if not with us, then with someone." For a moment she spoke more to herself than to me. "Who knows her schedule? Who would have accompanied her if not us?" Dame Guinevere blinked, her focus returning. "This wasn't a crime of opportunity. That means there is a plan, a purpose to be fulfilled. And since that purpose was presumably important enough to necessitate an attack on the princess, someone will try to execute that plan again."

My hands felt suddenly cold. Dame Guinevere was right. I should have made sure that at least one of the attackers couldn't even crawl away. But it had all happened so quickly, and I had been so dazed. Next time, I would do better.

And, if Dame Guinevere was correct, there would be a next time.

Chapter 3

When I finally climbed the stairs to the room Colleen and I shared, I felt like I had been on the receiving end of a thrashing, rather than having administered one. My muscles ached, and I had grown stiff. Far more disturbing was the sense that I had indeed failed the princess. I recalled the scene again and again in my mind. But the edges had gone all hazy. I seemed to remember Victoria's eyes being open as I lowered her to the ground and when I elbowed the first man. Did she know what had happened? If so, she hadn't let on by so much as a twitch.

In the unfamiliar hall, I passed my door and had to come back to it. Yawning hugely, I pushed it open. Five heads swiveled toward me.

"What took you so long?" Eleanor all but dragged me inside, kicking the door shut behind us.

I blinked as they all pressed close like they thought I might whisper my response. "Dame Guinevere wished to talk." That response was feeble. I ought to have demanded that they all leave, so I could get some rest. But for what seemed like the hundredth time that day, I didn't know what to do.

"No doubt. Now, tell us everything." Irene was nearly as bossy as Eleanor, but only if she knew her orders wouldn't be countermanded by her friend.

I played for time. "There isn't much to tell. Dame Guinevere was like she always is."

Eleanor narrowed her eyes. "About the princess you dolt. What really happened?"

I should have anticipated this. I really should. Nothing stayed secret for long at Saint Scholastica. They had taught us how to snoop and prowl far too well for that. I glanced at Colleen, and she shrugged. Did that mean she thought I should tell them, or not? Why wasn't she using our code?

I pushed past them and plopped down in front of the dressing table where I began unpinning my hair. "Can't this wait? I still need to dress for the opera."

Eleanor moved directly behind me and scowled at me in the mirror. "Stop stalling. We are all pledged to the princess just as you are, and whoever is added to her household needs to know what they might be up against."

She had a point, and Dame Guinevere had not forbidden me to tell anyone what had happened. I massaged my scalp gently. They were relentless. I'd have to tell them something though it went against the grain. I gave a very brief account of the events in the orangery but felt no need to share any of the theories I had constructed about the attack having been an aborted kidnapping attempt.

"Two men?" Plump fingers on her hips, Harriet stared at me. "You expect us to believe that even though you were drugged, you fought off two grown men. Why didn't the princess say anything about them when she awoke?"

My cheeks burned. "She may not have seen them. Why don't you ask her?"

Irene examined the perfect half-moons of her fingernails. "It seems odd that no one noticed these men. No one, except you, of course. We are all as well trained as you, though you never seem to think so."

"How do you know no one else saw them?" I shot back. "It isn't like we were able to question the household."

Eleanor shook her head. "We all knew you weren't going to gain a place with the queen because of your witty conversation or your family's prestige or wealth. I hadn't thought you would be so desperate that you would invent plots."

"You think what? That I somehow smuggled that contraption to the palace then drugged us both? How could I have known I'd have the opportunity to get her alone in the orangery?"

Marianne spoke up almost apologetically. "Well, with the drug in the diffuser, you could have knocked out twenty people as easily as one." She raised a hand. "Not that you did—"

Eleanor's blue eyes glittered. "And we all saw you practically dragging her along with you." She spun on her heel. "Come along, girls. I think we're finished here."

They sailed away under the steam of their self-righteous theories. Harriet had Marianne by the arm, marching her out to prevent her from staying and talking with us further.

I snatched up a shoe from the floor and threw it at the door as it closed behind them. It was only a silk slipper and sounded pitiful as it landed.

Colleen came to my side and touched my arm, managing to find the sore spot where I had elbowed the first fellow. "They're simply jealous. And their assertions hold no water if they are examined closely."

"I don't think they care."

"No, they don't. But if they try to share their ideas, others will care, and their opinions will count for far more." She coaxed me over to the wardrobe. "The maid will be here any moment, and we need to dress." She pulled out a jade gown and shoved it at me.

"This is yours," I protested.

"It would look better on you."

I seriously doubted that. Nothing looked better on me than it did on her. Not to mention her gowns were too long for me.

She grabbed one of my gowns instead, shrugged, and swapped me. "What did Dame Guinevere say? She believed you, didn't she?"

"I think so. But she was no happier about it. Raked me over the coals for not having incapacitated at least one of them."

"But you saved the princess and foiled their plan. What more does she want?"

"She wants whoever was behind it." As I spoke, I realized that so did I. The fact that Victoria had been attacked while in my company was a personal affront.

But how to go about it?

"Colleen?"

"Yes?" She looked up from a close examination of a stocking that had been partially eaten away by some noxious chemical.

"Tell me everything you can about that machine."

"What machine?"

When it came to Colleen and machines, one had to be very specific indeed. "The one you took away from the orangery."

"I didn't get to examine it minutely you understand."

"Yes." *Get on with it.*

"It was a perfume diffuser, but it had been modified with a larger motor and more vigorous fan than is typical. And that was no perfume in the scent bottle."

"Do you know where to get such a machine?"

"These particular models with the engraving are sold at a couple of shops in Burlington Arcade."

I almost crowed in triumph. "Then we have a trip to the Burlington Arcade in our very near future."

Colleen shook her head. "We can't go alone. Dame Guinevere would never allow it."

I flopped onto my bed and, ignoring the twinge of soreness, put my arms behind my head. I was going to redeem myself. "I will figure out a way, my girl. Just you wait and see."

Sneaking out was no mean feat. After all, we were in the care of those who had taught us presumably all we knew about sneaking. And despite having left half the teaching staff at the school, the remaining staff would be keeping a close eye on us in the wilds of London.

Still, I had a few ideas. The operation would call for subtlety. A light touch.

I put my plan into action the very next morning starting with a hint of rouge on my nose. A weak cough employed at strategic intervals during morning classes. The brave smile that showed I was game for a tour of the Royal Menagerie, even if I was at death's door.

As we sat at lunch, I let the conversation about the opera the previous evening flow about me. Even though I was ravenous, I only picked at my food.

Before ten minutes had passed, Dame Guinevere's eagle eye was trained on me from the head of the table where she presided in magisterial splendor.

Pretending I hadn't noticed, I pushed my roasted potatoes about with a listless movement of my fork. A few seconds more, and Dame Guinevere murmured something to Lady Amelia Pomeroy. Not only was Lady Pomeroy her right hand, she was Dame Guinevere's complete opposite. Lady Pomeroy loved bright colors, ruffles, lace, and all things frothy. She was plump and the school's dedicated shoulder to cry on. She was also the school's expert on botany, field medicine, and poison.

I wondered what she had made of the substance used to drug us.

Lady Pomeroy rose and circled the table to my side. She put a hand on my forehead. "My dear girl, you are running a fever. I'm afraid you won't be able to come to the menagerie today."

Of course, I felt feverish. I was wearing one of Colleen's inventions, a heated corset supposed to be worn in winter, that now served an even more desirable, if unintended, purpose.

I pasted a mournful expression over the glee in my heart. "Oh, but I'm sure it's a passing indisposition. I do so want to see all the animals."

"Poor pet, but I'm afraid it's out of the question." She motioned for me to stand, and I did so. "Off to bed with you. I will have cook send up a plate of dry toast and some tea in a while."

"Yes, ma'am." Shoulders slumped in the very picture of dejection, I left the dining room and climbed the stairs.

Safely in my room, I did a little jig of triumph. My plan had worked beautifully. I shed the corset that had me feeling as though I was being boiled alive and put on my nightdress. Then I waited impatiently for the others to leave. I stood at the window until I heard the chatter of the other girls as they milled about on the sidewalk in anticipation of leaving. When the steam carriage passed in the street below, I crossed to the wardrobe and searched for my simplest day dress. My head was deep inside when a knock sounded on the door. I cracked my head against an inner shelf.

The door swung open, and Dame Guinevere entered carrying a book. "Portia dear, you are looking quite flushed. I believe in being tidy too, but do come to bed now."

Numbly I did so, my mind whirling. What did she want? Was she onto me?

She tucked me under the covers then brought the straight-backed chair over from the vanity and set it beside the bed. "I thought you might be lonely if we left you to your own devices today."

"I wouldn't dream of keeping you from the sights, Dame Guinevere. Please don't feel as if you must stay. It will make me feel ever so guilty."

"Never you mind about me, I've seen the menagerie more than once. To tell the truth, I won't mind missing it." She settled into the chair, her spine so ramrod erect that it made the chair look as though it was slouching. She held the book up and began to read.

Horsefeathers.

I settled back into my pillows. It was going to be a long day, and I no longer had to pretend misery.

As Dame Guinevere droned on, I worked on a better plan. She might have foiled me this time, but I was by no means defeated.

By the next morning, I had made a remarkable recovery, which didn't seem to surprise Dame Guinevere at all. I watched her closely, but she never let on that she suspected I might have been anything other than ill.

My new campaign was based on the idea that if I couldn't sneak out to the arcade alone, I would bring everyone with me.

The opening volley in my next campaign arrived in the form of a thick, cream-colored envelope carried in on a silver tray with the morning post. Dame Guinevere's name was written across the front in bold copperplate script. It wasn't on the top of the pile, but it was there, nevertheless. I had made certain of it. It was a forgery I was proud of.

I'd have liked to turn it in to Mrs. Chauncey for credit. Alas, she was in the Outer Hebrides with most of our other instructors. I was careful not to stare as Dame Guinevere read and set aside the first two missives.

She frowned at the third, opened it, and unfolded the pages. She read the letter expressionlessly then tapped her spoon against the rim of her teacup. Silence descended instantly.

"I am afraid, ladies," she folded the letter back into its envelope, "that our plans for the day have been unavoidably upset. It would appear that Mr. Ninnian's gallery staff have experienced an unfortunate outbreak of the pox. We will not be able to visit them today and practice our sketching."

I made certain to look suitably crestfallen. "Surely, we could visit another gallery?"

Eleanor set aside her fork with delicate fingers. "We can't impose upon another gallery owner at such short notice. It would be unforgivably rude."

I couldn't have scripted a more perfect response for her, yet she still annoyed me. "Do you have a better suggestion?"

Colleen spoke up with the lines we had rehearsed before Eleanor could stick her oar in again. "Perhaps we could visit some of the shops. I could use a pair of evening gloves now that we are in town."

This immediately set Harriet and Marianne humming. They adored shopping of any and all kinds. To be fair, they knew how to put such outings to good use too. They'd made an art form of gathering intelligence from shop owners and clerks. Back at school, they had ascertained what was going on at all the farms within twenty miles of our little island, simply by regular visits to the local shops.

I shook my head. "It doesn't seem a good day for that. It could rain any moment."

Colleen was ready for me. "Burlington Arcade might serve."

I gave a tiny sideways bob of my head as if it didn't matter to me either way. Harriet and Marianne took up the cause with wheedling intensity and with support from Irene and Eleanor. This allowed me to finish my breakfast in peace. And considering the fact that I'd had little to eat the day before, I was starving.

Colleen returned her focus to her plate as well, almost as if she'd forgotten she had made the suggestion.

Dame Guinevere watched her speculatively for a moment before turning her attention to the other girls. It was out of character for Colleen to have suggested a shopping expedition, but I didn't want anyone else to know I was trying to investigate, and if I had asked to go myself, Dame Guinevere might have made the connection.

What I ought to have done was plant the idea in Harriet and Marianne's minds so that when the cancellation arrived they broached the subject themselves. Next time, I would do better.

Dame Guinevere endured the pestering for a solid ten minutes before she agreed. We were all sent to collect our pin money, so we might buy ribbons or silk flowers or some other trifle. Into my reticule I tucked a list Colleen had made for me of the stores which carried the diffuser along with a detailed diagram she had made of the modified machine.

Someone at the arcade would recognize it, I was sure. But whether they would know who had purchased it...? Time would tell.

Chapter 4

We arrived at Burlington Arcade in a belch of steam and splash of filth from the gutter. I descended last and nodded politely to the coachman who shielded me from the rain with a stout black umbrella. When we had each been escorted inside, we clustered around Dame Guinevere and Lady Pomeroy like chicks around broody hens.

The arcade bustled with shoppers. The high arched ceiling above protected all and sundry from the ravages of the weather, and those about their business looked suitably cheerful at having thwarted Mother Nature.

My classmates were rosy-cheeked and smiling in anticipation of the delights of frills and furbelows which they would select with great care. If I am honest, I likely had a similar anticipatory gleam in my eye. Mine was simply caused by another source.

I have often been accused of dawdling, but dawdling has its benefits. Dame Guinevere led the way to the first shop. I started out abreast of the other girls but lagged behind little by little until I slipped unnoticed into the first shop on Colleen's list.

I was back out within three minutes. The clerk was a ninny who could not recognize the drawing though he had the same basic model sitting on a shelf behind him. Not surprisingly, they could not recall selling any of the devices. I considered asking for the owner but didn't have time to wrangle. Not at the moment. If the attackers had bought the device there, they had chosen well.

At the second and third shops, I fared no better. I was beginning to think my parents had been right to mourn the decline in the British educational system. Surely, we had not become the most powerful nation on earth on the backs of such soaring incompetence.

I emerged into the arcade shaking my head and glanced up and down the row of shops. No hue and cry had been raised so far. I weighed the risk of rejoining my classmates in order to be seen among them, versus the difficulty of breaking away again.

Since only one shop remained on the list, I decided to risk a little more time. The final shop was located almost at the end of the arcade, and I glided toward it so it would not appear I was rushing, even though I wanted to run. I ducked inside, gasped with relief, and immediately sneezed. The atmosphere was cloying with incense. I sneezed again and fumbled for my handkerchief.

The whip-thin salesclerk had gray hair cut in the short Brutus style and buff-colored pants with creases sharp enough to cut anyone unwary enough to draw too close. His pince-nez reflected the lamplight so that on first glance he appeared to have flames where his eyes ought to have been. It occurred to me that the culprits behind the kidnapping attempt need not have bought a diffuser. What if they were in league with someone who supplied them the diffuser?

I smiled, though the clerk might not have seen it behind the handkerchief I was using to dab my nose.

"How might I assist you, miss?"

"Good morning." I injected my voice with sweet breathlessness. "I was wondering if you carry the Tonne Perfume Diffuser?"

"We do indeed." He gestured to one which sat in majestic display complete with a sign.

I had already seen that they carried the diffuser through the shop window. "Oh, how delightful." I sneezed again.

"Bless you." His words were bored.

I approached the machine and prodded it gently. "It is smaller than I expected."

"It works quite well, I assure you."

"But could it work for an entire ballroom, I mean without over-scenting one side?"

"That would depend upon the size of the ballroom?"

I dodged this obvious attempt to garner information about my financial status with a nimble, "Do you smell—I mean, sell many of them?"

"A fair number, it is a popular model."

Drat. "Have there been any recent sales?"

"Several. I believe the Marchioness of Hoyton was one of our recent purchasers."

Name dropping—a very good line indeed. "Anyone else I might know who could vouch for the excellence of the product?"

"Chevalier Ponce, the Bishop of Verney, Lord Bancroft, let's see." He pursed his lips in thought. "And Sir John Conroy picked one out for the Duchess of Kent."

I made my gasp into another sneeze and raised my handkerchief to my nose once more. I must not. Must *not* leap to conclusions.

"A friend of mine had hers modified to enhance its effectiveness." I pulled the sketch from my reticule. "Is this something you could do here?"

He accepted the drawing and pushed his pince-nez up his nose before peering at it closely. "An interesting design. But I am afraid we are not a mechanic's workshop."

"Is there someone you recommend for such work?"

"Does that mean you would like me to have one wrapped for you? We can have it delivered." He smiled thinly.

"I will have to speak to Papa about it first, but it does seem to fit all our requirements. Though if he wants the modifications, I will certainly want to know who could handle the work and how much they are likely to cost as that will figure into the decision."

His smile looked like it had curdled on his lips, but he went behind a counter and consulted a slim portfolio. "For such modifications we would recommend Xavier Mahlenbeau. His workshop is located near Kensington Palace in Butterleigh Close. Indeed, he is recommended by most of the shops in the arcade. His reputation is excellent."

I scribbled the information into a tiny notebook. "Thank you very much. I do believe that it would make the perfect gift for Mama."

Still uttering such reassurances, I swept from the shop. My mind was spinning. Was it possible Sir John Conroy was behind the dastardly attack? It was no secret that Victoria disliked the man. Still, what could he gain?

Unless…what if he had intended on making himself seem a hero by rescuing the princess? Perhaps it had all been mere playacting, at least for the villains. Could it have been a bid for the princess's favor?

I revolved the idea in my mind as I rushed back to the milliner's shop where my classmates remained happily ensconced.

The moment I appeared, Colleen thrust a length of scarlet

ribbon and a cluster of violently orange tiger lilies made of silk into my hands.

Dame Guinevere stood directly in front of us. She turned, sniffing the air. "There you are, Portia. Heavens, child, have you been sampling the perfumes? You smell like a—well never mind what you smell like."

Lady Pomeroy stepped close. "Let me see what you have picked out."

I held up the ribbon and flowers.

"An interesting color combination," she said at her diplomatic best.

Irene poked Eleanor in the ribs with her elbow. "Yes, Portia, were you going for eye-popping or merely garish?"

"It's cheerful," I said. *And would clash terribly with my gingery hair.*

"Looks like something Colleen would choose," Marianne whispered to Harriet loudly enough for us all to hear.

At my side, Colleen blushed crimson. She was color-blind, and they were forever twitting her.

We were straying far too close to the truth. I scrambled. "I hoped they would have some daffodils I could add to it, so there would be the gradations from red to orange to yellow."

Dame Guinevere tapped her lip with a finger and tilted her head.

I plowed on. "It was meant to be reminiscent of a sunset." *Perhaps if the shades were more subdued.*

Lady Pomeroy collared a clerk and soon had me fitted out with white velvet primroses and pale green silk ribbon instead. Then we were all on our way to the next shop and the next.

I was bursting to tell Colleen about my discoveries but there was no privacy. I had spent all I could spare of my scant allowance. So, while the others accumulated package after package,

I was free to analyze the problem which had begun to consume me. How could we protect the princess if the danger came from within her own household? A household to which we had no access?

When finally we arrived back at Cadogan Hall, I grabbed Colleen and practically dragged her upstairs to our room. It took hardly any time at all to recount my adventures, and in the retelling they didn't sound very compelling.

There was a pause when I finished. For once, I had Colleen's full attention without offering her some bit of machinery to examine. "But what would Sir John stand to gain from kidnapping the princess? His only path to power is through her."

"Aha!" I had saved my pet theory as the *coup de grâce*. "But what if he didn't really intend to have her harmed or kidnapped. His plan might have been to *appear* as if he had saved Victoria himself."

"Then why didn't he?"

"Because I did it first."

"But where was he? If he meant to put on a great show, why wasn't he with her? Surely he would have stayed near her so as to minimize the potential for interference."

I threw myself down on the bed. I loved it when Colleen turned her incisive intellect to my problems—except when she didn't agree with me.

The rain continued to patter against the window. Soon we would have to dress for dinner. I would much rather wrestle with my nice little knot than converse with Eleanor and her cronies around a dinner table. The silence was comfortable, though I had no illusions that Colleen was thinking about the same tangle I was. She was revolving some sort of cog assembly in her hands, and I would have laid money that she was inventing something.

Reining in my wayward thoughts, I tried to recall the precise sequence of events beginning with our arrival at the palace. As if my brain were a lamp show, the images flickered to life before my mind's eye. I went through it once and then again. On the second time through, I sat bolt upright.

Colleen paid me no mind.

I wracked my brain to make sure I had the details down. "It wasn't for himself. Not directly. I bet it was for his daughter, Louisa. You remember. She tried to take the princess's arm as if they were bosom friends, and the princess pulled away. The look on the princess's face left me in no doubt that she abhors the girl. Sir John might feel it incumbent upon him to improve relations between them and, in the process, his own standing." The more I spoke, the more plausible it became. "She might have been trying to get the princess alone in order to enact their charade. But the princess foiled them when she pulled free and walked away with me instead."

Colleen shrugged. "I don't know how you could ever prove it one way or another."

She was right. And in the meantime, if I was wrong, then someone out there really meant the princess harm.

There was only one thing to do. I needed to go back to the palace. The person best situated to give me real answers about her relations with the Conroys was the princess.

I sighed. "I have to break into the palace.

Chapter 5

It took me awhile to convince Colleen of the brilliance of my deductions. We took up the debate after dinner and once again in the morning, but this time I was convinced I was right. The only person who could answer my questions was the princess. The only way to speak to the princess was to go around Conroy's Kensington System.

I think Colleen could tell my mind was made up, and finally, though I don't know if I persuaded her to my view, she stopped debating the point. During our midday break from classes, I made a trip to the Cadogan Hall library and retrieved every reference I could find with a mention of Kensington Palace. I had plans to make.

After classes, I pored over the books. There would be fences to scale, locks to pick, guards to avoid, but the biggest obstacle was the fact that the princess was never alone. Either her mother or her governess, Baroness Lezhen, were with her at all times. Her mother even shared the same bedroom. Even if I could get Victoria alone, I had no guarantee she would talk to me. She might call the guards herself. And there would go my chance to improve my family's fortunes.

I gnawed on the inside of my lip. Maybe I should leave well enough alone. The only one driving me forward was me. I did not have to do this. Staring blindly at the book before me, I debated with myself.

Colleen poked her head inside our room. "Portia?"

I looked up.

"Would you have a moment?" She was wearing her thick leather apron over her tea gown, which meant she had been working in the laboratory.

She withdrew, and I followed absently. Colleen often needed a willing test subject for her experiments. I was well acquainted with the role and her persistence. For someone normally so mild-mannered, she could be relentless in the pursuit of her inventions.

In theory, the well-appointed laboratory at Cadogan Hall could have been used by any of the Saint Scholastica girls, but in reality, it remained Colleen's sole domain, just as the laboratory at school had been her exclusive territory.

Though I had acquired a passable education in the basics of chemistry and engineering, when I entered Colleen's realm I hadn't any idea what was occurring. The usual smell of hot metal, noxious chemicals, and brilliance felt like home. Brightly colored liquids followed tortuous paths from beaker to vial through glass spirals. Mysterious bits of machinery lay strewn about. I couldn't even identify some of the tools, much less what she intended to create with them. The stone walls were interspersed with gaslight sconces whose golden glow lent the utilitarian room its only charm.

Colleen beckoned me to join her at a long workbench. Several items were arrayed on it, and she gazed down upon them. After a long moment, she picked up a spool of slender ribbon.

"This I think." She handed it to me.

"You want me to…decorate something for you?"

She cut her eyes across at me. "You ninny, it's spider line."

"Spi…?"

She put her hands on her hips. "Do you ever listen to anything I tell you?"

I mustered as much wounded dignity as I could. "Of course, I do."

She plucked the spool out of my hand. "I told you about it before we left school." She unspooled some of the narrow ribbon. It was almost translucent. "This can be concealed upon your person, and even used as a decorative trim, which could be removed in the case of an emergency. It is as strong as a two-inch rope and can be used for all sorts of purposes. Such as climbing." She gave me a significant look.

My mouth dropped open, and I reached for the spool.

"The great advantage, of course, is its lightness. This spool contains a cable's length of line."

"That's 300 feet."

Her smile was smug. "Precisely." She pointed at the miracle in my hand. "But if you use it for climbing, you'll want to wear gloves. The one drawback is that it is thin enough that it will be difficult to grip. You'll have to wrap it around your hand like so," she demonstrated, "and it could cut your palms if you aren't careful."

"Noted."

Colleen reached for another item. With a flick of her wrist, she unfurled a folding fan, a delicate looking thing with a slim, carved handle, ornate silver spindles, and a painted scene of a stormy lake. It looked rather old-fashioned, but in a good way. An antique, as opposed to simply passé.

When she said nothing, I cocked an eyebrow. "This will be helpful if I need to flirt my way out of a situation?"

"I would never encourage that." She pulled a large chunk of firewood from a basket by the fireplace and put it on the table.

"Your flirting could end only in destruction." She waggled her eyebrows as she twisted the fan's handle and then bent it at a ninety-degree angle. Another sharp movement, something between a twist and a flick, and the blades began to spin. A faint whirring sound came from the device as they picked up speed until Colleen touched it to the log. Splinters spewed out as the blades bit into the wood.

I clapped my hands together. "Colleen, you are brilliant!"

"Surely, there was never any doubt about that." Her saucy grin made me certain I had not plumbed the depths of my friend's character.

She made a move with her thumb against the handle and the blades began to slow. She flicked it back up into place and handed it to me.

I examined the fan closely, but not so much as a scratch marred the delicate blades. "I'll never understand how you did that."

"You don't have to understand how it's made. Just how to use it." She demonstrated the movements required to extend the blades as well as the almost imperceptible protrusion in the filigree that activated and deactivated the internal mechanism.

It took a few tries but I soon mastered the motions. I sincerely hoped someone dastardly would challenge me so I could use the blades.

"Have I told you lately that you're brilliant?"

She ignored me. "One more thing." She handed me a pair of opera glasses. "These can help you see at night."

"At night?" I raised them to my eyes, but all I could see was a blur of white with violet edges.

"It's too bright in here right now. You'll have to take my word for it. They'll work. You'll be able to see regardless of the time of night or whether the moon is out. Oh, and that little dial on the side allows different lenses to be rotated into use so that these actually have a magnifying function as well."

I threw my arms around her. "You are the best friend a girl could ever have. I've been puzzling all day about how I could break into the palace, and now I've got an idea."

"Just stay safe, all right?" Colleen was fighting a losing battle against her grin of delight at the praise. "I have some other devices in the works, and if you come to grief, I'll have lost my best test subject."

That night I was ready for my foray. After an evening of dreadful German theater, Dame Guinevere and the other instructors shepherded us all back to the Hall. While the rest of the girls were slathering on face cream and wrapping their hair in rags, Colleen and I were preparing for the night rather differently.

I dressed in a dark gray dress. Perfectly respectable, perfectly nondescript, neither expensive, nor cheap, in short—invisible. Soft slippers with ribbons that laced up the ankles would allow me to walk silently and ensure I didn't lose them during a pursuit like some dim-witted Cinderella. A pair of neat, gray gloves, a poke bonnet with a brim made of a material that would obscure my face while still letting me see through it—another of Colleen's priceless inventions.

I also had the spool of spider line, Colleen's opera glasses, and the antique fan tucked into a deep pocket in my skirt as well as a few other tools that might come in handy. All of the items would look quite innocent to the uninitiated. I was as ready as I would ever be.

Colleen slid open the window and took a peek outside. A

steady drizzle made the city seem like a smudgy, amateurish watercolor. She looked back at me. "You're sure you want to do this?"

"I'm sure." To be honest, nothing would have stopped me. Something was wrong at Kensington Palace, and I meant to find out what it was.

Chapter 6

The rain proved to be a boon. Not even the usual pickpockets and cutthroats wanted to lurk about in such a depressing downpour. I walked briskly, eager to get on with things, and mentally making a note for Colleen. Illuminating opera glasses and lethal fans were all well and good, but what I really needed were waterproof slippers and a rain repellent dress.

From Hanover Square it was almost a straight shot west. As I was passing Binney Street, a stout constable in his instantly recognizable police helmet and glistening rain slicker came round the corner, smacking his truncheon lazily against his thigh as he strolled. The steady patter and splash of the rain had drowned out his footsteps, and I had no time to dodge for a shadow or some other cover.

"'Ere now. What's this?" His features were difficult to make out in the light of a guttering corner gas lamp, but there was no mistaking his tone. He'd had a dull uncomfortable night and was delighted at the idea of making someone else's night even more uncomfortable—not to mention having an excuse to haul someone into his station house, where he could get a good hot cuppa and a dry pair of socks.

If his features were difficult to make out, I knew he could see nothing of my own, shadowed as they were by the brim of my bonnet. "Oh, officer!" I made the words shrill, layering them with every ounce of nasally aristocratic accent I could muster. "Thank heavens. I've had the *most* trying time this evening. You simply can't imagine."

The accent made him stand up straighter and relax his grip on his truncheon. "What seems to be the trouble, miss? What's a young lady doing out alone on a night like this?"

"It's all been too much, really." I was scrambling for an explanation that would satisfy him. Dame Guinevere had taught us to lean into the truth. I drew a handkerchief from my sleeve and sniffled into it, doing my best to convey distress in every move. "This is my very first trip to London you see. The road can get very crowded."

On and on spilled out a jumbled and confusing tale. The poor officer's eyes began to glaze over. Perhaps I could bore him to sleep where he stood then be about my business? No. Better to have him send me on my way.

"And as you know a hansom won't usually stop for a lady alone. And now I can't even seem to find any. I've been walking for simply ages, and I am quite dreadfully tired."

The poor constable blinked as I concluded my rapid-fire assault on his eardrums. "It'll be a pleasure to help, miss. What's the address of your friend's home?"

I let out a wail and buried my face in my handkerchief again. "I just tell the coachman who I want to see, and he manages the details like addresses and so on."

"Ah. Well. What's the family name then, I know the families in the neighborhood."

"Do you know the Parsley-Greenthorpes?"

"Parsley-Greenthorpes?" His lips turned down, and I wondered if I had perhaps gone too far.

I needed to find a way to shake this fellow without him

escorting me anywhere. I could hardly walk up to one of the houses lining the street and ring the bell expecting to be admitted at such an hour.

"How long have you been walking?"

"Oh, ages and ages."

I could practically see him pulling on his thinking cap to help me solve my dilemma. "Hmm. Yes, cabs won't often stop for single young women. They don't want anything to do with"—a sideways glance at me—"not that this applies to you, miss, but they don't want to take a chance on admitting a woman of low moral character."

I let my shoulders droop. Then I straightened. "It's come to me! I need to go to number six, Gloucester Terrace." The address was in the general direction I wished to travel and would be well outside this frustrating fellow's beat. I vowed never again to complain about Dame Guinevere's insistence that we maintain an encyclopedic knowledge of London's streets and byways. It could indeed come in handy.

"Oh, ah. Well, I'm glad you thought of the address, miss." The constable's look was eloquent, and I could see him wondering what sort of ninny I had to be to have wandered so far afield.

"Is it very far away, officer?"

"Well now, miss. It's…I'm afraid it's not in my beat, and I'm not allowed to leave my beat for an errand like this you see."

"Certainly." I let my voice falter and turned as if to set off for a trek into a vast wasteland, which in some ways, London certainly is. "I quite understand."

"Now, now, miss. I'm sure we can come up with something."

Blessedly, at that moment, a cabbie's distinctive lamp floated into view from the direction I had come.

"Here comes another cab, but I'm afraid he won't take me

up, either." My tone implied a death of all hope and resignation to a life of hapless wandering.

The policeman's face became so relieved and happy I felt quite ashamed of myself. "You leave this fellow to me, miss. We'll get you sorted right quick."

And he did. In under a minute, I was tucked under a rather musty traveling rug and trundling along toward Gloucester Terrace.

I'd have preferred not to leave such evidence of my passage through the streets, as both constable and cabbie would remember the daft young miss they had encountered tonight. But with any luck, no one would have any reason to question anyone about a young woman walking alone, and as they say, needs must.

At the address I had supplied, I hopped out and paid the cabbie his fare and a generous tip. "Thank you, sir."

"I'm surprised no lights are on. Didn't they wait up for you? In fact, I'm surprised there aren't people scouring the streets looking for you."

I considered briefly. Normally, one of my class wouldn't deign to answer such an impertinent question from a cabman, and I wanted to avert suspicion, not invite it. "Are you American?"

"Close enough, miss." He touched the brim of his cap. "I've only been here a short time. Kind of you to notice."

"Not at all. Well, good evening to you."

"I'll just wait here until you get inside safe and sound."

Drat the man.

Undaunted, I opened the gate, marched up the walk, and pulled a pair of lockpicks from their concealed pocket at my waist. It took no longer than if I'd had a key before I was inside the door. Thank goodness they didn't have a bolt, though I had a device that could have handled that if necessary too.

I gave the cabbie a little wave and stepped inside the darkened house, closing the door softly behind me, hoping mightily no vicious dogs waited within. A curious cat came to twine around my ankles. Otherwise, the house remained shrouded in deep quiet aside from the ticking of a clock somewhere. I counted out sixty seconds before I chanced a peek outside. The cab had gone, and sighing in relief, I slipped back outside.

I headed due south, and in a moment came to the palace grounds. Not even a fence set the house apart from the gardens and Hyde Park beyond. I shook my head at such notions of "security." God willing, the nation's future monarch resided here. They ought to be more careful.

Carefully. Carefully. I cautioned myself. Perhaps appearances were deceiving.

Time to pull out Colleen's miraculous opera glasses. As I slid them before my eyes, the world changed from an indistinct mosaic of black and slightly less black, to a vivid purple. Shadows were banished, and I could see at least four guards standing watch that I had been blind to previously.

Luckily, none of these guards had spied me either.

Taking care to maintain absolute silence, I skirted the building until I came to the wing which housed the princess. I stared at the expressionless brick façade. Such a shame there were no convenient balconies, but at least, I had a good idea of where to find the princess.

There had been quite the flap in the newspapers early in the year when the king learned the duchess had expanded her living quarters by appropriating the King's Gallery for herself and the princess. Not only that, but without so much as a by-your-leave she had made alterations that turned it into three rooms: a bedroom, dressing room, and maid's room.

I slipped the opera glasses into my pocket. Time to put the spider line to the test. Crouching low in the shadow of some shrubbery, I quickly fashioned a loop in one end of the line and, after unfolding a little grappling hook that had a pulley rigged to the back, fed the bulk of the line onto the pulley with an intricate knot of Dame Guinevere's devising. I should have done this part in the comfort of my room. It was cold standing in the steady drizzle and patiently loading the line through the pulley. I risked discovery every moment I remained on the grounds. But if the spider line worked correctly, it would make an easier way for me to scale the building than finding a drainpipe and prove safer than trying to break in and wind my way through a maze of corridors and servants. I would be able to get precisely where I needed with as little fuss as possible.

I checked to make sure no guards were near then stepped from my concealment and moved close to the building. I took careful aim, spun the grappling hook experimentally a few times, then let it fly. The first time, it clunked against the brick and fell back to the ground. I held stock-still, hardly daring to breathe, waiting to see if anyone had heard the sound.

After a moment, I inhaled a deep breath and gave my hands a little shake. I'd try once more, and if it didn't work, I would figure out another plan. Once more, I spun, and then tossed the grappling hook. For a heart-stopping moment it sailed straight at the window. But then a small *thunk* as it bit into the wood of the windowsill of the room above the princess's. I gave the line a solid tug to make sure it was secure.

With my foot settled in the loop I had formed, I began to haul with all my might. Inch by inch, I ascended toward the window. This next bit was the trickiest part of the whole evening. I had to wake Victoria without alerting the duchess who slept in the same room. It would be best if I could get in the room, but how to manage that with both hands fully occupied keeping me aloft could prove...troublesome. Particularly if the window was locked.

My arm muscles were screaming, and I determined that I had been far too free with the tea cakes lately. Even my leg was starting to cramp from the tension, although all it had to do was stand secure in the foothold. I would have to ask Colleen to invent something else for such situations. By the end of the evening, I would have enough ideas for new gadgets to keep her occupied for some time.

It took a solid ten minutes for me to reach the right window. I pulled on the spider line until I could step onto the narrow windowsill. The relief to my arms was enormous. I perched there recovering the feeling in my fingers and rubbing my arms vigorously.

Joy and raptures, the German sense of discipline had asserted itself and, despite the rain, the window had been left open a crack—probably in the belief that it was healthy.

Inside, I could make out the two beds containing the sleeping royals. There was no doubt in my mind that the narrow bed contained the princess while the opulent carved affair mounded high with pillows and a thick comforter must belong to the duchess.

Hanging on to the spider line to help me maintain balance, I leaned down and slowly wiggled the window up. Slowly, slowly I worked to make sure I made no sound. I aged about ten years but finally coaxed the window open enough that I could slip through. The opera glasses made everything as clear as if it had been day.

Silent as smoke, I stole toward the princess's bed and bent over the huddled figure. "Prin—"

A flash of light, white and searing. I reeled away, nearly dropping the opera glasses.

Clad in a voluminous nightgown, the princess was out of bed, holding an instant candle in one hand and a knife in the other. "I knew you villains would strike again." Her words were an outraged hiss.

I held my hands up, palms out. "Your Highness, it's me." My whisper was frantic, as she advanced on me with the weapon. "I apologize for the strangeness of my approach, but I needed to speak to you."

The avenging fury slowed her steps. "Lady Portia?" she too kept her voice low. Interesting that she should be so anxious to bypass her mother's control that even in such circumstances she had not cried out for help.

"Yes." Relieved, I dropped my hands. "Your Highness, I needed to ask you some questions."

"Surely there are more conventional methods."

"Of course, you're right, but I needed to talk to you alone."

Her chin tilted up at that. "I assume this is about the attack on my person?"

So, she *had* been conscious enough to realize what had happened. "Yes, ma'am. I believe it was a kidnapping attempt. I want to make sure no stone is left unturned."

"Who are you, Lady Portia?"

She already knew my pedigree. That wasn't what she was asking. "I'm a friend, I swear it. I explained before the purpose of our school."

She looked at me for a long time, her gaze steady in the waning light of the dying fire in the grate. "What are your questions?"

The duchess's soft snoring stopped and she rolled over fitfully in her bed.

I reached out and grasped the princess's hand, drawing her farther away from her mother. It was no time to be tactful or circumspect. "I got the sense that you don't care for Louisa Conroy or her father."

Another long silence. "When I am queen, I will certainly organize my household differently."

Her self-containment was admirable. "I will take that as an affirmation. Your Highness, there is a possibility that Conroy was behind the abduction attempt. It's only a theory," I cautioned. "I think Louisa meant to be by your side. If she had foiled the attempt, it might have placed you in her debt so to speak."

"I should rather be kidnapped." She looked so fierce even in the watery moonlight that I believed she meant it too.

"Is there anyone else you can think of who might wish you out of the way?"

She shook her head. "I know almost no one. Conroy has seen to that, keeping me locked away from the court."

"Have you received any threats?"

She was relaxing now, her body language shifting. She slid the knife she had wielded into the sleeve of her nightgown. "If I had, I would not have been told. I have no more privacy in my correspondence than I do in my sleeping arrangements." A jerk of her chin indicated her mother's bed.

"Have there been any other attempts, or has anything odd occurred?"

"No."

"Please think carefully."

"My days are so regimented that the slightest abnormality stands out like a beacon. I'm not likely to forget."

She was not making this easy. "Your Highness, I beg your indulgence. I'm convinced something more is afoot than a single attempt on your person. I fear the same assailants could try again."

For the first time, I detected something aside from aplomb from the princess.

Her front teeth caught at her lower lip briefly before releasing it. "I think so too." She peered past me into the darkness. "I honestly have no idea who could be behind this attack, nor who would wish to do me harm. While the king yet lives, I am no use to anyone."

"While he yet lives."

"Do you fear a plot on the king's life as well?"

"I don't know what I fear. I am simply plagued by unease with the situation."

The princess's chin twitched up ever so slightly. "I agree. I hereby commission you to continue investigating until you discover some answers."

My eyebrows fair flew right off my forehead. "You do?"

"I need someone I trust to look into this. If Conroy is behind it, I want to know. And if he would dare such an insult on his future sovereign, I want his head." Her shoulders lifted slightly in the chill. "If it's someone else, then I must be equally assured that the person investigating has my interests at heart, not simply political expediency."

"With pleasure."

"Wait here." She stepped away from me and returned a moment later.

She held something small out, and I automatically reached for it. Something cold and hard landed in my palm.

"I believe it is customary that a signet ring be given to an agent of the crown as a token of authority."

I cleared my throat. "Yes, ma'am, I believe that is tradition-al."

"Good. I trust you can see yourself out then?"

Taking my cue, I sat on the windowsill, my legs dangling over the edge as I sought my foothold. I gave her a little salute. "Cheerio, Highness. I'll find a way to report back when I have more information."

For a second, I thought I heard her laugh at that, but then I was sliding a little too rapidly down the spider line.

I slowed my descent and was moving at a moderate pace when I heard a rustle below. I stopped, frozen in place. An A Division constable stood perhaps six feet below me. He looked right and left. He must have heard some noise I'd made.

I dangled.

He didn't move.

I waited. He waited.

The muscles in my arms and legs began to tremble from the strain as time stretched on and on.

I had almost concluded that I would have to fall on him and try to silence him before he could bring other guards running, when he at last walked a few paces. I began allowing the line to slither through my gloved hands again.

He paused once more.

I couldn't stop. With a very unladylike expression, I dropped the final ten feet or so to the ground, turning it into a roll as I had been taught. There was no question of "if" he had heard me this time. I popped to my feet and ran for all I was worth.

"Oi!" The shout was followed by a blast on a policeman's whistle and the thud of heavy feet coming after me. In an instant, the sound of pursuit echoed from other quarters as well.

Just my luck.

I sprinted as I had never sprinted before. Neither the lawn

made marshy by the rain, nor my sodden skirts which were determinedly clinging to my legs, slowed me. I was as fleet of foot as winged Mercury himself, scarcely touching the ground as I sped toward the relative safety of Hyde Park. The bridge would be the choke point, so that was out. The only option was to go around the Serpentine. Cutting north would be the shortest way out of the park and into the anonymity of the streets.

They would certainly expect that.

South it was.

I redoubled my speed, sprinting for all I was worth. My breath rasped and sharp pain arced through my side. Perspiration prickled my skin despite the chill. I would have to make certain Dame Guinevere never caught wind of this escapade, or I would receive enough penalty points to choke a horse.

The sounds of pursuers had grown quite faint when I began to cut left around the tail of the Serpentine. Just as I made the move, I glimpsed shadowy movement and a pair of arms reached for me. My training kicked in, and I pirouetted away as if I was waltzing.

The man stumbled and fell to his knees when he failed to make contact. They were obviously prepared and had placed men strategically throughout the park. I would have to make a break straight for the streets and hope to find a hole in their perimeter.

I slowed my pace a tiny bit. I had to be careful, to watch and listen for the snares that no doubt awaited.

Lights bobbed behind me from handheld pyrogenes. The phosphorescent glow cast an eerie illumination that was sliced apart by the shadows of tree trunks. The result was a disorienting kaleidoscope world.

But I was almost home free. London's welcoming streets with their innumerable alleys and offshoots lay just a few hundred feet away. The blasted pyrogenes had at least one benefit: they also revealed the waiting guards to me. Two of them converged from north and south on the very spot toward which I was running.

I must be very fast indeed.

They would be right on my tail all the way through the city at this pace. My mind raced as fast as my legs.

The final bit of turf passed under my feet, and I reached pavement. To both right and left, the police were a mere fifteen feet or so away.

A steam carriage careened in front of me. "Get in!" a voice commanded.

Without hesitation, I launched myself for the door and simply held on, one arm hooked through the window, my feet scrabbling for the step.

Loud swearing erupted from the police officer left behind.

I had barely managed to plant my flailing feet when the other officer snatched at me and caught my free arm. He held on, and I could not quite restrain a cry as pain exploded in my arm and shoulder. The officer tried to dig his heels in but the carriage had too much weight behind it. The momentum wrenched me free of his grasp.

Eyes watering, it was all I could do to hang on as the carriage slewed into one turn after another. After what seemed a minor eternity but was probably ten minutes or so, the carriage slowed to a more sedate pace.

For a moment I rested my forehead against the side of the carriage but the jarring of the rough road was too much.

My rescuer looked down from his perch, and our eyes met briefly. If I wasn't much mistaken, it was the same American cabman. He had shaggy brown hair, a wide nose, and an expressive mouth.

He had the effrontery to wink at me. "We meet again. Imagine getting lost a second time in the same night."

I hadn't any idea who this man was. I would find out, but in my own time and my own way. Instead of replying, I offered him a jaunty salute before jumping free of the carriage and slipping through one alley and into another before he could rein up the vehicle.

My shoulder ached fiercely as I trudged home, my every sense vibrating with the possibility of pursuers.

I heard and saw nothing to alarm me further, so after taking a circuitous route back to Cadogan Hall, I didn't hesitate to haul myself up to my window. The climb hurt like the dickens, but the fact that I was able to accomplish it reassured me that the shoulder was not broken or dislocated.

"Do be quiet." Colleen's anxious face peered out of the window as I scrabbled for purchase on the sill. "What kept you?" Her urgent whisper was at least as loud as any noise I'd made.

"Complications." The response came out more as a grunt than a word.

She tugged on my arm, attempting to help me in, and I gave an involuntary hiss.

"What have you done?"

I waited until I had clambered through the window before trying to respond, but by that time she was making her own assessments.

She helped me undo my bodice and eased it over my shoulder. Cold fingers prodded at me and she made me raise and lower the arm. "I think it's just muscle strain."

Wearily, I accepted her diagnosis then told her of my evening's activities before showing her the signet ring. Finally, I broke the bad news.

She didn't rant. Colleen never ranted.

A part of me wished she would. I'd had to leave behind the grappling hook and spider line. It was now no doubt in the hands of A Division. I had succeeded in obtaining very few answers but had accumulated a great number of additional questions and at least two new problems.

Chapter 7

At breakfast the next morning, the chatter at the student's end of the table was all about a second attempt that had been made to assault the princess. For an instant, I was confused since I had been there, and no one had attempted anything of the sort. Then the other shoe dropped.

They thought my visit to the princess was an attempt upon her person. The other girls were eagerly poring over the morning papers and exchanging tidbits of information. Overnight, my cohort also had concluded that I had been correct and there had been an attempted attack on the princess earlier as well. Not that there were any apologies forthcoming. That would have been too much to hope for.

"Listen to this," said Harriet, waving for Irene and Marianne's attention. She gave the newspaper a little snap and began to read. "A Division has refused to provide a statement citing their ongoing investigation, but this reporter spoke to an officer who claimed the would-be assailant was dressed as a female, possibly in order to throw off suspicion."

"Men are always so blind. What if the assailant was actually female?" Eleanor reached for Harriet's paper, and her acolyte meekly handed it over.

It was a good thing none of the students or the teachers

at the far end of the table were paying any attention to me. I could feel my cheeks going pink.

Marianne paused in buttering a scone. "Surely not."

"Well, why not. We've been trained to do such things."

"We have not." Irene sounded offended. "We have been trained to protect the queen and make sure no one has an opportunity to harm her. Not to sneak and spy."

Had we been attending the same school for the last six-and-a-half years?

"Besides." Irene thrust the paper at Eleanor. "I think the papers are just trying to be sensational. This article says the person, whoever it was, was outside and pounced upon an officer. No one who wanted to gain access to the palace in order to attack the princess would go about it that way. It sounds like some lunatic who has a grudge against the police."

"Why were they on palace grounds then?" Eleanor demanded.

"Why should it have anything to do with the princess when she wasn't present?"

Bravo, Irene. She rarely voiced disagreement with Eleanor.

Eleanor sniffed and tossed the paper aside. "I don't think it was a coincidence, and I'm going to ask Dame Guinevere to be allowed to enter our guard duties early."

"They'll never agree."

Surprised, I looked at Colleen as did all the other girls. She wasn't usually paying enough attention to the table conversation to take part. "The Praetorienne have fully-fledged members. If they believe the princess is in danger, they would dispatch someone with more experience. Not a bunch of students." Colleen's gaze flicked to me for the barest instant. "Besides, I tend to agree with Irene. Just because an altercation occurred on the grounds of Kensington Palace, doesn't mean it had anything to do with the princess. It could have been a lover's quarrel between the officer who was attacked and his ladylove. His colleagues may not have understood, and if he didn't want to confess..."

She really was the very best of friends.

I stood and moved to the end of the table to pick up one of the discarded papers. It would be interesting to know if the reporters had gotten anything correct. As I returned to my place, I spotted the seal on the top letter in Dame Guinevere's stack of correspondence and lost my appetite. It was from the Duchess of Kent. Once the hue and cry for me had been raised, the princess must have been questioned and revealed the details of my little visit.

Colleen's diversion had been a noble effort, but it could only accomplish so much.

My head ached as if the American's cab had run it over. In fact, I was acutely conscious that every inch of me felt as if it had been trampled, buried, dug up, and trampled again. I was sure I looked as ill as I had previously claimed to be.

Dame Guinevere's considering gaze weighed upon me longer than I would have liked.

I made an effort to act normally as I resumed my seat. Allowing not the faintest grimace to twist my lips, I reached for the marmalade.

Eleanor carried on as if Colleen had never spoken, enthralled by her own opinions. "I think it's shameful the way the police allowed this miscreant to escape, regardless of whether the individual meant to harm the princess. A person like that should never be allowed within her vicinity. It certainly lends all the justification we could ever need to our program of education. Although..." here she glanced in my direction, "when given the opportunity at the first, I'll admit we did not make best use of the chance to catch these blackguards, either. But we at least had the excuse of being incapacitated by gas."

"You are too kind." My voice was even drier than the largely untouched toast on my plate.

With a smile as smooth and chilly as iced cream Eleanor continued. "I do try to be fair, Portia dear. I'm sure none of us could have done better than you had we been so honored as to be at the princess's side at the critical moment." Her tone made it clear she thought the opposite.

I opened my mouth to retort, but Dame Guinevere forestalled me with a light clap of her hands. "Finish now, ladies. Master Nathaniel will be here momentarily, and I want everyone in proper dancing slippers. No clomping around in boots or walking shoes, if you please."

This was the signal for a general exodus, though most of us were already wearing slippers. I'd had to employ the maid mechanical to help in lacing my slippers and in dressing that morning. Mechanicals had been all the rage among the upper crust when they had first been deployed during the regency, but as the novelty had worn off and the price had come down, the fashion among the well-to-do had perversely shifted back to human attendants. Mechanicals were all well and good for out-of-the-way jobs, but if one could afford the wages of good upper servants one did.

The school employed two human lady's maids who were shared among the students. I didn't care much and would have used a mechanical all the time, except that Eleanor and Harriet were always hogging the maids' time, and it nettled me. But that morning, it had been all I could do to drag myself out of bed, and I couldn't risk Brigitte or Annie bearing tales back to Dame Guinevere about the multicolored bruises that had blossomed across my body overnight.

I gingerly sat in the only comfortable chair in our room and tried to devise a plot that would get me out of dancing. I normally quite enjoyed dancing, certainly more than learning a formula for knockout drops that could be derived from *eau de parfum* and carbolic, but the mere thought of it made me moan. I didn't know how I would keep up my pretense.

Colleen came in and settled herself on her bed. Her skirts puffed to perfection around her. She was the picture of genteel beauty until she let out a snort. "What was that all about do you suppose?"

"All what?"

"Guinevere's patent attempt to distract us and get us all out of the way quickly."

I gaped at her like a codfish, because, of course, that had been what the old girl had been about. I had simply been to ninny-witted to notice. "Why do you suppose?"

"That's what I just asked you."

"I haven't the foggiest." The gears in my mindbox finally started churning. "I'd wager it was a sudden thing. Her excuse was flimsy. Most of us weren't even done with breakfast. And it's no mistake that only the teachers have a decent view of the street from the morning room without craning their heads. I bet either a visitor had arrived or they were about to, and she wanted us all out of the way."

"But who do you think it is?"

I deflated a bit. "I haven't the foggiest."

Annie poked her face around the door. Her eyes were even wider than normal in her round, good-natured face. "Dame Guinevere and Lady Pomeroy sent me. You have a visitor, and they say for you to come smart like."

"A visitor?" I glanced at Colleen, and she shrugged. "Are

you sure you're supposed to fetch me and not one of the other girls?" I hadn't had a single visitor in all my years as a student.

"She asked for you specific, miss."

Carefully, I untucked my legs from under me and stood. "All right then, lead on."

Annie's nose quivered like a rabbit's, and her face turned red.

"What?" I demanded.

"Well, miss, it—you—that is, you might want to tidy up a bit before you go down."

I frowned at her, then looked in the glass. She had a point. My hair drooped, I had a smudge of something on my cheek, and my dress was thoroughly wrinkled. In short, I looked disreputable. But then who could possibly be visiting me that wouldn't expect me to look at least a little disreputable? In fact, who could be visiting me at all?

Annie pinned back up my errant locks. In the interest of time (Annie's reason) and secrecy (my reason), we decided against changing my gown. Colleen left reluctantly for dance class. I blessed this unexpected visitor for getting me out of that today at least. I figured the only likely culprit was a distant cousin who worked in the city. He might have felt it incumbent upon him to visit his titled cousin, now that she was in town.

Freshly scrubbed, I headed downstairs. I recalled almost nothing of my cousin Geoffrey. This meeting promised to be stilted.

The drawing room door was closed, and I had to tug hard on the heavy old handle to pull it open. Dame Guinevere set aside her teacup at my entrance. A man sat with his back to me.

Dame Guinevere smiled at me thinly. "Lady Portia, I believe you've met Sir John."

I froze.

The man stood and turned. A chilly smile lifted one corner of his mouth. "It's delightful to see you again, Lady Portia."

I didn't believe him for a second, but the social nicety activated my ingrained good manners. I approached and extended my hand for a brush of his lips. "Sir John, this is an unexpected pleasure."

I withdrew my hand from his grasp as quickly as polite, then settled into the seat beside Dame Guinevere, all the while shooting questions at her with my eyes.

Sir John reseated himself and crossed his legs. "It seems that the princess royal was quite taken with you." It should have sounded like a compliment. It didn't.

I accepted the cup of tea Dame Guinevere handed me. "I was quite taken with her as well. She is such an engaging personality." I smiled blandly. "And such charming manners."

Sir John's return smile was so artificial he looked for a moment like a mechanical. It really was no surprise that the princess disliked him. "The duchess would like to invite you to call upon her again."

Poppycock. The duchess had been all too relieved to see our backs. I looked to Dame Guinevere for guidance, but her expression was as neutral as Sir John's. "I will be delighted to attend the princess at any time she and Her Grace would desire."

"If you do well, there is the possibility of further connection." He rose and moved to the fireplace where he stood hands clasped behind his back as if in contemplation of the flames, though nothing was burning at the moment. "I need hardly tell you how beneficial this connection could be for your family."

My jaw tightened and so did my fist. He acted as if royal favor were his to bestow. Even worse, as if he knew of my family's straitened circumstances.

Careful to strip every hint of what I felt from my voice,

I said, "It is a signal honor. I am eager to do whatever is required."

He wheeled. "Excellent. Then I must make the expectations clear."

Whose expectations did he mean? I said nothing.

"Her highness's constitution is delicate. I do not wish her to be upset by difficult conversations or upsetting topics."

I nodded slowly, anger seething under my skin like lava boiling beneath a volcano.

"Following any and every visit with the princess you will report to me the substance of your conversations."

"To you? Not the duchess?"

He smiled thinly. "I have her utmost confidence, and she assigned this task to me as I am most able to judge what is best for the princess."

I choked back a hot rush of words and looked to Dame Guinevere for help.

Her tone was as neutral as her expression. "Thank you, Sir John. It appears your requirements are admirably clear."

"Good. We shall expect your visit tomorrow afternoon." He pulled out a pocket watch and glanced at it. "I must dash. Good afternoon, Dame Guinevere, Lady Portia." He gave us both a punctuated bow and hurried from the room before Dame Guinevere could ring for a footman to show him out.

When the door had closed behind him, I collapsed back in my chair. I stared at Dame Guinevere. "I have no intention of spying for that man."

"Of course not." Unperturbed as ever, she raised her teacup to her lips. "But you must give the appearance of compliance, or he shall shut you out." She paused ever so slightly. "And I shall require reports of both your encounters with the princess and what you report to Sir John."

I sighed. This was not going to be easy.

Dame Guinevere apparently read my thoughts. "Nothing worth doing is easy."

If she only knew.

She excused me, and I achily dragged myself up the main staircase toward dancing class. The front bell sounded, and I paused on the landing to see who it could be. The Hall's butler, Larkin, answered the door to a fellow wearing a tweed jacket and bowler.

To Larkin's raised eyebrow, he tipped his hat. "I'm from A Division. A..." he consulted a slip of paper, "Dame Guinevere asked that I call about the attack on the princess."

I perked up. A Division was the unit of Scotland Yard assigned to the security of the royal family. This fellow spoke well and, interestingly, he hadn't called at the servants' entrance.

Larkin sniffed. I happened to know that he wasn't nearly as stick-in-the-muddish as he was acting, but he gave a good appearance. "Please wait here. I will see if Dame Guinevere can receive you now."

As Larkin turned to go, the inspector glanced up. I hurriedly pulled back and headed regretfully to dancing class.

There was a great deal to think about. Did Dame Guinevere intend to tell the inspector about the first attack on the princess and the fear there was a kidnapping scheme in the works. If she did, she'd probably turn the perfume diffuser over to him as well. I hoped we had gleaned everything we could from that source and wouldn't need it again.

Then there was Conroy's visit and request, no, make that his demand. His high-handedness was aggravating. Juggling regular reports to him and Dame Guinevere would be challenging, especially when I wanted to draw as little attention to myself as possible.

But as I turned the situation over in my mind, I noted definite bright spots. The princess had not snitched on me. She had kept our secret, which to my way of thinking meant she wanted me to complete her commission. Beyond that, my access to her and Kensington Palace had been unaccountably smoothed. I had to chalk that up to her wiles. She had understood that I would need a chance to investigate the goings-on at the palace in order to determine whether Conroy or anyone else was behind the kidnapping attempt. She had given me something to work with, but I had a feeling that formidable young woman also would be expecting updates on my progress and swift work.

Aside from Conroy himself, my only glimmer of a clue lay in Butterleigh Close. Much as I felt like crawling beneath the bedclothes and sleeping for a month, I would have to investigate today.

I considered my options. Following dancing, codes, and French, we were going to be shuttled off to the Chelsea Physic Garden for a botany lesson from Lady Pomeroy—the only woman I know who can make even poison seem frilly and girlish. Colleen would certainly allow me to copy her notes afterward, but it would be risky to slip away. Lady Pomeroy would likely call on me to answer some question, and my absence would be noted immediately. And that was assuming I managed to slip away unobserved in the first place. After this excursion we were scheduled to attend a lecture on some new archaeological discovery at the British Museum. I let the facts percolate in my mind. Yes, that would be my best chance.

I needed to talk to Colleen.

Chapter 8

It was all I could do to stroll sedately through the Apothecaries' Garden. My sketches were more than a little flurried and my notes were practically nonexistent. The whole was proceeding far too slowly for my tastes, although I was sore enough to be grateful that I was not obliged to do any running, jumping, or climbing. A sedate stroll wasn't the worst thing that could happen.

After a lengthy lesson on poisons and remedies, many of which were also poisons if improperly dosed, we were shepherded to the nearest flying train station and the day began to improve. We climbed up to the platform, and while we waited for the next car, I leaned over the rail to see all I could of the city life spread out like a living tapestry at our feet.

As the car chuffed into the station, we were advised to mind the gap by the mechanical attendant who wore a jaunty blue conductor's cap and vest. Before boarding, each passenger had to hand over a ticket of heavy stock paper with holes punched in one end. The mechanical fed this into a slot in his chest which somehow told him that ticket's validity and destination. He then handed the ticket back to the passenger and allowed them to board.

It would be handy to have one of the tickets that allowed for an unlimited number of trips during a month.

The car swayed slightly as I boarded. I took a seat on a wooden bench next to a window, and Colleen soon joined me. Away to our right, the Thames lay sullen and windblown, as if simply waiting for the rainstorm promised by steel gray skies. Then we rounded a curve and headed north. We disembarked at the Montague Place Station practically on the doorstep of the British Museum. Dame Guinevere was always admirably efficient. The flying train was much faster than driving through the clogged city streets, and it made it feel more like an outing than another steam carriage ride ever would have.

The museum was a bit dingy in the afternoon's feeble light. We filed up the stairs behind Dame Guinevere, feathers and frills fluttering all the way. Nothing could have looked less threatening.

We were ushered to our seats, and Colleen and I maneuvered so that we sat at the end of the row. The moment before the lights were dimmed for the presentation, I stood. Dame Guinevere sat at the far end of the row, and I signaled that I was going to use the facilities. She gave a stiff nod, no doubt unhappy about the request but unwilling to make an issue of it.

I strode away. Time was of the essence. Colleen would take care of her part of this caper. If I knew anything about these lectures, it was that time passed much slower within the lecture hall than it did in the rest of the world. Butterleigh Close was in Clerkenwell, about a mile away. I all but flew through a side door of the museum and down the street into the fading daylight. It still took me a good ten minutes to wend my way to Mahlenbeau's workshop.

The street on which I found myself was a generation removed from gentility. From the amount of rubbish in the lane, the street cleaning mechs had not been through the area in weeks. Among all the shabby shops and peeling paint, Mahlenbeau's establishment shone like a new penny. A gleaming front window glowed from within and a well-crafted sign hung over the door, the letters deep and painted with gilt to stand out. I could see a man inside, working at a counter covered by bits of machinery.

I pushed through the door and a small bell chimed.

The workman glanced up, the light winking off the elaborate monocle he wore. It made his eye look enormous. "Good evening, miss. How may I help you?"

"Are you Mr. Mahlenbeau?"

"Certainly." He gave his head a slight incline and politely removed his monocle, placing it squarely within a chalk outline of the device.

In fact, everything on the counter had been placed in precise outlines, from the bits of metal he was working with to the tools lined up beside him. This man valued precision.

I decided to change my plan of attack. "Yes, sir. I was hoping you could help me identify a recent customer of yours. He came to you to have a perfume diffuser modified."

He studied me. "I believe I know who you mean. A gentleman from A Division was here earlier inquiring about the same customer."

Drat it all. That was certainly quick work on their part. It confirmed that Dame Guinevere had handed over the diffuser though. Unencumbered by the need for subterfuge since they had arrived before me, I tried for a smile. "Yes, sir. That is likely the same man. Would you have any objection to telling me about him too?"

"Perhaps." He regarded me steadily. "I do not know you."

"Is there something I can say to reassure you?"

He gave me another long speculative look. "Would you care for some tea?"

My gaze sought the clock mounted on the wall behind him. I didn't want to offend him, but... "I am, unfortunately, pressed for time."

A beatific smile touched his lips. "I'm glad. I hate the ritual of tea. It is an inefficient use of time." He straightened a screwdriver that sat askew in its outline. "I will make you a deal. If you will tell me what this is all about, I will tell you what I know of my customer."

"The police didn't tell you?"

"Refused to tell me a blessed thing."

"Oh." It was my turn to study him. Then I turned to examine his shop. Everything had a place and everything was in its place. There was nary a cobweb or a neglected corner. Despite that, objects abounded. There was simply order to the madness. He took pride in his work and his workplace but knew how to hoard things too. Perhaps he would do the same with information. "If I tell you, could you keep it secret?"

He spread his hands. "I have few friends. Who would I tell?"

"The temptation will be great."

"You intrigue me." He did not continue to protest his trustworthiness.

I decided to take him at his word. I explained briefly that there had been an attempted abduction of a highborn young lady. Even if he tried to sell the story to the papers, it would be difficult to cause too much of a sensation. The princess would simply be produced and the story could be denied or exploited as the powers that be saw fit.

I could see him putting the pieces together with his visit from A Division and drawing conclusions about the identity of the potential kidnap victim. "I see. That explains why an aristocratic young woman might also be requesting information."

It was my turn to play enigmatic. I considered showing him

the signet ring which I had strung on a chain and hung around my neck but decided against using it unless I absolutely had to do so.

He tapped the side of his nose. "What do you wish to know?"

"Did you get a name?"

He raised an amused eyebrow. "Mr. Smith."

"Can you describe him?"

"Average height and weight. Late twenties to mid-thirties. Fair coloring. He was dressed respectably, not extravagantly."

"When did he first visit your shop?"

"Ten days ago."

"And when did he pick up the altered device?"

"A week ago."

So, he'd had the device for a couple of days before finding an opportunity to deploy it. I cast about for something else reasonably intelligent to ask. "How did this gentleman speak?"

Mahlenbeau nodded. I seemed to be going down a list he'd already established in his head. "He sounded educated."

"Accent?"

"Good question. One the police did not ask." He pushed his lips together. His eyes grew distant for a moment. "He spoke precisely. It's possible he was concealing his natural accent, but I couldn't say for sure."

It was the first time he had been anything less than definite in his response. I filed it away. "Was there anything out of the ordinary about him?"

Now he smiled. "Two things in fact. The first was that he carried an elaborate walking stick. The head was figured into a three-towered castle in red enamel. I noticed it because it looked like it would be uncomfortable to use. One certainly wouldn't want to lean on it."

"A castle?"

"In a medieval style with crenellations. The center tower was higher than the others. It could serve only a decorative purpose. He didn't seem to carry it for any reason but ornamentation. He was not infirm in any way."

I nodded, mulling this over. I couldn't think of any three-towered castles offhand. Most medieval castles were square with a tower in each corner. Mr. Mahlenbeau let me muse.

After a moment's woolgathering I shook my head. "What was the second thing?"

"A ruby ring."

"He was wearing a ring?"

"No, not wearing it. It was in his pocket. He had removed his gloves to examine a piece of machinery and when he drew them back out of his pocket, the ring came with them. Made an enormous clunk when it landed on the counter and disrupted my workspace." He made a gesture at the small tools, gears, and so on arrayed before him.

"Was it gold?"

"Yes."

"Engraved?"

He nodded.

"Did you recognize the insignia?"

"I'm afraid not."

"Did you have the completed diffuser delivered?" It was a long shot but perhaps he had given an address.

"He picked it up."

"Did he pay in ready money or ask to be billed?"

"He paid when he picked up the device."

There went the chance of finding another address for this fellow. I was running out of things to ask. The fellow had obviously taken pains to cover his identity. Except for that walking stick.

"Is there anything else you can remember about your dealings with the man? Did he arrive on foot?"

He raised a long, thin finger. "Ah, yes. He did arrive on foot."

My shoulders began to slump.

"But only because his carriage had been parked at the end of the lane. I don't know why he chose to walk the last few blocks."

I had a guess. "Did you notice anything about the vehicle?"

"It was a steam rig hired from a livery owner I know. I recognized his mark on the back, and I've done work for him in the past."

In a trice, I gathered the livery owner's name and place of business. Maybe he would have more information about this all-too-average customer.

After thanking Mr. Mahlenbeau profusely for his assistance, I exited the shop and headed rapidly toward the British Museum. It would be just my luck to have the first ever short-winded lecturer when I had been compelled to sneak away.

As I glided along, mindful of Dame Guinevere's instructions on ladylike bearing, I turned over the information Mr. Mahlenbeau had imparted. What could that cane have meant? Why carry such an ostentatious article when so careful to make everything else about oneself neutral?

Could the castle emblem point to someone with a connection to royalty? Perhaps it had some other meaning. Was there a reason it was red?

As I wrestled with this somewhat futile speculation, I became aware that I was being followed. Had I not been preoccupied, I would have noticed sooner as, despite my rush,

I was taking the usual precautions, pausing to glance in shop windows, and so on.

The fellow following me was dressed inconspicuously in a dark gray suit and black felt hat. I might never have noticed him except he was quite tall and strutted with square-shouldered confidence in a street where most people walked hunched, with their heads lowered against the wind.

I flicked my wrist and palmed the tiny, scalpel-sharp knife that I stored in my right sleeve. As I passed a woman carrying her string bag of produce home from the grocer's, I casually brushed up against it. Two steps later, the poor woman realized her sack had inexplicably split on her as a cabbage and three potatoes tumbled to the ground.

The woman let out a cry and scrabbled to collect the items which only caused her to lose other things and send them skittering out of her reach. Several gentlemen stopped to help her creating an effective roadblock, while a street urchin grabbed up a potato and legged it.

I ducked into an alley, darted around a corner and into a side entrance. Pushing my way past a pair of startled millinery assistants huddled over their workbenches, I plunged through the workroom, slipped out to the shop, and from there out the front door.

I returned to the same street, but this time behind my would-be follower. I paused in the doorway. The man was peering suspiciously into the alley I'd just vacated.

The lady with the vegetables passed me going in the opposite direction. One of the men who had stopped had her wayward produce piled high in his arms and strolled beside her. They were deeply engaged in conversation, his head bent attentively toward hers.

Smiling, I decided that I didn't need to feel guilty for my trick with the knife after all.

My quarry gave a quick glance up and down the street. He made up his mind and headed into the alley.

I followed.

Quiet as a wraith I crept up behind him and jabbed the end of my parasol into his back. "Don't make a move."

He groaned. Not like a man in pain, though. More like a schoolboy who had been bested in a game of hide-and-seek.

I gave him another jab. "Hands up, please."

"All right. All right."

I blinked. That American accent sounded suspiciously familiar. "Who are you and why are you following me?"

"Following y—"

"Don't bother denying it."

He sighed and began to turn. "Miss, I'm afraid you've made a mista—"

I planted the tip of my parasol at the base of his neck which arrested his movement nicely. "Either you tell me the truth right now, or your head is going to be separated from the rest of you. I'm growing impatient."

"You are charming, aren't you? What sort of young lady are you anyway?"

"The sort who is asking the questions."

"Well, we could have started this interview off much more pleasantly. For example, you could have thanked me for my help last evening."

"I don't know what you're talking about." I used my very best simper, even though it was lost on him since he had his back to me. "I'm an ordinary helpless schoolgirl."

He snorted. "And I'm the Archbishop of Canterbury."

"I really don't want to have to kill you."

"Then we've found at least one point we can agree on whole-heartedly." He was far too casual about my threats, and I didn't like it.

"Where are you from?"

"Toronto."

Not an American then, a colonial from Upper Canada. That was interesting, although I didn't know what it might mean. "Did you follow me from my school?"

He hesitated. "Yes."

"Why?"

"I understood that you thwarted an attempted kidnapping on the princess royal."

"Why would you think that?"

A shrug. "It's my business to know. I'm a reporter."

"For what paper?"

"Freelance."

"Pish. Tell me the truth. Who do you represent?"

"Before I forget, that trick with the woman's shopping was very slick. Quite effective. I never suspected a thing. Thought you'd only taken advantage of the situation, right up until you got the drop on me."

"Flatterer. Now who—"

A sharp gun-like report came from the right, and I jerked my parasol around to face the threat as if I could actually fire back. There was nothing there, but in the second I was distracted, he was gone. I might have chased him, but I doubted I would get anything out of him, and I needed to get back to the museum. I bent and picked up a small twist of paper. Partially blackened, a wisp of smoke still rose from it. I took a sniff. Gunpowder and something else. I pocketed the little squib for Colleen to examine later. It would be a handy device for my arsenal if she could figure out how to replicate it.

The interview hadn't been very productive, although, it did confirm others were watching the royal goings-on. And rather concerningly, my own doings.

But why a colonial?

I pondered this as I hurried to the museum, but had come to no satisfactory answers by the time I arrived. I wasn't even sure I was asking the right questions.

I paused at the rear of the lecture hall to catch my breath. From a distance, I admired Colleen's tissue paper construct of me. She'd explained its principles—something about the Japanese art of paper folding. Ori—something or other. I was less interested in the origins of the device, than its results, and from where I sat, it provided a lifelike replica of me in shadow to anyone who didn't look very closely. As we'd planned, in the final moments before the houselights were brought up again, Colleen collapsed the decoy.

As the gaslights flared to light and everyone blinked, I swooped in and reclaimed my seat. Our timing was slightly off as I ended up sitting on the remains of the decoy, but not so off that anyone remarked my absence.

Colleen and I stood and followed our classmates from the hall at a dignified pace and with our hands folded primly in front of us. Like the animals trailing onto Noah's ark, we all marched two by two to the flying train. As I was waiting at the end of the line to board, someone tapped my shoulder, and I turned.

"A fascinating lecture, wouldn't you say, Lady Portia?" Dame Guinevere's glacial expression was cold enough to freeze the blood in my veins.

"I certainly would, ma'am."

"I was pleased to see you so attentive for once. Usually, you have such a deplorable habit of fidgeting." She cocked her head and gave me a long look.

"Yes, ma'am. Thank you." I swallowed.

"Well?"

"What, ma'am?"

She raised an eyebrow. "I believe it's your turn to board. You're holding up the queue."

I hurried after Colleen.

Dame Guinevere suspected. She definitely suspected. Then again, she'd be a very poor teacher if she didn't suspect her students of something at all times.

What I needed to do was give her something relatively harmless to suspect me of.

Chapter 9

"So Conroy thinks I'm spying for him, but I'll actually be spying for the princess and feeding him misinformation, while I also investigate him for the kidnapping attempt." An interminable dinner had finally wrapped up, and Colleen and I had retreated to our room for the evening. Or at least until it was dark enough to go in search of more answers. I continued musing. "His daughter, Louisa, could potentially have come up with the scheme on her own if the princess is right about the motive. Or, I hate to say it, the duchess could have. She desperately wants her daughter to reconcile with Conroy. And I still need to figure out what Upper Canada could have to do with any of this."

"You ought to write it all down. It's becoming a lot to keep track of." Trust Colleen to recommend taking notes in any given situation.

I sighed. "So that Dame Guinevere or Eleanor can find it? No, thank you. First things first. What shall I use as my decoy infraction?"

Colleen considered. "Knowing Dame Guinevere, it won't be enough to have a single decoy. You'll need a decoy for your decoy."

I gnawed on my fingernail. "You're right. She'll never settle for the easy answer. She'd keep digging."

"As she's taught us to do."

"Wouldn't she be proud if she knew. We ought to be earning extra credit." I grinned and flipped in my bed so that my head hung over the side and my legs stretched above me against the wall. I needed all the blood flow to my brain I could get in order to scheme.

"The obvious decoy would be a beau."

"Do you think she'd believe it? Besides, wouldn't I need to have some sort of male in the picture to do that justice?"

"If it's the first decoy, she wouldn't have to believe it. In fact, if there's no believable male, it will allow her to discard decoy one and focus on your true misdeeds sooner."

"And what shall my true misdeeds be?"

"Don't take this the wrong way, but with you she's apt to believe almost anything."

"Actually, I will take that as high praise."

"You would." Colleen leaned forward and extended the box of bonbons she'd been picking through.

I accepted one as an aid to creativity.

She was sitting cross-legged on her bed. Around her, as usual, sat piles of books. I'd come to think of books as Colleen's version of armor. Without one close at hand, she felt vulnerable. "I suppose treason is out?"

I spoke around the sticky sweet. "Right out. I do still want to graduate."

"All right. I had to ask."

"Not every thought must be voiced." I quoted Dame Guinevere with relish.

Colleen threw a pillow at me. Which, given the vulnerability of my position, was quite unfair. "Perhaps not treason, but what if you let her believe you are getting orders from someone else?"

"Who could that be? I mean, that isn't going to get me chucked out of school?"

"Only two possible people."

I swallowed. "The king or queen?"

"Precisely. You could make it look as if you were investigating on their behalf."

"But Dame Guinevere is never going to believe that they would commission me directly. I haven't been presented to the court yet, and why would they go to a student when they must have access to all the fully trained Praetorienne? Besides, they wouldn't know me from Adam. My parents were never courtiers."

"But they are aware of our school and what we do. And you hold two trumps. One, we were there at the behest of his majesty when you foiled the kidnapping."

"Yes?"

"And two, the princess asked for you. So, you have access to that very small circle of hers that others would have great difficulty penetrating." She grinned, very satisfied with herself. "Ooh, and didn't you once tell me that your mother and the queen were cousin of some sort?"

"A very distant relationship."

"Doesn't matter. Blood is blood. That will be a third point for you."

"But we have no evidence of such a commission."

"If we can manufacture a whole love interest," Colleen said, "it shouldn't be too difficult to fake some convincing evidence that you have been called upon by the highest authorities. I'm thinking of some mostly burned correspondence to begin with."

"The brilliance of this scheme is that it's nearly true. I am investigating by royal request, just not the queen or king's."

"And when you're caught, as you inevitably will be, you *may* avoid expulsion for disobeying a direct order."

"You inspire me, Colleen, you really do." I righted myself, nabbed another bonbon, and popped it in my mouth then licked my fingers.

"I have some news of my own." Her smile was small but proud.

She had my full attention. "You do?"

"This afternoon I searched Lady Pomeroy's quarters."

I gaped. "You...what?"

"You know as well as I do that she would have tested the drug that was used before giving the device to A Division."

She was correct.

"I found her notes and the drug was a distillation of poppies."

"Like opium?"

Colleen nodded. "Very similar."

"Interesting. What does it tell us?"

"Well, it suggests that the attackers weren't trying to kill anyone with the drug. They must have had a targeted purpose. I believe it supports the hypothesis that this was a kidnapping attempt."

It was my turn to nod. "So, we are on the right path?"

"We seem to be."

I grinned.

"What?"

"I can't believe you broke into Lady Pomeroy's quarters. I'm so proud of you."

She looked around. Probably for another pillow to throw.

Before she could find a suitable missile, I changed the subject. "Did you have any luck at the library figuring out what the three-towered castle might mean?"

"Not so far." She gestured to the books around her. "I borrowed a few references so we could keep looking."

I refrained from groaning or sighing. I loathed research, though I knew it was necessary, and it wasn't fair to expect Colleen to do it all, even though she loved it. Colleen tossed me a book from her pile, and I grunted when I caught it. It was heavier than it looked.

I flipped through pages listlessly, my mind whirling far too much to focus on the words properly. I gave up after several minutes and turned to the index. No mention of castles with three towers or otherwise. I gladly set the book aside, but Colleen was ready for me and tossed me another.

I yawned. It was clearly going to be a long night.

I was on book four or five when Colleen gave a little squeal. I immediately cast my book aside. "What've you got?"

"All right, listen to this." Her face was aglow with the light of discovery. "The three-towered castle is a symbol of Gibraltar."

"Gibraltar? Why would someone from Gibraltar bear a grudge against the princess?"

Colleen didn't answer right away, as she was busy rooting through her piles of books. "Here it is," she said at last, holding up a very large flat volume.

"What is it?"

"It's a bound copy of all the *London Times* for the month of January in 1803." She was turning pages gleefully. "The princess has led such a sheltered and inoffensive life that I figured whoever was behind the kidnapping either wanted money, championed a political cause, or held a grudge. If it was the latter, then it might be a grudge against her parents rather than her."

I moved to sit beside her.

"Here's the first article." Her fingers traced along the lines of newsprint. "Victoria's father was appointed the Governor of Gibraltar in 1802. According to the *Times*, it was because there was a complete lack of discipline among the troops stationed there at the time. So, Mad King George charged Edward, the Duke of Kent, with putting things in order. Edward made a mess of things though, coming in too heavy-handed. He put in place more than a hundred and fifty new regulations overnight. Men were flogged for the smallest infractions. A few even died due to the severity of the beatings. Then three men were hanged because they were suspected of theft."

I leaned over so I could peer at the woodcutting of the Duke of Kent from the article she was summarizing. He had been a portly man with a receding hairline and a hooked nose, but that hadn't restrained him from wearing the flashiest military regalia with about six-dozen medals and ribbons adorning the jacket.

"Finally, on Christmas Eve, the Royal Scots showed up and demanded that he listen to their grievances. Another regiment came to the duke's defense and they clashed. One of the Royal Scots was shot and died. They eventually dispersed, but the next day, another Scottish regiment went rampaging through the town. They didn't get the support they needed from other units for their mutiny, so they returned to their barracks, but not before two of them were killed."

"What happened next?"

Colleen turned the page. "Court martial. Twelve men were sentenced to death and a couple of others to floggings." She winced. "A thousand lashes each."

"Can someone survive a thousand lashes?"

She shrugged. "The duke commuted nine of the death sentences to transportation to Australia."

"Not a happy fate, either." I nibbled my lower lip. "You think one of the old mutineers would be seeking revenge on the dead duke by kidnapping his daughter?"

"Not when you put it that way."

"They'd have to be in their sixties or more by now."

She brightened. "What if it's not one of the mutineers? What if it's someone related to one of those who was killed or punished for the mutiny?"

"A son or something?" I considered. "It's possible. I have to make sure that I don't focus on Conroy to the exclusion of all other possibilities. With the king ailing, they may not want the daughter of their nemesis to claim the throne."

It all came back to that: not what the princess was now, but what she would be soon. In a matter of days, she'd turn eighteen. If the king died after that she would be queen in her own right. There would be no regency that would allow the duchess to rule in her place.

Maybe that had something to do with why Conroy would try kidnapping the princess. What would happen if she was in the clutches of villains at the time of a transfer of power? Would a regency be established to ensure the continuation of government until she was either recovered or they knew that she was dead or something?

When I asked, Colleen didn't know the answer either. She made a note to look at some dusty old legal books. "Of course, if Victoria dies without issue, the British throne would go to the next in line, which right now, is her uncle Ernest, the Duke of Cumberland."

I sat upright. "He's the one who murdered his valet."

"Allegedly. There's not really any evidence it was him, and he received serious injuries in that attack."

"Everyone knows the verdict made no sense, though." I

thought about swiping another candy, but decided against it. "There's no way that valet committed suicide by slitting his own throat."

Colleen rolled her eyes. "It could have been a mechanical at his command. That's ancient history anyway. Now, focus."

"There's also the convenient death of his wife's first husband."

This elicited a full-blown sigh. "If we go by your rumor-mongering, wouldn't it make more sense for Victoria to have been assassinated rather than kidnapped? The only way he inherits is if she's dead."

"Ah, but Ernest is the most hated man in England. If Victoria died in mysterious circumstances the Whigs would try to blame him for sure."

"Then why risk it?"

"He may not care so much for himself as for his son, George's, future."

"He did originally hope George and Victoria would form a marriage alliance. But when George had that accident and was made blind, Prince Ernest seemed to relinquish the idea that he could tempt Victoria in that direction. Maybe he proceeded to Plan B."

For some reason, now that she was giving the idea serious consideration, I felt compelled to point out its weakness. "But if King William dies, Ernest will become king of Hanover because their laws don't allow a female to inherit the throne. He will have a crown of his own without resorting to kidnapping or murder." I scrunched up my nose. "Also, why would an agent of Ernest's have a cane with an emblem of Gibraltar on it?"

"Maybe it was meant to be noticeable in order to lay a false trail. And Great Britain's crown is a much bigger fish to fry than Hanover," Colleen shot back.

I bit my lower lip to keep from breaking out in a grin. It wasn't often that Colleen got agitated enough to mix her metaphors that badly.

She could tell what I was thinking and bopped me with a pillow. "Or it could just as easily be anarchists who want to disrupt the government, Irish rebels, or merely a criminal gang that wanted her for ransom."

"We are suffering from an excess of suspects."

"We need data. We must know more in order to eliminate anyone."

I stood and rolled my neck. "I'm on it."

Chapter 10

That night, I only took a few twists and turns to shake my pursuer. I reckoned by how easy it was to lose him that it wasn't the colonial tonight. He was far more tenacious. I made my way to the livery stable and took measures to shake any tails I hadn't spotted. By the time I arrived, I was fairly certain no one could have followed.

In the murky light of a gas lamp, I checked the address. This was definitely the place. All locked up for the night, and everyone had gone home for the evening. Which was to say, no one to interview. I should have found a way to come in the day. If I hadn't had to escape the attentions of Dame Guinevere at every turn in order to investigate, I probably would have already figured out who was behind all this. I sighed. One day, I would have more independence.

All right, when in doubt, reconnoiter. I made a careful circuit around the building. No lights shone anywhere and none of the ground floor windows were unlocked. But behind the building that fronted the street and which I decided must be the office was a courtyard and a larger building.

That would be where the carriages were housed. As I stared at the dark windows of the office wondering whether it would be worthwhile to break in on the chance of finding some sort of paperwork, a soft whickering drifted from the direction of the courtyard. I straightened. The company must keep horses and old-fashioned carriages available for more traditional clients. And if there were horses, there was probably a groom to care for them.

Light dawned both figuratively and literally. A glimmer of light trickled from a crack at the bottom of the stable door. Good. That meant someone was here, and I wasn't waking them. Grinning, I marched up to it and knocked.

Then knocked again.

A scowling face popped out. The man was tall, with close cropped somewhat greasy hair, and a nose that looked like someone had flattened it in a fight. "Yeah, what's it?"

"Good evening. I need to ask you some questions about a recent customer."

At the sound of my voice, the suspicious squint vanished. The fellow opened the door wider, lounged against the doorframe and tucked his hands up under his armpits. I think the smirk he adopted was meant to be charming. It was really no wonder that crime was rampant in the city. If a female voice was all it took to make a man drop his guard, it was a wonder that more people weren't robbed blind nightly. "What do you wanna know?"

"I want to know about a man who rented a carriage about a week ago. He was driven to Butterleigh Close but let down at the end of the street." I described the unusual cane he had carried.

A slow smile spread across his face. "It so happens that I might have been the fellow who drove that bloke. How much is it worth to you?"

Why did I have the sudden sense that I was the one about to be robbed? "I have a shilling."

He shook his head with a sad smile, like I'd told a tired old joke.

I considered my options. We had been taught a variety of techniques for getting information out of people, but while I would have enjoyed wiping that smile off his face, I was in a hurry. "Half a crown is the best I can do."

He scrunched his lips up while he considered, then shrugged and held out a hand.

I dropped the coin into his palm.

He moved away from the door. "All right. Come on in."

He led me inside to a small table where someone had been interrupted in a game of patience. The door was at the end of the building and opened onto a small living area. A couple of cupboards graced the back wall beside which stood a small pot-bellied stove and, standing in the corner behind a half-closed curtain, a cot covered in rumpled blankets. Stretching away in the other direction a line of three stables stood in an orderly row, beyond those the old-fashioned carriages, and finally the steam carriages.

He gestured me to the other chair at the table. Then he reclaimed what had clearly been his seat and pulled the cards toward him, stacking them into a neat pile and shuffling them. "So, what do you want to know?"

"Anything you can tell me about the man."

He kept shuffling. "He was about average, I'd say."

"Average?"

"Yeah."

"How old was he?"

"Oh, uh." He paused briefly in his shuffling. "He wasn't old and he wasn't young. Maybe in his thirties or thereabout."

After careful questioning the picture that emerged was similar to the one Mr. Mahlenbeau had painted.

"Was there anything at all unusual about him?"

"Well, he had that cane."

"We established that."

"He talked kind of funny."

I perked up. "What do you mean? He had an accent?" I had a hard time imagining a world where this fellow would have picked up on something the old clockwork maker had missed. But he also described a man less prosperous than the picture painted by Mr. Mahlenbeau. To the point that he'd made the fellow pay up front.

He started laying out the cards in front of him. "It wasn't an accent really. More like, he mixed in foreign words sometimes when he was talking."

"Did you recognize the language at all?"

"I think it was Spanish maybe."

"What made you think that?"

"I knew a Spaniard once. When he talked his foreign lingo, it sounded like this fellow."

"Did you take him anywhere besides Butterleigh Close?"

"Just where he had me let him down after he was done."

"Where was that?"

"Scarlet Lane. In front of number twelve."

I culled through my mental map. "That's a fairly poor part of the city, isn't it?"

He shrugged. "None of my business."

"Was the address a house or a business of some kind?"

"It was a house. He said he was renting the garret room."

None of this was adding up. Why would someone trying to hide his identity, provide that kind of information?

"He told you that?"

"That's what he said."

Now that I thought about it, why hadn't the fellow simply

hired a cab? Usually, a livery service would be used by people who wanted to drive themselves or had several stops and wanted a price for the whole day. Why go to the trouble of hiring a driver from a livery service for a single trip if he was trying to remain anonymous? Why not just take the flying train? It would be far more anonymous and much cheaper.

This story had more holes in it than Irish lace.

My informant laid his cards down and reached across the table to brush the back of my hand. "You know, you could have your money back if you wanted to trade in kind."

I snatched my hand away. "I don't think so."

"Come on now. There's no call to be like that."

I stood, and he stood as well.

"Good evening." I gave him a brief nod. "I'll be leaving now."

He reached for my arm but I evaded his grasp and moved toward the door.

"I say you ought to stay." He grabbed my arm and jerked me back against him.

I spun in his grip, my free hand wrapping around his wrist. In an instant, I was standing behind him, with his arm twisted behind his back.

He grunted and attempted to move.

I pulled up on his arm, demonstrating why that was a very bad idea, and elicited a little gasp. "All right. All right. I was only trying to be friendly."

"Friendly, is respecting a lady's no." I gave his arm another tweak.

"All right." His voice was growing breathless.

"I think I deserve a refund for my inconvenience."

He muttered something inarticulate, but with his free hand fished in his pocket for the half crown I had given him earlier.

He held it up, and I snatched it from him. Then with my forearm administered a sharp blow to his neck.

He crumpled to the ground.

I let myself out, tucking the coin away. *Waste not, want not.*

The great oaf would wake in a few minutes with a headache and, hopefully, a new lesson burned indelibly into his consciousness.

I, meanwhile, had a new lead in number twelve Scarlet Lane. I didn't think for a moment that I'd find all the answers I sought there, but someone had gone to a great deal of trouble to lay a trail to the place. It would be rude not to at least take a look.

Chapter 11

Upon arriving at Kensington Palace the next afternoon, we were ushered into a sort of receiving room, made our curtsies, and took prim seats across from Baroness Lezhen and Victoria. Dame Guinevere exchanged meaningless pleasantries and society gossip with the baroness for an eon. I wondered if it was possible to get a cramp in one's cheeks from smiling too much.

Realizing I was committing the great sin of fidgeting, I released the fabric of my skirt, which I had been pleating. As I raised my gaze, the princess caught my eye and gave an infinitesimal shrug.

I had things I needed to talk to her about. Being so near and yet unable to speak was exceedingly trying. Dame Guinevere could not have devised a more vexing exam if she had tried. I glanced at that lady as I thought this. Surely this wasn't…No. Ridiculous. We were here at Conroy's behest, which is the very thing I needed to discuss with the princess.

Restless, I turned my head, taking in the room in detail.

A chess set on a little side table near the window grabbed my attention. It wasn't strictly proper for me to invite the princess to a match. It was her prerogative to initiate a game if she chose.

As Dame Guinevere recounted some amusing anecdote for

the baroness, I caught Victoria's eye and tilted my head toward the table twice. Her brow furrowed.

"Do you care for chess, Your Highness?"

Her lips popped apart then she smiled. "Enough, although I find stimulating conversation even more to my liking."

I nodded like I was just being polite.

Her smile broadened into a positive grin. "Lady Portia, would you care to play a game of chess?"

I agreed instantly, and we moved away from the prying ears of our respective guardians.

The princess sat with a graceful movement. "Do you prefer white or black?" On the side of the table away from the others she held something out to me.

"Either, Your Highness." I reached for it and touched smooth metal. I looked down surprised.

The princess smiled. "Yours, I think?"

It was indeed. I closed my fingers over the folding grappling hook and spider line I had used to scale the palace. She'd had the presence of mind to retrieve and hide them before any investigators arrived.

I took the items as if she'd given me a precious gift and shoved the hook into one of the concealed pockets in my skirt. I had been worried about it somehow leading back to me or Colleen, but had concluded nothing could be done. Now, I was in the clear...for that infraction at least. "Sir John Conroy paid me a visit yesterday."

Her mischievous grin flattened and she raised an eyebrow and moved a pawn in her opening gambit.

"Ostensibly, he came on behalf of the duchess to invite me to become better acquainted with you." Paying little attention to the game, I moved my knight out.

"Ostensibly?"

Quickly, I explained that he wanted me to befriend her then act as a spy for him.

The princess's face went pasty white except for two spots of furious red in her cheeks. Her eyes bored into me.

"I accepted." I wound up my report in record time. "I thought we could use the opportunity to turn the tables on him. But I will rescind my acceptance, if you prefer."

"No." The word was clipped short like the end had been bitten off. "He would try to use my few friends as spies against me. How dare he!" She too kept her voice low, but its vehemence made me look to the older ladies to ensure we weren't drawing undo attention.

"Is there anything particular you want me to learn?"

Her approximation of a smile held no humor. "Everything. If he was behind that attempt, I want to know so that I can crush him with it."

"There is more." I filled her in on Conroy's purchase of a diffuser of the type used in the attack, supposedly for the duchess. "Did your mother order such a diffuser, or has he perhaps presented her with one?"

The princess scowled. "She did actually. Decided that the large receiving room needed one with a stronger motor."

"Oh." Well, there went that theory.

The more I thought about Conroy, the less he seemed like a viable suspect. Colleen had been right. If he had planned the kidnapping attempt, he would have made sure he or his daughter were on the spot to catch all the accolades. Not only that, it dawned on me that if the princess and her companions were knocked out, they would have missed the grand climax of his little drama. Why go through all the trouble of arranging such high theater if his audience was going to be asleep?

I started to explain my thought process. "He is a tempting

suspect, but I can't see why he'd have you kidnapped. His only hope of power is through his relationship with you."

"He has no relationship with me. I'd have him horsewhipped out of the city if I could." She wasn't joking. Not even a little bit. "He is devious. I can see him thinking to make me more reliant on him by a foiled attempt." She slammed her rook into place with such force that the other pieces on the board hopped and my queen toppled.

Absently, I straightened my pieces. "But——"

"No. I think you were right before. His odious daughter tried walking at my side. If I hadn't taken your arm instead, she would have been with me when the attack came. I bet she would have tried to take credit for running the kidnappers off. He is always foisting her upon me, and he would love to put me in her debt." She squeezed the pawn in her hand. "It is either that, or he is playing some even deeper game."

I couldn't help trying to make her see reason. "Your Highness, the drug used by the kidnappers would just as likely have knocked Louisa out too, and if you were drugged, you wouldn't be able to witness her bravery on your behalf."

"Or lack thereof. I would have had to accept whatever story she chose to tell me."

I didn't reply. She had a point but I was far from convinced, though I had a feeling it might be difficult convincing Victoria that it could be anyone other than her mother's comptroller. Her resentment was implacable.

I wondered if he had any idea. "I'll have to tell Sir John something if I'm to gain his trust. What shall I say?"

A real, if bitter, smile tilted the princess's lips. "Tell him I'm terrified by the attempts on my person but putting a brave face on things. One day soon, I'll be turning the tables on Sir John."

The ladies were coming our way. I'd been paying no attention whatsoever to the game, and as I looked at the board it appeared that the princess had been as distracted as I.

I dropped my handkerchief then jostled the board with my shoulder as I straightened up. The pieces tumbled to the ground. I was full of apologies for my clumsiness as I scrambled to pick up pawns and royalty alike.

I didn't enjoy looking like a clumsy fool, but if Dame Guinevere had glanced at that board, she would have known we'd not been playing a real game. I couldn't risk it.

Chapter 12

The mechanical chambermaid rattled in with the newspaper over one arm and her basin of hot water steaming merrily on the hob in her belly. I stumbled from bed, bleary eyed and headachy. I considered popping right back under the covers, but as I pulled a towel from the warming drawer my gaze landed on the headline screaming along the paper's front page: "DASTARDLY ATTACK ON PRINCESS."

I snatched the paper and jumped onto Colleen's bed. "Look at this."

She groaned. "Go away."

"No. Look!" I shoved the paper in her face. "They've tried to kidnap the princess again."

Colleen struggled against the covers.

I pulled the paper back and devoured the article. "Ha! Listen to this. A man broke into Kensington Palace and actually entered the princess's former bedchamber. However, just the night before her apartments had been changed."

"That's down to you," Colleen said.

I waggled my eyebrows. "I rather think it is." My misunderstood nocturnal visit to the princess had probably prompted the change. Not to mention an increase in surveillance from A Division. "Ooh, the fellow made a daring escape to the roof and got away in a small airship which was steered by some sort of newfangled rotor design."

Colleen grabbed the paper from my hand. "Rotors? How…" She chewed on her lower lip for a moment then tossed the paper aside in disgust. "They don't give any other details about the machine."

"More importantly, they don't give much information about the crime." I stood and crossed to the clothes press. "I'll bet the police have more information that they chose not to share with the public."

"I doubt they'll share it with us, either. Even if we say 'pretty please.'"

I chose a dress and held it up, considering. "Then we'll have to take it."

Colleen paused in the act of taking the ewer and basin from the mechanical. "You can't burgle a police station."

"Why not?"

"It's not like a shop that closes up for the night."

"I know."

"They're not going to let you wander in off the street and start looking around."

I pulled a fresh chemise over my head. "I'll dress up as a street doxy then get myself taken up for brawling or something."

"You can hardly expect to move freely if you're locked up for brawling or being hauled before the magistrate."

"Well, what do you suggest?"

"You go as the victim of a crime, not its perpetrator."

The idea didn't appeal to me. I hated assignments where I had to be weepy and weak.

"Don't look at me like that. You need the practice anyway." Her next words were muffled as she scrubbed her face.

"What?"

"I said, 'you could pose as a respectable young woman whose brother is missing or something.'"

I brightened. "Not my brother. My betrothed. They won't want to break it to me that he's probably left me at the proverbial altar." I began to nod as a story developed in my head. "If I can get the detective to leave the room for a few minutes, I ought to be able to locate the file and read what it has to say."

We refined the idea as we dressed. It was going to be another late night. But with luck, I could find the crucial clue that would lead us to the culprits.

Bolstered by the fact that we had a plan, I hurried downstairs to breakfast with a spring in my step.

Harriet and Eleanor sniffed as we entered and took our places. They'd had very little to say to me since it had become known that I had been asked to attend the princess on a regular basis.

"You are always rushing around and still always late." Irene was none too happy with me either. She stabbed an inoffensive sausage violently with her fork. "It's disgraceful in someone who's supposed to be a lady."

"Better than always talking and never saying anything." I returned her smirk with an acid smile of my own.

"As if you're so interesting. You—"

Whatever else Irene meant to say was cut off as Dame Guinevere swept into the room. "Good morning, ladies. I've received some exciting news." She paused, allowing anticipation to build. "I congratulate you all on the positive impression you made. As we had hoped, we have received an invitation for you all to attend the princess's birthday ball at Saint James's Palace."

A squeal just one note away from glass shattering pierced

the air and the other girls all started talking at once. Colleen and I exchanged glances.

I know the princess hated the Kensington System, but her usual strict supervision did at least provide some protection. Public appearances posed a whole new level of risk when it came to guarding her from potential assailants.

Marianne and Harriet launched into a campaign for another, more extensive round of shopping. I sighed. Then it occurred to me that Eleanor was uncharacteristically quiet. Her head was lowered, and she ate steadily from her bowl of oatmeal. Normally, she would have been leading the pack demanding that we hie off to this expensive modiste or that exclusive milliner, finding a way to poke fun about my family's scant resources in the process. Interesting. I filed the tidbit away for later consideration since I had more important things to think about at the moment.

Dame Guinevere clapped her hands. "Girls. I see no reason to disrupt today's schedule. You have not graduated yet, and I'll thank you to remember that before you start presuming to order me about."

A chastened silence fell around the table.

"Miss Yancy will continue our instruction on the use of hatpins as offensive weapons then Mrs. Dutton will be conducting our bartitsu session. We have been deplorably lax in our training regimen since arriving in London. Master Nathaniel will be doubling up on our dancing classes in anticipation of the ball, and he will also be holding our regularly scheduled fencing lessons. If you wish to remain in a condition to actually protect our queen you must continue to train even after you've left Saint Scholastica's behind you."

I let the rest of the lecture drift around me without actually absorbing any of it.

Colleen and I were going to have to come up with a plan to keep the princess safe at the ball. I could voice my concerns to Dame Guinevere but since it was she who had taught me tactics, I doubted I would be telling her anything she didn't already know. The best thing for everyone would be if we could discover who was behind the kidnapping attempts before the ball.

I spent most of the day toddling along like a mechanical and going through the motions expected of me. It would probably have been better if I had set thoughts of the princess aside and focused on something else for a while in order to come back to her later with a fresh perspective, but like a bulldog with its jaws around a juicy bone, I couldn't seem to let the situation go.

It wasn't hard to imagine how the princess must chafe under the Kensington System. The restrictions on my life weren't nearly as oppressive, and I found them almost unbearable at the moment. Since I had limited freedom of movement, I had to decide whether to prioritize Scarlet Lane or seeking information from the police at A Division. Which path was more likely to yield useful information?

The man at the livery had either been lying, or the fellow had specifically asked to be dropped off in Scarlet Lane in order to obscure his trail. Whereas, the second attack might have given the police fresh evidence that would lead to more productive lines of inquiry. I would be able to see what they had gleaned on the first real kidnapping attempt, and on my own little visit as well.

I dithered for a time, but the choice was obvious.

That night the door to our room had barely closed behind us before I was changing into an eminently respectable dress of gray serge and a lace cap over a wig of dark brown curls from the school's stash. Colleen covered my freckles with a thick layer of makeup, and I changed the shape of my face by stuffing cotton pads in my cheeks. She saw me out the window and within minutes I was on my way to the A Division police station. I made sure no pesky colonials were on my trail as I hurried along.

A little raw onion in my handkerchief did the trick, and my eyes were authentically red and brimming as I approached the sergeant who sat at an elevated desk just inside the station door.

When he looked down from his perch at me, I summoned a timid chirping voice. "Excuse me, sir. I was told to ask for Chief Inspector Ogden." At least the papers had given me the identity of the man in charge of the investigation into the kidnapping attempt.

"What's it about? He's a busy man."

I gave a despairing little wail and buried my face in my hands to renew the onion effect on my streaming eyes.

"Here now. Here now. There's no call for that."

"Oh, but sir there is. He's disappeared you see."

"Someone's missing?"

"I fear foul play. It's the only possible answer."

"Now, miss, I'm sure it's not as bad as all that."

"I wish I could think so." I sniffled once more into my onion-filled handkerchief. "Would—do you think Mr. Ogden would see me? I would feel so much better if he could tell me what might have happened to my dear John."

I could see the conflict in the worthy old sergeant. My instinct was to say something more, but mindful of Dame Guinevere's training I bit my tongue and focused on looking pitiful.

After a moment he sighed. "Have a seat, miss. I'll check if he'll see you, but mind you, he may not be able. Like I said, he's a busy man."

"Oh, thank you. You're very kind." I settled in a graceful swirl of skirts on the chair he indicated. Then I waited.

And waited.

I caught myself tapping my foot impatiently and stilled the motion immediately. It didn't fit with the sweet, mousy little character I was creating.

Nearly an hour went by before I was ushered to the detective's cubbyhole of an office. Everything in the place was at right angles. I'd never seen anything like it. Even Mahlenbeau's workshop had nothing on this detective.

He half stood as I entered and gestured to the chair in front of his desk. It was the same fellow who had come to see Dame Guinevere. "Please have a seat, miss."

I took the chair he indicated, my whole frame trembling delicately. I dabbed at my eyes which gave me a perfect opportunity to study this officer. His hair was every bit as coppery as I remembered, rivaling my own. He was younger than I'd realized, but I wasn't sure if it was because I was now viewing him up close, or perhaps it was the effect of the late hour. Fine stubble covered his cheeks. He had a narrow chin, a full lower lip, and serious gray eyes.

Eyes that were regarding me neutrally.

I gave a final sniffle and lowered my handkerchief.

He didn't speak immediately. And the way those eyes continued to examine me, I knew I was going to need to tread carefully. It would be foolish to underestimate this man. I decided to say as little as possible. "Thank you for seeing me, Inspector."

"The sergeant tells me you're concerned about a young man who's gone missing."

"Yes sir."

"How long has he been gone?"

"I—I'm not entirely sure. He—we were supposed to meet last night. But he didn't come, and I've had no note from him today. It's so unlike him. I went by his home, and I didn't see him."

"He wasn't home? Did his family say where he was?"

"I couldn't ask."

His brows drew together. "Why not?"

"I—we're not acquainted."

His expression shifted ever so slightly, but it was hard to interpret what he was thinking. "How did you meet your young man—what's his name?"

"Reginald Garland. We met about a month ago outside the draper's shop."

"Were you introduced?"

I cast my eyes down and caught my lower lip between my teeth. "No."

He waited without saying anything. A very effective tactic for interrogations. I figured my persona would never be able to withstand the silent pressure. I babbled out a vague and jumbled story that amounted to a fairy-tale hero who had come to my rescue when a street urchin stole my purse. He'd caught the fellow and retrieved my goods, then helped me to a tearoom until I calmed down. He was not of the same class as my family, and I knew they wouldn't understand, though I could see the nobility in him. So, we'd begun to meet secretly.

This paragon had asked me to marry him a week ago and was going to speak to my father, but I figured the best thing to do was to elope to Gretna Green. Then we could return and the deed would be done, and my family could do nothing about it. I had a trust from my grandmother, and I had withdrawn a goodly sum and given it to him to make the arrangements for our travel, a special license, secure a place for us to live, and so on. Now, I was desperately afraid he had been injured or attacked because he hadn't shown up to collect me at the appointed time and place.

Inspector Ogden did a pretty good job of maintaining a neutral expression, but as I brought the tale to a rambling close and broke down in fresh tears, I caught a flash of mingled pity and exasperation.

Next, he would have to decide how to tell me that I had fallen for one of the oldest frauds in the book.

He glanced at the spotless desk and cleared his throat. "Perhaps you would like a cup of tea?"

Perfect! As I had hoped, he was giving me time to collect myself before he broke the bad news. I kept my face buried in my handkerchief but managed a nod.

He rose and left the room.

As soon as he was gone, I sprang to my feet and began searching for the right file. The princess's case had to be the most important he was handling at the moment, so it would be close at hand.

Sure enough, the file sat directly adjacent to his blotter. I mentally shook his hand as I snatched it up and combed through the contents. The meticulous Inspector Ogden had made my job far easier than anticipated. The file was arranged chronologically with the most recent information on top. I sped through the pages. At the end, my eyebrows were about level with my hairline. Was it possible that the officer I had believed to be so shrewd was even more credulous than the character I was masquerading as for the evening?

I bit my lip reconsidering but went ahead and slipped in the note that Colleen and I had worked out with the anonymous tip about twelve Scarlet Lane. Since they hadn't gleaned the bit from Mahlenbeau about the livery service, we had thought they might not yet have gathered that lead. And after all, fair was fair. Information for information.

I slapped the folder closed, scooted it back into perfect alignment with the blotter, and had just resumed my seat when he returned with the bad news that my one true love was a heartless confidence trickster. I had the onion ready.

Colleen was waiting impatiently for my return. "What did you find out?"

"Hello to you too."

"Pish. You're usually happy enough to dispense with niceties. Now, spill."

"They think a monkey's behind it."

She jammed a hand against her hip and cocked her head. "No more games, or I might stop helping with your little escapades."

I raised my hands. "I'm serious. They found tiny handprints in some dust at the palace. The chief superintendent was pushing a theory about fairies. Then Inspector Ogden brought in an expert from the London Zoo who stated that they were from a monkey. Probably a Barbary macaque."

Her mouth drooped open.

Relishing my story, I smiled. "Guess where those particular little monkeys come from?"

"They're indigenous to Gibraltar."

I hated it when she did that. Robbed of my revelation, I turned so she could help me with the lacings on the back of my dress. "The theory at A Division is that the furry little menace was trained by someone to climb up and enter through an open window then make its way downstairs where it unlocked a side door, allowing the would-be kidnapper to enter the palace."

"Doesn't that leave a great deal unexplained?"

"It certainly does, but they are focusing their efforts on finding suspects with a connection to Gibraltar." Freed of my gown, I sat on the bed and took off my shoes.

"I see. I suppose we can't dismiss the evidence. Apparently there *was* a monkey there." Colleen was coming to grips with the outlandish theory.

"If the perpetrator is some random Gibraltan—Gibralta-nese—"

"Gibraltarian."

How *did* she know these things? "Whatever. If it's a matter of looking for a needle in a haystack, the police are far better suited for the pursuit than we are."

"You're giving up?"

"Don't be absurd. I'm just thinking if the police are covering that angle, then we need to focus our efforts elsewhere."

"What elsewhere are you specifically thinking of?"

"I still have to follow up on Scarlet Lane. Who knows how long it will take Inspector Ogden to find the note I left him? Then there's Conroy and his daughter. We have access to them, and the princess is convinced they're the culprits. We need to either rule them in or out."

"Anyone else?"

"I want to know why that blasted colonial is snooping around all this. Someone must be backing him, and I'd like to know who."

"I guess that's a start."

I arched an eyebrow. "Do you have other suggestions?"

"No." She shook her head. "I'll focus on our other suspects like Prince Ernest and see what I can gather."

"You'll be careful?"

"As careful as you."

Swathed in my nightdress, I climbed under the coverlet. "That's not particularly comforting you know."

"I do." She blew out the lamp.

It dawned upon me that it would be hard to have the job of staying behind and waiting for someone else to return from daring adventures. I would certainly hate it. I would have to think of a way to actively involve Colleen.

Or I would have a mutiny on my hands.

Chapter 13

Eleanor bested me at fencing the next day, which put me in a foul mood and made her gloat. I blamed it on the fact that I was tired, but the truth was, she hadn't been at her top of form either. The circles under her eyes were at least as shadowed as the ones under my own.

What was she up to? Was she secretly investigating the kidnapping attempts too?

I made a note to be extra vigilant about being followed and swore to myself that, if she prevented me from fulfilling my promise to the princess, I would run her over with a steam carriage.

A lovely dense fog settled in that evening as we sat at dinner, and the other girls complained of the unseasonable chilliness. I on the other hand began to cheer up. It was exactly what I needed to conceal my movements.

The trip to Scarlet Lane was too far to manage quickly on foot, so as soon as I was certain I had not been followed, I headed to the nearest flying train station and purchased a ticket from the mechanical conductor. Only two other passengers sat inside. One who looked like a rumpled clerk in a suit whose trousers and sleeves were slightly too short. He was probably returning home after a long day at work in a dusty office somewhere. The other was a young man who was dressed spiffily and who kept running a finger over his upper lip which sported a slightly patchy mustache as if it was a new effort. In his other hand, he clutched a bouquet of spring flowers. Someone was going courting.

Neither of them was Eleanor in disguise or that wretched colonial.

Scarlet Lane turned out to be, as I had thought, about a half step up from a slum. None of the gaslights on the street were working. The globes had probably been broken by whichever gang controlled the neighborhood. The better to hold sway over the night.

I took care to move swiftly and quietly.

Number twelve looked like it had been around long enough to have defied The Great Fire of London. Three stories tall and claustrophobically narrow, it butted up to the neighboring house as if trying to pass along a secret. On the top floor, a single window nestled under the eaves. The good news was that it wasn't barred. The bad news was that there was no convenient drainpipe. Nor did I have the grappling hook device. I would have to chance going in through the front door.

I stood in the shadows staring at the building. If this was some sort of trap, I might very well be caught in it.

I could turn around and go home.

Right.

Dealing with the cheap lock on the door took no time at all. Once inside, I carefully closed the door behind me. To my relief, it didn't squeak. Despite the neighborhood and the shabby atmosphere, someone clearly cared for the place and the hinges were well oiled.

The smell of boiled cabbage and mutton permeated the atmosphere, and I listened hard for any sounds of movement. All was still.

Before proceeding, I pulled Colleen's opera glasses from one of my pockets and raised them to my eyes, blinking a little at the sudden purple glow that illuminated everything.

The door opened directly into the sitting room and beyond that, I could see the kitchen. The furniture was sparse, but the sofa and two chairs were covered with crocheted antimacassars while lace doilies shrouded every flat surface.

Praying no dogs were in residence, I crept toward the stairs. The house remained silent. The stairs again hinted that, even if the owners were poor, they expended care on the house. Not a one squeaked. At the first landing, I paused. I could hear snoring in at least two different pitches, but otherwise nothing. Not even a mechanical trundled about. Maybe they couldn't afford one.

I headed on up again. The third set of stairs was narrower than the others and steeper. The smell of cabbage had faded to be replaced by the scent of cheap tallow candles. No gasogenes, pyrogenes, or gaslights here. What if these people were Luddites? Could the desire to halt the progress of technology be the political drive behind a move to kidnap the princess?

If so, we had a whole new realm of suspects.

A single door stood on the top landing. I wrinkled my nose. Drat. As happened more than I cared to admit, I had not foreseen all the eventualities.

What if my quarry was still awake? If that was the case, my only option would be to silence him before he could raise an alarm.

Which meant I would need my hands free.

I put away the opera glasses and waited impatiently for my eyes to adjust to the darkness. Without Colleen's device, it was very dark indeed. I needed to remember to praise her ingenuity more.

I stayed completely still trying to reach out with my other senses. Now that was a thought. A device that amplified sound in the same way the opera glasses amplified light.

Someone below snuffled in their sleep. Outside, a nearby church steeple struck eleven o'clock. I'd better get moving.

With infinite care, I turned the doorknob. It moved easily. Not locked then. This did not bode well for my hopes of finding a criminal mastermind.

Unless he was simply overconfident.

Or it was indeed a trap.

Crouching low, I pushed in the door. If someone waited on the other side to attack, I hoped they would aim too high. Light from the street filtered through threadbare curtains, making it easier to take in the small room. There wasn't much to it. A narrow, canopy bed that had clearly seen better days and looked lumpy even from where I stood. A desk that was just a table with a single drawer was pushed up against the wall. A wardrobe and a single straight-backed wooden chair.

What was noticeably missing was a person.

Where could my suspect be at such an hour?

At least it meant that searching would be easier. I straightened and stepped into the room, closing the door behind me in case its occupant returned. Retrieving the opera glasses again, I made straight for the wardrobe, almost the only place where anything could be concealed.

Here again, the doors opened easily without even the hint of a lock. Inside hung a man's suit, one workaday pair of pants, and two shirts. A single pair of boots sat neatly on the bottom. The shelf held a quilt and a few odds and ends. Tucked back in the corner was a walking stick. I pulled it out. Sure enough, a three-towered castle was carved into the top. Mahlenbeau had been right. It wasn't the sort of thing anyone would actually want to lean into.

Nor did it seem to match anything else in the room. It was too elaborate. Too gothic. If it belonged anywhere, it fit a windswept manor house full of secret passages and breathless heroines. Not in this prosaic rented room.

I replaced the cane as I had found it and stepped back to close the doors. There was a rustling then a sort of chirping that sounded as loud as a scream in the silence. Even as I gasped and spun toward the noise, a dark form pounced. I dropped the opera glasses as something struck my shoulder, and I flailed out at it blindly. My hands met fur, and I recoiled.

The chirping sounded again, louder this time. A tiny hand tugged at my hair.

The *monkey*.

I panted from the fright the little demon had given me and put a hand to my chest as if I could slow my heart rate from its gallop. I stooped and picked up the opera glasses, tucking them into a pocket. He must have been asleep somewhere when I entered, perhaps on the bed, or even on top of the canopy. As the monkey continued to pull at my hair and pat my face, I chuckled. I was intensely relieved there had been no one else present to see my reaction.

"Hullo, you monster," I murmured.

He answered with a *chirrup* and plucked at my sleeves.

I needed to remember that the little beast was a thief through and through. Sure enough. He had my opera glasses in one hand. I pried them free of his grasp and set him on the bed. He wasn't interested in remaining where I placed him and immediately hopped back onto my shoulder. Of all the aggravating—I shrugged, trying to dislodge the rascal as he scrabbled around my back to my other shoulder like we were playing some delightful new game.

I pulled out the single desk drawer and found a few sheets of writing paper and a couple pencil nibs. A penknife and a handkerchief were the only other occupants. Certainly no ruby ring hid inside, although maybe the fellow was wearing it, wherever he was.

I was about to turn my attention to searching the bed, when out in the street came the chugging chuff of a steam carriage. Odd that. Such flashy, modern vehicles could not often venture into neighborhoods like this. Although I knew of at least one time recently when one had. The day my mystery man had picked up the perfume diffuser from Mahlenbeau.

I tried again to remove the blasted monkey from my person, but he clung to me. Abandoning that particular effort for the moment, I slipped over to the window and peered through a crack in the tatty curtains.

A wash of light swept like a flood before the vehicle as it trundled down the street. It pulled up smartly in front of the house in which I stood. Two men hopped out. As the one passed around the front of the carriage, his face was illuminated. Not my quarry at all. It was Inspector Ogden of A Division. Heartily sorry I had slipped the note about Scarlet Lane into his file, I watched as he and his companion marched toward the front door, disappearing from my line of sight.

I once again tugged at the monkey trying to get him to let go without hurting him in the process. Below, a hard, steady hammering began on the door. At the blast of sound, the monkey screeched and released me. He launched himself from my shoulder toward the bed, hiding on top of the canopy. The poor beastie was obviously terrified. I started to go after him, but someone in the house had begun swearing up a storm and was blundering about, probably striking his shin on things.

There was only one way out. I threw up the window sash and, before the householder had even admitted the police, I was perched outside on the eave, my cheek pressed into the shingles and my ear attuned to what was occurring below.

A disgruntled voice demanded to know what the fuss was all about. In polite, official tones, Inspector Ogden explained his identity and desire to speak with the tenant of the garret flat. I didn't quite catch the grumbled response. Something about law-abiding folk being rousted from their beds in the middle of the night for foolishness.

Despite the litany of complaints that continued, the officers were admitted and shown up to the room I had just searched.

First the sound of a light knock reached me then the creak of the opening door. Candlelight spilled through the cracks in the window. "Andrew, these fellows from the police wants to speak with you." An indrawn breath. "Why, he isn't here."

Sounds of hurried movement.

"Martin, check to make sure he didn't go out the window." Inspector Ogden's tone was decisive.

I pulled back farther into the shadows, trying not to make a sound. I should have legged it when I had the chance.

Turned out, I needn't have worried. The officer stuck his head out the window, looked up and down the street, then retreated inside. "No sign of him, sir."

Inspector Ogden merely grunted. "Look at this. I'd say it matches the cane described by the witnesses."

"Yes, sir. I'd say so."

"All right. Let's see if we can find the ring as well." Rustling sounded as the search was presumably undertaken. Inspector

Ogden was apparently not part of this effort, his attention being focused elsewhere. "Sir, I didn't catch your name."

"Who me?" The landlord no longer sounded as grumpy, more bewildered. "Farraday."

"Mr. Farraday, what is the name of your lodger?"

"Andrew Reese."

"When did he take lodgings here?"

"Oh, goodness." He paused. "I'd say it's been nigh on seven months or thereabouts."

"Do you know where he hails from?"

"Gibraltar as I understood it."

"When did you see him last?"

"Why, this morning. He was heading off to work, and I wished him a good day. He tipped his hat to me, polite like, and said the same, like always. Usually, he's home at half past six like clockwork. I was out this evening, but I assum—"

"And do you know how he is employed?"

"He's a bricklayer with a yard over to Whitehall way."

"Has he ever expressed any sentiments against the crown or the royal family?"

"The roy—well, no. Not in my hearing."

There was a sort of thump and a muffled shriek. "What the dev—!" The unflappable inspector sounded thoroughly flapped.

I clamped a hand over my mouth, stifling the giggle that threatened to escape. I had a good idea what had happened.

"It's a monkey, sir." The voice sounded awed.

"I see that now." Inspector Ogden cleared his throat. "Can you remove him from my back, please."

"A monkey!" Once more, the landlord sounded aggrieved. "My tenants all know there are to be no pets in the house. I never would have rented to him if I knew he kept a monkey. And I check the rooms regular like. I don't understand it."

"Mr. Farraday, do you know when your tenant will return?"

"It's former tenant now, and no. I didn't even know he was gone."

The inspector sighed heavily. "Martin, in light of the evidence we've found, I'd say we have enough to make an arrest. You stay here and arrest the fellow when and if he returns. I will take the evidence back to the station."

"Including the monkey, sir?"

A pause. A sigh. "Including the monkey. Oh, and finish a thorough search for that ring."

That was my cue to leave. If an officer was going to be stationed there, I wouldn't be able to get back inside and do any more searching myself. I'd have to turn my attention elsewhere.

Chapter 14

The next afternoon I curtsied to the princess and duchess, as Dame Guinevere and I were once more shown into the drawing room where they were seated. I was improving now that it mattered. I neither wobbled nor stepped on my hem.

Sir John was there as well, insufferably smug in a high collar that had points so sharp they looked like weapons. I examined him closely, trying for the umpteenth time to make up my mind about him. He was no dandy, but he took care with his appearance. And he was not unhandsome though his forehead was quite high and would probably continue to get higher as he aged. His dark hair was close-cropped but he had balanced out the lack of hair up top with enormous muttonchop sideburns. His nose was narrow. His eyes fine. His manners were nice enough. Why had I always found him odious?

I don't mind disliking people. I just prefer to have a reason for my dislike.

As soon as I got sufficiently close to the princess I spoke under my breath. "We need to talk."

Her chin dipped in a gracious nod as if I'd complimented her dress.

We spent some ten minutes in desultory small talk with Sir John and Baroness Lezhen while the duchess and Dame

Guinevere sat a little apart from the rest of us deeply engaged in conversation. Somehow, in our few visits, the old girl had managed to entirely win over the princess's mama. She no longer regarded us as unwanted interlopers.

Just as my impatience was about to brim over, the princess turned to her mother. "Mummy, I'd like to show Lady Portia the doll clothes Lezhen and I have been making."

The duchess looked up. "I suppose we can go."

"Oh, no. We mustn't disrupt your lovely chat. It's just in the sewing room and Lezhen will go with us."

After several moments and multiple reassurances, we were allowed to withdraw. The princess conducted me to a light-splashed room with enormous windows and shelves full of dolls and dollhouses. It contained a couple of worktables with piles of pretty silks and brocades and a spindly sewing mechanical whose head was crowned in spools of brilliantly colored threads and which wore a sash of minute silk flowers. It seemed to hold every possible tool which might be required for sewing. A sweetly smiling china doll's face had been painted on, but the whimsical contraption also had scissors in place of fingers on one hand.

It may have been irrational, but I was careful not to present my back to the device.

We had no sooner entered than the princess sent the baroness on an errand. That lady looked as if she was about to protest, but she changed it to a nod and left.

The door scarcely clicked shut behind her before the princess spoke in a clipped tone. "I expected you sooner in light of the second attempt on my person."

"With the increased security, I thought that waiting for a more…orthodox means of seeing Your Highness was warranted. But I haven't been idle."

Her eyes flickered, and I could see frustration at her dependence upon others. "Then what progress have you made? No one will tell me anything."

I described the substance of my investigations thus far, including my adventures of the previous evening and Inspector Ogden's intent to have the Gibraltarian, Andrew Reese, arrested.

She listened, but I could tell she was no more impressed by the idea of a trained monkey than I had been.

The only thing I held back was information about the mysterious colonial who dogged my steps because I still had no idea what to make of him.

"Gibraltar, pah!" She stood and paced, her hands clasped behind her back. "I still believe Sir John has had a hand in this." The frustration simmering below her placid demeanor was in danger of boiling over. She needed something to do.

"Highness, with your assistance I could perform a thorough search of Sir John's office and apartments."

An altogether different gleam entered her eye. This proposal was definitely to her taste. She wanted him to be guilty and wanted action taken against him. "What can I do?"

"I need you to remain here and explain my absence if anyone else should come in." Her stony expression made me hasten on. "I'm sorry, Princess, but Baroness Lezhen won't be gone long and if you are not here she will start searching and we can't risk it unless you want to take her into your confidence?"

She huffed but considered. "No. I don't think so. Lezhen is very dear, but she could never keep it from my mother if she thought I was in real danger."

"All right. Whatever excuse you devise for me make sure it is something that won't put Sir John on his guard."

She nodded slowly, and I could see she wanted something more active to do.

"I also need your help in deciding what you'd like me to tell Sir John when he inquires about you. I'll have to have some story to fob off on him."

A wicked grin curled the edge of her lips. "I will come up with something appropriate."

"And Baroness Lezhen?"

"I will explain only that I asked you to inquire with Sir John about something. That way if anyone mentions seeing you near his quarters no one will think anything of it. I detest him, so I often send intermediaries if I must communicate with the man. It won't seem strange to her."

"Excellent."

The princess described for me the least used passage to Sir John's office and I slipped from her sewing room. I made no effort to slink as I was firmly of the opinion that the best way to creep about during daylight hours was to look as if one was not creeping at all. I was in luck, and the man was not in his office.

Conroy's apartments within the palace were, well, palatial. Everything was made to a kingly scale. The draperies and upholstery were made of richly vibrant velvets the color of fine claret. In the outer chamber a desk of highly polished, inlaid wood sat in pride of place with two armchairs at attention before it. This was my first point of attack.

But with the best will in the world I could find nothing incriminating among the man's papers. It was a stretch to find them even mildly suspicious. He had made plans for more of the "progresses" he periodically pressed upon the princess. These were trips around the country for the purpose of ingratiating her to the people.

I knew she loathed these jaunts, feeling as if she was being put on display for his sake. Despite her feelings, these forays could hardly be said to be opposed to her interests. They worked. She was easily the most popular royal.

I found some notes on how he meant to make the princess more disposed toward his daughter, but nothing that appeared nefarious, in fact, it seemed more burdensome to Louisa who was required to take an interest in anything that caught the princess's fancy as well as being unfailingly pleasant, courteous, witty (but not too witty), ladylike, and engaging.

Goodness, if I were she, I would want to do away with the princess simply to be free of my father's unreasonable demands.

I searched for hidden drawers in the desk and came up with nothing. Then I began a careful circuit around the rest of the chambers.

Nothing. Nothing. And nothing.

The princess wasn't going to be happy, but I had largely convinced myself that Sir John probably didn't belong on the list of suspects. His only path to power was through Victoria. It made no sense for him to take any chance on jeopardizing what ought to be a sure thing. He would do better to make himself agreeable as he wanted his daughter to do, rather than trying to rule Victoria's life. As things stood, I had a feeling that once the princess took the throne, Sir John was in for a rude awakening, but if he couldn't see that for himself, I wasn't going to try to educate him.

I took a last look around, making sure things were as they had been when I entered. Then I ducked out of the suite.

I had taken no more than a half dozen steps when Sir John rounded the corner and stopped short at sight of me. "Lady Portia?"

I bobbed a shallow curtsy as he came abreast of me.

"What are you doing here?"

In response to his poor manners, I became icily polite. "Sir John." I gave a grave nod as if to acknowledge his nonexistent courtesy. "I've come to report on the princess and also to see if you had any particular directions."

He glanced wildly about then seized my arm and all but dragged me into his rooms. "Your use to me is limited to the number of people who know about our connection."

"Oh, but surely everyone knows you have the princess's best interests at heart?"

"They do. But—well…unfortunately the princess, like many young people of this generation, sees the extraordinary care taken for her well-being as interference. She isn't always as appreciative as one might expect."

"I see."

He seemed to expect some sort of commiseration. When I didn't offer it, he proceeded. "Did you have something to report then?"

"Not much. The princess is quite upset about these attacks on her person, as I'm sure you are."

He dropped into the chair behind his desk though I was still standing. "Yes, as well she might be. I've made my dissatisfaction with the police handling of this known to his majesty."

I heartily doubted that the king paid any attention whatsoever to Sir John's correspondence. There was no love lost between the court and the duchess's household. They disliked the way Conroy had secluded the princess from the court, taking it as an insult.

I pushed. "Have they found anything out?"

"Certainly not enough to compensate for all their fumbling about and interference. Do you know they actually tried to speak to the princess?"

Keeping this man on track was a task worthy of Hercules.

Perhaps I could provoke a response that would tell me something. "I heard that there might be an arrest forthcoming."

He gave me a long look. "You are well-informed."

"You know how quickly gossip can spread." I smiled as sweetly as I could. "Then it's true?"

"Yes. The police have identified the young man whom they believe to be the culprit."

"*A* young man? But what about the airship? Surely, there's more than one person involved."

Another long look. I was being too obvious. Dame Guinevere would have been appalled.

"I'm certain the A Division officers have considered everything."

So now he was advocating for the bobbies?

"Of course. I'm sure it was some madman. There can be no other explanation."

"No doubt."

He turned the conversation back to what intelligence I had gathered from the princess. I fobbed him off with a number of choice tidbits about hat trims, her excitement about her upcoming birthday ball, and a desire for a trip to the seaside. In a display of just how disconnected he was from the princess's true feelings and desires, he accepted my report with equanimity.

"You need to get closer to her and find out why she refuses to be friendly to Louisa."

As if the answer to that wasn't painfully obvious to everyone in the world but himself. I nodded and tried to look diligent. I was soon dismissed and hurried back to Victoria.

At my arrival, the baroness tactfully removed herself to a corner of the room supposedly to look for some buttons. The princess wasn't happy with my assessment, or as she termed it, "my failure to discover any evidence," but I was reasonably confident that there was at least a possibility someone else was behind the attempts on her person. It cheered her up when I pointed out that we had not yet investigated Louisa.

By the time Dame Guinevere and the duchess came to retrieve us, we were fully occupied in fiddling with tiny scraps of cloth and lace to fashion a doll's dress. Dame Guinevere gave me a long look. She knew me too well to think I could possibly be interested in such a pastime. It had taken her a great deal of time to drill into me the importance of proper dress for people. And her arguments hadn't worked until she had pointed out how useful dress was for manipulating expectations and for concealing weaponry. She knew full well I would be bored to death by dressing a doll.

I gave her a tiny shrug. It was, after all, the princess. I could hardly override her wishes on what activity we would undertake.

Chapter 15

Dame Guinevere wasn't satisfied with that explanation. She insisted on my report as we returned to the townhouse. Nor was she as accepting of my flimflam as Sir John had been. I stuck to the truth as much as possible, reporting the princess's concern about the kidnapping attempts. It would have been unnatural had she not been somewhat worried. I also told her of the princess's belief that Sir John was behind it, now that I had ruled him out to my own satisfaction. The princess's dislike of him was too palpable. Not mentioning it would have alerted my headmistress that I was hiding something.

She assumed I was hiding something anyway, and only after pointed questioning, did I break down and admit to infiltrating Sir John's quarters in a search for any evidence that he was connected to the kidnapping attempts in an effort to put the princess's mind at ease. This last admission finally satisfied her. As indeed it should have. I was, after all, being almost entirely open.

She really ought to have been proud of me. She had long taught us that the best lie was the truth.

When at last she released me from her clutches, I had to hurry to dress for dinner. After which we all piled into the steam carriage for yet another trip to the opera. I have honestly tried to like the opera. I really have. But with the exception of one or two songs, I've never enjoyed it.

Colleen said it's because I'm a cultural Philistine. She's probably right.

But truly I'd much rather hear some silly ditty that makes my toes tap and brings a smile. I'd have paid good money to be able to come up with an excuse as to why it was vital for me to be doing something else. Unfortunately, my brilliant inspiration didn't hit until the warbling was over.

I had wracked my brain all evening for my next course of action. It was possible that the officers of A Division were correct in their belief that Andrew Reese was the culprit. But I didn't see how the attempts could have been the work of a single man. Certainly, I had seen two men, and if Reese and his monkey had been inside the palace trying to abduct the princess, then who had been piloting the airship?

At the very least, he had an accomplice. At the worst, there were several involved in a conspiracy. That thought made me very nervous indeed. If the police only locked up one person, then the others would be free to go about their business.

The question was, what could I do about it? Even if I eliminated Sir John as a suspect, which I wasn't entirely able to do, we still had plenty of other suspects. I didn't even know where most of them were likely to be.

I gnawed on the problem, which at least gave me something to take my mind off the caterwauling onstage. It wasn't until we stepped into a mist-dampened night and saw the line of hopeful cabbies ready to offer rides to tired operagoers that I knew precisely what to do.

What was good for the goose was good for the gander. Or rather, reverse that, what was good for the gander was good for the goose. Specifically, that dratted colonial cabbie might have answers to some of my questions—including why he was poking around in this affair which was clearly none of his concern.

Yes, indeed. He did have some explaining to do. And this time he wouldn't avoid my questions so easily. But first, I needed to know more about him. Time for the watched to become the watcher.

I pulled my evening wrap closer, inwardly cursing the demands of fashion which prohibited wearing anything comfortable or sensible. From the vantage point of the opera house stairs, I had a good view of the throng and the waiting cabbies, but I couldn't see my—the—colonial anywhere.

Typical. When I actually wanted to see the pest, he was nowhere to be found.

I would have to find him wherever he lurked.

I caught Colleen looking at me with narrowed eyes and raised my eyebrows in question.

She bent closer so only I could hear her. "You're scheming."

"I?"

"Just don't be so obvious."

I gave her a look of injured innocence and returned to surveying the crowd. Despite my best efforts, I did not spot the annoying cabman. I didn't believe for a minute that he'd decided to leave me alone. He was simply living up to his billing. I wouldn't let that stop me. I'd find him some other way.

By the time we had returned to Cadogan Hall, I'd concocted a plan. It was risky and whether it would work or not... we'd see.

Luckily, I had slept through the majority of the four-hour opera, so I had replenished my energy stores. Colleen wasn't for it, but she eventually came round to my point of view.

The biggest problem was finding another method of egress. I suspected that my window was under surveillance. Or if not my window specifically, at least in the line of sight from wherever he lurked. It was the only explanation I could think of for how the blasted Canadian had been on my tail so quickly.

I managed the difficulty rather handily.

All the activity of the past several days had provided invaluable practice of skills which up to now had largely been a product of classroom study. Practice makes perfect as they say. In any event, I was able to avoid the security mechanicals and weasel out through the laundry without waking up the household.

I crept to the corner and with the opera glasses caught sight of the watcher. He was not obtrusive, tucked into a sort of alcove between houses across the street.

Truthfully, I might not have spotted him except that, as I watched, a burly fellow strolled along the sidewalk, hands in his pockets. He could have been the servant of one of the nearby houses headed home from a half day off, except he stopped ever so casually at that little alcove and spoke to the shadows while lighting a cigarette.

I was too far away to make out what he said but his intonation implied a question. The reply a short string of sentences and an overall negative.

With this brief exchange complete, the burly fellow traded places with the shadowed man.

It was my lucky day.

I had managed to catch the watchers at shift change. The now unshadowed man continued on the way the other fellow had been going. A casual observer from any of the nearby homes would have noticed only that a man had paused to light his cigarette before walking on.

I withdrew and plotted a course parallel to my quarry as there was no other way to get past his replacement without being seen. I raced along and was rewarded for my haste when I came to the end of the mews a couple of blocks down, peeked out, and found him but a few meters away.

As he passed, the light from windows opposite illuminated his profile. Between that and his jaunty walk, I grinned. I hadn't just found someone who could lead me to my erstwhile colonial. I had found the man himself.

Good. Let's see how he liked being followed.

I bet I could do a better job of tailing him than he had made of pursuing me.

I let him get well ahead of me, then stepped from my concealment. He obligingly led the way with nary a turn of his head. As it turned out, we didn't have far to go.

Without taking a single evasive maneuver or checking once for the possibility of pursuit, he headed toward Trafalgar Square and the Admiralty, passed them and marched up the stairs of a sedate Georgian mansion with grand front columns. He pushed through the imposing door as if he was arriving home.

Now, this was interesting indeed. Not many cabbies bedded down in a mansion.

I didn't think for a minute that he owned this palatial space. Who was my Canadian nemesis's sponsor? Was there some colonial conspiracy brewing against our soon-to-be queen? But if that were the case, why had he helped me?

I hesitated, eyes fixed on the building. A pyrogene flickered to life in the front rooms, and I watched, trying to follow its progress as it moved through the building. I shifted around the corner then to the back of the building where, at last, the lamp came to rest in a second-floor window.

A quick glance to left and right assured me no one was watching, and I quickly crossed the street. Once more, I scanned the area for passersby, bobbies, or any other inconveniences. Reassured, I shinned up the drainpipe. It was a fairly easy climb.

As my head was about to come level with the lit window, I heard voices and slowed my ascent. I edged to the side of the window and raised my head until I could peek inside.

My nemesis stood at attention before a man who was seated at an enormous table with his back to me.

"Yes, sir. Surveillance on Cadogan Hall has continued as well."

"Then why are we no closer to an answer? I want answers."

The only reaction from my Canadian was a cool nod. "As do we all, sir. We are doing everything in our power. My sources at Scotland Yard indicate that an arrest is imminent. The only reason it hasn't already occurred is because Reese hasn't returned to his lodgings."

A snort of disgust that sounded like a horse huffing came from the man in the chair. "The only thing the young man is guilty of is being a sap, but it could be helpful. With police attention diverted, the kidnappers may try again."

Expression still neutral, my fellow's hand clenched into a fist at his side. "Surely, we do not want them to try again. We should see them caught before the princess could be endangered."

"The tensions in Upper Canada are growing daily more fraught. The mob is goaded on by those rabble-rousers from Lower Canada and emboldened by America."

My colonial spread his hands. "Unfortunately, we have no official status before Parliament and the Tudor days are gone. We cannot simply seize anyone we suspect and put them to the rack until they confess."

"More's the pity," grumped his inquisitor.

"There is no proof. I am investigating, but there isn't much to go on."

The shaggy gray head shook. "It's gone on too long, Jack." He sighed. "We can't afford to delay any longer. We must know if he is involved. If we can at least eliminate him as a possibility, then we could leave the rest to A Division in the knowledge that whatever happens has nothing to do with Upper Canada."

"We could simply take our concerns to A Division and let them sort it out. That would also alleviate Upper Canada of any culpability."

"We've already had that discussion. It's not feasible."

My arms and legs were starting to quiver with the effort of maintaining my position.

With a rustle and groan from the tired chair, the gray-haired man stood. "I don't want to have this conversation again, Mr. Harding. You know what needs to be done. I expect you to do it."

The older man left the room, leaving my Canadian alone. I was about to climb down when the window sash was thrown open and the fellow I now knew was Jack Harding, stuck his head out. "Did you get all that?"

For a moment, the power of speech left me as my face burned, and I actually considered letting go of the pipe and dropping to my death. "There's no way you knew I was following you," I finally choked out.

He grinned. "I made it easy enough. I even walked in the outermost hallways so that the lamplight would lead you to me."

"Come on." He extended a hand out the window. "Your arms must be about to give out."

Since I really was at risk of falling to my death, I took the proffered hand, and he helped haul me inside the room. My final tumble over the sill was somewhat inelegant. "What was all that about? Who do you suspect of trying to kidnap the princess, and why on earth would it implicate Upper Canada?"

"You can't guess?"

I glared at him.

Laughing, he held up a hand in mock surrender. "All right."

I massaged my upper arms one after the other. "And who are you?"

"I am an…investigator. I often work for the Upper Canadian government and others on issues of a sensitive nature."

"You're a spy."

"I am not."

"What other term is there?"

"I'm a private enquiry agent."

"Sounds like a spy," I grumbled under my breath.

"Do you want to know about my suspect or not?"

Trying my best to look penitent, I nodded. "I do."

"The princess's father was marginally more sober than his brothers, but he had his share of indiscretions throughout the years."

"I'm aware."

"Many years ago, well before his marriage to the duchess, he served as Commander-in-Chief of British North America. He was the first royal to tour Upper and Lower Canada."

This was hardly news.

"While he was in Quebec and later in Halifax he set up house with a woman named Julie de Saint Laurent. They had met while he was still stationed on the Continent and begun an affair, though she was already married." Jack paused to make sure I was still following. "When he was given the post in Canada, Madame de Saint Laurent joined him after her first husband died. They kept house together quite openly and many

Canadians had no idea that she wasn't his actual wife. Two rumors have persisted about their relationship. The first is that during their early days in Quebec they were married in a Roman Catholic service. The second, even more persistent rumor is that she bore him two children during this time, a boy and a girl."

At this my eyebrows shot up.

"Are you saying—?"

He nodded ruefully. "Exactly. If it can be demonstrated that Edward was legitimately married to Madame de Saint Laurent, then her firstborn, the son as it happens, could argue that he is the rightful heir to the throne, not Victoria."

"But Victoria's presence or absence would make no difference to such a claim. She would be irrelevant."

He gave a single shake of his head. "Perhaps on the surface it seems that way. But without Victoria, the next in line is…"

"Prince Ernest."

"Edward's younger brother isn't well-liked or trusted in England. Many still believe he murdered his valet. If people are given a choice between an illegitimate usurper and sweet young Victoria, they will obviously side with the princess. But if the other choice is Ernest…well, the powers that be may decide a little fresh blood in the Hanoverian line isn't such a bad idea after all."

It made a certain amount of perverse sense. As I thought about it, it could explain why they were trying kidnapping instead of outright assassination. They didn't want a dead body. If she was dead, then the crown would simply pass to Ernest. They needed uncertainty about her status and time for a rival to make his claim. At least initially, they couldn't afford a public death.

I chewed on the inside of my lip. "Who is this would-be king?"

"William Fennick. He was adopted as a baby by the commissary general of the British garrison at Halifax. He just happens to be in London currently, staying with Lord Bancroft."

I considered. "He's been somewhat overlooked by society, but I've heard he's incredibly rich. Bancroft, I mean. Not Fennick."

"He's been more than overlooked. He's been shunned because of the way he would always retreat before Bonaparte. He became an object of scorn and ridicule. But that's not all."

I waited for him to continue.

He glanced over his shoulder as if to make sure again that the door was closed. "There is a great deal of unrest in Upper and Lower Canada both. Less so in the other provinces. But the ideals of America and their success as an independent nation have many reconsidering their loyalties."

I frowned, trying to absorb this. "So, Fennick has the backing of these rebels for a sort of coup that will put someone with Canadian interests on the throne?"

"To be honest, I don't know the source of his backing. All we have are suspicions. Nothing concrete, and that's the problem. Someone definitely is playing at kingmaker."

"Why are you telling me this?"

His gaze skittered away from mine. "The princess has taken a liking to you, and you have access to her. I presumed you would wish to protect her interests."

"You are well informed," I said coolly.

He shrugged modestly.

"I don't believe you."

His jaw fell open as if offended. "I assure you—"

"Your sponsor or patron, or however you would classify that

LISA KARON RICHARDSON

gentleman who just left, clearly didn't want us British to know of the possibility of a Canadian threat. You've told me anyway."

He grimaced. "He's wrong. Our priority should be protecting the princess. His strategy puts her at risk, prioritizing Upper Canada's reputation above her safety. For all of his concern for Upper Canada's good name, he is doing nothing to address the trouble brewing there. It's as if he is hopeful it will all just die down. But if Fennick's sponsor is an organization, his reach could be far more extensive than we have considered. They could have influence in any number of ways over parliament's members. Influence that could be traded in for votes regarding the succession plan."

I wasn't sure I believed everything he had told me, but here at least I agreed with him. "Why have you chosen to confide in me?"

He sighed heavily. "I don't know who you're working for, but it's clear you have specialized training. I..." He cleared his throat. "I happened to be near the orangery working in the guise of a gardener at the first attempt. We didn't know there was going to be a kidnapping per se, but we were investigating. The men entered the orangery but before I could even get inside, I saw you take them both down. You singlehandedly foiled that plot. That's why I placed you under surveillance. I wanted to know more about you." He grinned. "You're certainly resourceful. Who do *you* work for?"

"You could say I work for the princess."

He narrowed his eyes.

I smiled beatifically. "Didn't the Royal Marriages Act prevent any of George III's descendants from marrying without the express consent of the crown? There are oodles of illegitimate royal offspring. The mere fact of his parentage can't be

151

the only reason you're so concerned. Not even in light of the republican rumblings."

"He is said to have evidence that George III did sign an official document agreeing to the prince's marriage to Madam de Saint Laurent."

This surprised me. "If the king consented, why the need for secrecy?"

"King George wasn't always…lucid."

I pushed my lips out as I thought. Caught myself and stopped. Dame Guinevere said the habit made me look like a fish. Poor old mad King George. Someone could have gotten him to sign something when he wasn't quite himself.

Jack had paused to allow me to think through the ramifications.

From deep in the recesses of my mind a memory of one of Dame Guinevere's lectures surfaced. "Doesn't the Royal Marriages Act require the crown's consent be entered into the records of the Privy Council as well?"

He looked mildly surprised that I knew that. "A search has been made. That particular volume of the Privy Council records happens to be missing."

I raised an eyebrow.

"Precisely."

"What else?" I crossed my arms and waited.

"Fennick has a bit of a history of…self-aggrandizement and wanting to manipulate politics. He's greedy and not above unscrupulous ways of accessing cash. It's rumored that he's dabbled in blackmail—which he used to control political votes."

That was a surprise. I hadn't suspected outright criminal behavior. "Blackmail is an ugly business."

"Almost as ugly as kidnapping."

"But surely, with that kind of history Fennick can't really

expect he'll get the sort of backing he'd need from the House of Lords to make a claim."

Jack shrugged. "Nothing's ever been proven. In fact, no charges have even been filed. Local officials were certain he was guilty but were unable to find any evidence. He's cagey."

I waggled my eyebrows. "So am I." With that, I returned to the window and began lowering myself down.

Jack leaned his head out the window. "I could have let you out the front door."

I chose to ignore this unnecessary remark. I had a great deal to discuss with Colleen and, I suspected, not much time to plan.

Chapter 16

I turned my head as if fascinated by something outside the steam carriage window, but really, I was trying to hide my yawn from Dame Guinevere. It didn't work.

Her riding crop came up within a second to tap my chin closed. "I hope you don't intend to gape like a fish in the princess's presence."

"No, ma'am."

"I have noticed a great deal of yawning from you lately. Clearly you are not getting the rest you need."

"I'm quite rested. Thank you."

She simply stared at me.

I bit my tongue to keep from babbling something and making her even more suspicious. The only way I could conceal information from Dame Guinevere was to say absolutely nothing, and even that wasn't foolproof.

Luckily, we turned into the palace drive at that moment, and her interrogation was cut short.

The duchess greeted us more cordially than she had previously. In fact, she seemed to be in very high spirits. Victoria also looked pleased about something.

"I suppose you've heard that A Division has finally made an arrest," the duchess said as she settled herself in the best chair.

Dame Guinevere's expression gave no hint as to whether she was already aware of this development or not.

I certainly had not been aware, even if I had been expecting it. "Who was it?"

"Some dreadful little person from Gibraltar apparently. Completely unhinged, of course."

"Of course." I accepted a cup and saucer. "Just one man, though?"

"You don't think there could be more than one fiend out there seeking to harm the princess?"

The toe of Dame Guinevere's pointed boots made sharp, but discreet, contact with my ankle.

I did not spill my tea.

"No, of course not," Dame Guinevere said. "What a silly idea."

Despite the duchess's announcement, I didn't think that news of the arrest really accounted for her good humor.

I was right. When the princess and I managed to get away, she told me she'd had a letter from King William. He meant to get Victoria an allowance from Parliament of 30,000 pounds a year just for her.

It was a fortune.

"Your mother must be quite pleased by the compliment paid you," I said.

"She's pleased because she thinks she's going to have it all at her disposal. But that is not going to happen. As soon as I turn eighteen next week, I'm turning Conroy out on his ear."

"Isn't he your mother's retainer?"

Victoria didn't like the gentle reminder that she might not have the power to rid herself of Conroy quite yet. There was a bitter twist to her lips. "Since hearing of the king's plan for my income, he has been browbeating me constantly. I really thought he might strike me last night. He wants me to make him my private secretary or keeper of the privy purse. As if I would ever. No. Either he goes, or I do. I shall move to Saint James's Palace to be near my uncle and aunt. The king has spoken before of wishing that I would. Mother would hate that. She is always fearful someone else may win some influence over me." The princess shook her head. "If she only knew that her attempts to keep me trapped here and dependent on her make me more determined to escape."

"Shall I make another search of his quarters?"

"Yes. I think so." She nodded. "I feel the need to get a bit of my own back."

Within moments, I once more found myself outside the door to Sir John's domain. This time I could hear voices in the room. No one else was in the corridor, so I paused to listen.

If that tweedy, placid voice was anything to go by, Lord Liverpool was ensconced in the office with Sir John, though I could not make out his words.

A bang reverberated through the door making me jump and Sir John's voice rose, reaching me with ease. "If Victoria will not listen to reason she must be coerced!"

Lord Liverpool's voice rose correspondingly. "I could never condone such a course. The princess is well within her rights in this matter, and I do not feel that the king would look kindly on any such attempt from you or the duchess."

Well, well, well. Conroy very much wanted one of those positions. He was trying to enlist aid from other quarters. No doubt, he could feel his grasp on the princess slipping.

I could scarcely search the room while Sir John was inside and I was about to turn back the way I'd come when a thought occurred to me. What about Louisa?

Of all people, I should know not to discount the potential

of a young woman to get up to trouble. I'd been meaning to look into her more.

I reversed course. Surely, her rooms would be located near her father's suite?

At the next door, I tapped lightly before poking my head inside. It was a smaller room with no personal effects. Probably a guest room. The same was true of the next room I tried and the one after that. As I emerged from the latter, a maid entered the hallway.

She paused and bobbed a curtsy at the sight of me, but a small frown puckered her forehead.

I smiled as charmingly as I could. "I seem to have gotten muddled. Can you direct me to Miss Louisa's rooms?"

"Yes, miss. Just this way." She led me back through the hall the way I'd come and to the door on the other side of Sir John's suite. "Shall I announce you?"

"I don't think that will be necessary. I'm hardly the princess." I raised my hand to tap briskly.

The maid nodded and hurried on her way, obviously glad not to be distracted any further from her tasks.

No sound came from inside and, once the maid was out of sight, I opened the door. This room was large and airy with a pretty view of the gardens. Pink damask covered the walls and the furniture was decorated in needlepoint flowers. I tried to imagine Louisa Conroy's life here—despised by the princess, but pressured by her father to pursue a friendship with her future queen. It was possible she was even lonelier than Victoria.

I began a thorough search of the room, starting with the writing desk that stood adjacent to one of the windows. Her letters from her few friends were full of trivialities about ribbons, laces, minor household happenings, and gossip from around town.

The novels on her shelf were of the type designed to instill virtuous character in young women, most sappy romances full of rainbows and happy endings. I checked under the bed, under the mattress, behind picture frames unsure what I was looking for, but wanting to make sure I didn't miss anything.

Where would a young woman secrete something when maids were constantly about? I checked her sewing box. Sure enough, buried at the bottom was a small pile of half a dozen letters bound together with a blue, silk ribbon. They were the real kind, not the sort carried by the pigeon force.

I sat on the settee situated under the window and pulled out the first one. I gasped when I deciphered the signature at the bottom: William Fennick.

The letter was full of compliments and endearments. The man was clearly paying court to Conroy's daughter. Was it with Sir John's knowledge?

I refolded the first letter and removed the second. More of the same. The third professed himself devoted to her. This letter was slightly different. It was full of questions about things at Kensington Palace, professing he wanted to know everything he could of her life since they could not yet be together. The others were similar in nature to this one.

When I'd read the last letter, I folded it up, slipped it back in the ribbon, then replaced the stack in her sewing box. Was Louisa aware that Mr. Fennick might have designs on the throne? Or was he simply using her to gather intelligence about the princess and operations at Kensington Palace that could be used, for example, in a kidnapping attempt?

I was so lost in thought that when the door opened, I jumped, startled.

Miss Louisa paused on the threshold, a bonnet and parasol clutched in her hand. "What are you doing?" she demanded.

She and the princess looked alike in some ways, but objectively, she was prettier than Victoria. Her hair was a glossy brown, parted in the middle and formed into two wings that covered her ears. Her nose straight, her lips the sort of rosebud pout that was all the rage among sentimental poets. She was taller than the princess and me, her bearing erect.

I stood and straightened my skirts, summoning a smile. "The princess was hoping you would join us for a nice chat and perhaps some refreshments." Victoria was going to be furious, but she'd have to back my story. At least, until I was able to tell her what I had learned.

Louisa snorted and stepped into the room, tossing her bonnet and parasol onto the bed. "I find that unlikely."

"Why?"

She put a hand on her hip. "The princess and I take little enough pleasure in one another's company."

I continued to play the role of naïve outsider. "I'm sure that's not true."

She pulled off one glove then the other. "Oh, but it is. I don't understand her at all. She has all my father's attention and devotion. He does everything to make certain she is provided for and comes to no harm, yet—despite all the care lavished on her—she remains ungracious and quarrelsome." She flung the gloves on the bed as if punctuating her sentence.

This was interesting. Louisa did indeed resent the princess almost as much as the princess resented her. Not only that, but she was jealous of the way her father bent every energy to advance Victoria's interests while virtually ignoring Louisa.

I gaped as if at a loss for something to say, which, in fact, I was.

This girl seemed deeply unhappy. I had a feeling she wouldn't mind too much if Victoria keeled over dead, but would she involve herself in a kidnapping scheme? Especially if that would mean her father's ambitions would be crushed?

She sighed and her shoulders slumped. For a second, I thought I saw the sheen of tears in her eyes. Then she straightened and projected a smile. "Please excuse me. I've had a trying morning. I would be more than happy to attend Her Highness."

I nodded and smiled and moved to join her.

Her smile grew a little tentative. "I would appreciate it if you wouldn't mention my unkind words to the princess. I don't mean it."

"Certainly," I murmured.

It didn't seem likely that Louisa would have the resources to have hired men and an airship to do her bidding. Not just financially, because there were other ways of gaining loyalty. I didn't think Louisa had the gravitas or wherewithal to be a criminal mastermind.

However, she could be an effective pawn.

Chapter 17

Colleen shook her head when she saw my getup for the evening. "Really?"

I nodded. "It won't do much good for me to be arrested if I'm put in the women's lockup. I'm going to need your help though."

Her eyebrows rose. "In the field?"

"Of course, in the field. You're going to have to rescue me."

"That sounds about right."

"Very funny. Ha ha." I mimed a laugh. "Do you want to construct a plan?"

She gave me an enigmatic smile. "Don't worry about it. I will get you out."

The very idea of trusting someone else to control my escape made my heart beat a bit faster. But this was Colleen. If she said she'd do something, she'd do it.

I finished tucking the last stray strand of my red hair under a short brown wig. "All right. Give me a couple of hours at least. It may take me a bit to find an opportunity to speak to Mr. Reese."

"You should give yourself the illusion of stubble as Miss Yancey taught us. It will help sell your character. Otherwise, your face is too feminine."

I whirled to peer into the looking glass again. "Drat. I was afraid of that."

Once I finally got my disguise to pass muster, i.e. Colleen's caustic gaze, I splashed a bit of purloined brandy on my shirt. That should help sell the story. Then I slipped into the night.

This was going to be fun.

As I rounded the front of Cadogan Hall, a small scraping sound came from the front door. A dark figure stepped out then turned back to do something with the lock. I watched from the shadows. The person moved toward me, definitely a person rather than a mechanical. I held completely still and stared with all my might.

She passed within a few feet of me. Eleanor. I knew from the expensive perfume she wore and the silver buttons reflecting from the front of her jacket as they caught a hint of moonlight.

Well. Well. Well.

I positively itched to know what she was up to. I started to follow, but she was going in the opposite direction from A Division. I sighed. An image of the princess's determined face rose in my thoughts and I stopped. If Eleanor was investigating, she was following her own lines of inquiry, and I should be happy about that. I should leave her to her investigation and keep on with my own. So long as the princess was kept safe, it didn't matter who would ultimately be responsible for that.

It was going to be me though.

Maneuvers to make sure I was not being followed were becoming rote, but conscious of what Dame Guinevere termed my tendency to err on the side of "economy of effort" and wanting to make sure I wasn't interrupted, I took a few extra precautions. Once I was certain I was free of any followers, I made a beeline for A Division and lay in wait.

It didn't take as long as I feared before a couple of bobbies

emerged and walked my way. There wasn't much to choose between the two of them, they were both of a size and shared similar coloring except that one sported an enormous moustache
while the other had opted for truly luxuriant muttonchops.

I began my performance with low muttering as I emerged
from the alley where I lurked. I staggered then launched into
song, raising my arm as if in a toast. "Here's a health to the
king and a lasting peace—" The old drinking song ought to
immediately make them think of low pubs and previous in-
cidents with public intoxication. They slowed and, as if they
had choreographed the movement, each placed a hand on their
truncheons.

I slurred a couple of lines into illegibility. "For there's no
drinking after death. And he that will this health deny." I grew
louder and more expansive in my movements. "Down among
the dead men, down among the dead men, down, down—"

"'Ere now lad, what are you about?" They had come within
a dozen paces or so.

I squinted at them as if trying to bring them into focus.
"Down among the dead men let him lie!"

"You sound as if you've been in your cups, young sir." Moustache cocked his head.

Nine feet.

I halted and thrust my chin up. "I? I! That...I'll tell you." I
waggled a finger in their direction. "That's an insult. I demand
satisfaction, sir."

"Now, laddie, there's no call for that." Muttonchops sounded as if he was trying to hold back a laugh. "Whereabouts are
you headed?"

"I fail—fail to see what business that is of yours." I swayed.
Six feet.

"You need to—"

"No. No. You need to leave a perfely—a perf—a good fellow alone. You bobbies." I spat out the last word as if it tasted bad.

Moustache rolled his eyes.

I was within an arm's length now. "I could do a better job of keeping the safe city." Lightning fast, I snatched the helmet from Moustache's head and pulled it toward me. Cackling, I turned as if I meant to patrol the city in his place.

"Oi!"

Muttonchops' heavy hand landed on my shoulder. "Now you've done it. You need to settle down."

I staggered. "I'm a free Englishman." I started singing more loudly yet and made a feeble attempt to pull free from his grasp.

Moustache seemed to have recovered from his outrage. He retrieved his helmet and popped it on his head.

I started yelling. "Police! I've been robbed! Police!"

Moustache had had quite enough of my shenanigans. "That's it. You're coming with us."

I kept yelling as they hauled me into the police station. I accused Moustache of stealing my helmet and insisted I was the real bobby. I refused to tell them my name, telling them they could call me Constable. Within moments, I was given a good cuff to the head and tossed into a holding cell. The two officers retreated to the more civilized spaces beyond. It was a good thing they left too, because as soon as they were gone, I developed a fit of the giggles. Luckily, no one else was there to hear me.

Although that raised the question of where they were keeping the Gibraltarian. I craned to see down the hall. The cell in which I had been tossed had bars, but was otherwise open to the hall. So was the cell next to it. But at the end of the hall was a door with a couple of metal covered hatches. That had to be where they would keep a treasonous, would-be kidnapper. No matter. I could make it work.

I removed my decorative cravat pin and slipped my thumbnail into the crack that looked like filigree. In a moment, it came apart, and I had an admirable pair of lockpicks. I moved to the cell door and had just inserted them into the lock, when a thump against the inner door to the station made me jerk back. I thrust the picks into my pocket as the door opened wide and another drunk was brought in.

"I'm glad to see you've come to your senses." I slurred for all I was worth and swiped at my nose with the back of my hand.

"Not so hasty there. We've brought you company." One of the officers unlocked the cell door. The man they were dragging along with them seemed to find something hilarious. He was laughing and mumbling to himself.

Well, this could complicate things, but Colleen and I had planned for such an eventuality. I patted my pocket for the vial of drops that would have him peacefully snoozing within a matter of minutes. Then, I caught a glimpse of the fellow's face. Irritation surged through me.

My new companion was heaved into the cell, landing in a still-chuckling heap. The officers withdrew, shaking their heads. I was sorely tempted to roll my eyes.

As soon as the door closed behind the bobbies I rounded on the fellow. "What are you doing here?"

"Me? What are *you* doing here," he eyed me up and down, "sir?" Jack sniggered as he sprang up with an alacrity that left no doubt his drunkenness had been as much of a ruse as mine.

I raised my chin. "It would seem that we are both here for the Gibraltarian."

"Well, where is he?"

"You don't know?"

He looked around. "I can guess." He bent and pulled a pair of lockpicks from his boot.

"If you do that, I will raise the alarm and say you were trying to escape."

He looked at me with a wounded expression. "You wouldn't."

"I would. I came to interview him. I can't have anyone muddying the waters."

"Well, what do you propose? Maybe I'll call for the police if you try to sneak out of this cage."

In retrospect, I may have used the wrong tactic. We glared at one another for a long moment.

At last, I broke the silence. "Do you know of any connection between Mr. Fennick and Sir John Conroy?"

This seemed to take the Canadian aback. He tilted his head. "Conroy?"

"Yes. The duchess's comptroller, and some claim more."

"What makes you ask that?"

I shrugged and offered a surface-deep explanation. "The princess loathes Sir John. Since you've been investigating Mr. Fennick longer than I, I wondered if you had come across any connection."

He gave me another look.

I sighed. He'd been forthcoming with me. "I've come across an indication that Mr. Fennick may have some sort of attachment to Sir John's daughter."

"Louisa?" Jack nodded thoughtfully a V puckering his forehead. "That's interesting. Do you think he's using her, or do you suspect the opposite?"

I shook my head. "I don't honestly know."

"Is Sir John aware?"

"I don't know that either." My thoughts resumed the treadmill they had worn smooth during the last day. "Sir John could be more aware of Victoria's dislike of him than he lets on. It's possible he decided to hedge his bets through his daughter? Father-in-law to the king would be a much more secure position than advisor to the queen's mother."

I wasn't sure if I was happy or frightened that he didn't reject the possibility out of hand. Our gazes locked. "How could we prove or disprove it?"

"There again, I don't know. I've searched his suite in the palace and didn't find anything incriminating, but a smart man would be careful not to keep anything incriminating. I may not like the man, but he's not stupid."

Jack took a moment to respond and when he did it was with an apparent non sequitur. "Are we agreed that Mr. Reese is an innocent?"

"I don't think he's guilty of anything, but I wanted to speak to him before ruling him out," I said.

"Agreed. I don't think the conspirators would have laid a trail to anyone who actually had anything to do with the plot." He did not break eye contact. "Look, we'd get further working together."

I waited for his speech about how men were better equipped for this kind of task—blah, blah, blah. I would set him straight on that score if nothing else. Instead, he astonished me.

"You know all about this court stuff and these players. If he knows anything, you'll get more out of him than I can. Or at least more that we can make sense of."

All of the starch and vinegar I had been about to pour out drained away. "I—well, yes. I agree with you." *Pathetic.*

"All right. Then what can I do to assist?"

"I could use some cover."

The door opened again and an officer stuck his head in and gave us a squint.

Jack winked at me. Actually winked.

He turned to the officer and doffed his hat. "You're jus' in time. We will serenade you." He clapped his hat back on his head and at the top of his voice launched into an alcohol-soaked rendition of "Spanish Ladies."

I smothered the giggle welling up in my belly and joined him with gusto. "Farewell and adieu unto you, Spanish ladies!"

The bobby rolled his eyes in disgust and closed the door with a bang.

Jack grinned and waggled his eyebrows as he continued to sing. I kept it up too as I plucked my lockpicks back out and went to work on the lock. In a trice, it opened. Still singing, I stepped into the hall and pulled the door so that it didn't quite catch behind me. A moment later, I was at the end of the hall.

While Jack kept singing, I eased open the hatch in the door that would allow me to look in. The cell that was revealed had plain whitewashed walls and a cot with a flimsy mattress, pillow, and blanket. On the cot lay a young man. He was unshaven and thin. His wrists and hands protruded from his shirtsleeves looking knobby and overlarge. In short, he looked like they'd had him on the rack. He sat up at the sound of the flap opening and laid aside the book he had been reading. He gazed at me with red-rimmed, soulful brown eyes set above a prominent nose.

"Are you Mr. Andrew Reese?"

He nodded. "Who are you?"

"It's unimportant."

He frowned.

I continued. "What is important is that, if you are innocent of any attempts on the princess, I want to help you."

He stood and came closer to the door. "You're not with the police, are you?"

"No."

"I'm not sure I should talk to you."

"Do you have anything to lose? If I'm not able to help, then you're no worse off than you are now." I continued as if assuming his agreement. "Why does Inspector Ogden believe you are behind the kidnapping attempts?"

"He found some sort of cane in my room." His accent was very slight, only discernible with certain sounds.

I acted as if I knew nothing of it. "I see. Where did you get this cane?"

"I never had a cane. I don't know what he's talking about." He rubbed a hand through his hair in frustration.

"That's it? He found a cane?"

"That and I'm from Gibraltar." His gaze slid away from mine.

I followed up on the point. "Just that you're from Gibraltar?"

He sighed, his gaze still lowered. "My father was a soldier. He was killed under the Duke of Kent's charge when he was Governor of Gibraltar."

"He was a mutineer?"

Head still lowered, he nodded.

"Do you blame the duke for his death?"

"I don't even remember him, but the way I understand it, the duke didn't want the men hanged and was sorry for it."

If hatred of the duke was his motive, he had just passed up a perfect opportunity to climb up on his soapbox and expound upon his grievances. People are rarely able to let such a chance slip by even if a little discretion could save their lives. "Is there anything else which they think makes you guilty?"

He huffed. "They claimed they found a monkey in my room too."

Again, I played ignorant. "A monkey?"

"As if I had time or money for a monkey. I work all day every day to save enough money to send back home to my mother and sisters. How could anyone think I had a monkey? The landlord doesn't even allow pets."

"Do you own a ruby ring? Perhaps an heirloom?"

"A ring? No."

"Do you know if the police found such an item in your room?"

His brow furrowed again. "Not that they've said. Why? Is it important?"

I bit my lower lip. "I'm not sure." I tried to focus. "What kind of work do you do?"

"I'm a bricklayer. I used to dream of apprenticing as an architect, but there's no way that's going to happen now. Who's going to provide for my mum and sisters with me locked up in here?" He sounded so forlorn at the idea of his family being destitute that, if I had not already been inclined to believe him, I would have been persuaded.

"Where were you three nights ago?"

"Home sleeping. That's where I am most every night."

"Was anyone with you?" I could feel the pressure of time speeding away. Jack was still warbling, but the police could return any moment and there would be nowhere to hide.

"No. Not even a dashed monkey."

I smiled at his adamant attempt at a joke.

"What about ten days ago in the afternoon? Where were you?"

He shrugged. "The police didn't ask me about that day. I'd have to think about it, but I work every day but Sunday until seven."

Interesting. That had been the day of the attack I had

thwarted. I didn't recognize him as either of the men who had made that attempt, which wasn't conclusive, but it was something. "Do you think your boss would be able to swear to it?"

"I'm sure he would." An eager expression crossed his face. "Is it important?"

"It could be."

He gave me the name of his foreman, the company he worked for, and described the location of the worksite. "Do you think you can help me?"

"I'll do everything I can."

Jack's singing changed. "Come away! Come away!"

"Gotta go." I smacked closed the hatch and raced back to my cell.

Jack had the door standing open. When I darted in, he pulled it shut.

The outer door swung in again, and Moustache stuck his head in. "Shut up already, or I'll ask the magistrate to add a week of hard labor to your sentences."

When he had gone, I recounted my conversation with Mr. Reese for Jack.

He was a good listener.

When I was done, he rubbed his chin. "I can check at the worksite to see if he was there as he claims."

I nodded and gave him the details. Although it went against the grain, since he was being so open, I decided to do the same. "I will be researching the gentleman who is hosting Mr. Fennick."

"Lord Bancroft?"

"Yes. I can't quite imagine what that man believes he is about. His whole reputation rests on cowardice. But a plot to kidnap the heir presumptive is not for the fainthearted. It's possible he's not aware. Perhaps if we can get to the bottom of that question, then we can determine who is actually pulling the strings."

"I understand the fellow is—"

The door swung in hard enough that it hit the wall. I jumped as Officer Moustache stood framed in the doorway. "C'mon, laddie. Looks like Mummy is here to save the day."

I thought at first that he must be talking to Jack, then remembered my disguise.

Mummy? I didn't know what he was talking about, but I obligingly staggered to my feet.

He approached the cell door, pulled out a large ring of keys, and unlocked the door.

I stepped through, and he grabbed hold of my upper arm and spoke low in my ear. "If it had been up to me, you'd be doing some hard labor for your stunt, young sir. I suggest you cut back on your drinking and make yourself useful to your mother and the nation."

"Yessir. You betcha." I gave a clumsy salute with my free hand.

Sighing, he led me away.

"Farewell, chum," I caroled to Jack. "I hope you get outta here soon."

He shook his head and offered a crisper salute than the one I had given Moustache as I was escorted from the holding area.

"Mummy" turned out to be Colleen. She was wearing a fine dress of black moiré, an impressive string of pearls and various other jewels, as well as a veil which obscured her features. I assumed that her gray hair was a wig. At my appearance, she gave a shudder and raised a handkerchief to dab at her eyes beneath the veil. "Oh, Charles. What could you have been thinking? I can't even begin to think what your father would have said if he could see you now." I was impressed. Her voice sounded like a matron's, rather than a schoolgirl's.

I was paraded over to the desk of another officer. This fellow was ruddy with the sort of windblown coloring that comes either from being in the outdoors too much or heavy drinking. He had both muttonchops and a moustache. "Now, sir. Your mother has informed me of the recent loss of your father." He cleared his throat. "It is for her sake that I have agreed to overlook the disgraceful conduct you exhibited tonight." He was looking at me with the same gimlet glare Dame Guinevere often adopted.

I looked to "Mummy" and then back at the officer. Blinked twice. "Thank you, sir." Then I yawned widely.

As expected, the lecture had only begun. He was off in an instant waxing eloquent about the dissipation of modern young people at large and myself in particular. I nodded penitently when he paused to draw breath. It took a solid quarter of an hour, but he eventually ran out of steam.

"Now, I expect you to apologize to the officer whose helmet you took, and then you can be on your way." He wagged a finger at me. "But don't let me catch you in your cups again, young sir. You go home and take care of your poor mother."

I was led to where Moustache sat at a desk. "Sir." I worked my jaw a bit. "I offer my 'pologies for the insult I did you." In a grand gesture I swept off my hat and made a low bow, appearing to almost fall over for my efforts.

Moustache and Mummy steadied me.

Colleen shook her head and held tightly to my arm as we made our way toward the door. "You ham," she muttered in a low voice.

Just as we reached the door it swung open and Inspector Ogden stepped into the station. He looked exhausted, with dark circles under his eyes. He did a double take. A questioning expression came across his face.

I lowered my head as we passed, and we left him behind, gazing after us curiously.

Chapter 18

The next morning, lessons started promptly with a dis-
section of the London papers. As Lady Pomeroy kept
telling us, we could learn a lot about the power of
the various political factions by paying attention to the gossip
columns. Though much of it might be mean-spirited twad-
dle, gems could be gleaned that would inform a careful Praetorienne when someone might be switching sides or allianc-
es forming or breaking. Then there were the agony columns.
These could be encoded, and Lady Pomeroy shared a number
of anecdotes about how the personal ads had been the lynchpin
in solving one conundrum or another for a queen. She chortled
merrily when she came across one she was certain gave all the
details of a planned elopement. At the end of her lecture, she
set us to *Debrett's Peerage* to see if we could figure out to whom
the ad referred.

Normally, I was quite good at such puzzles, but I had no
patience with the practice today. I was tired, a bit cranky, and
most of all aggravated that I still had no solid answers regarding
the princess's would-be kidnappers. It was all well and good to
eliminate suspects, but I would much rather catch someone.

Eleanor raised her hand then tossed me a smile over her
shoulder. She gave her answer.

I smothered a yawn.

And what had she been up to? Colleen and I had discussed that little mystery at length to no avail.

After our morning lesson, we were bundled into the steam carriage and taken on a sightseeing excursion to the Tower and Westminster Abbey. All our instructors accompanied us and they took it in turn to lecture us on various points of interest. Although, *their* lectures went a bit beyond the common tourist patter.

I tried to pay attention. I really did.

Finally, much to the delight of the other girls, our agenda for the day took us to one of the most fashionable modistes in the city for final fittings on our gowns for Princess Victoria's birthday ball. I hadn't been able to afford a new gown, but I was having an old gown made over so that it was *au courant*. As the customer spending the least, I was at the end of the line for my fitting. Which was fine with me. While everyone else was busy, I sat quietly in a plush chair with my thoughts.

Before I knew what had happened, I was awakened by something hard prodding my shoulder. I started and blinked. Dame Guinevere was standing over me, hands clasped loosely in front of her. "It's time we talked."

I sighed inwardly. I was too tired for this right now. "Yes, ma'am."

She led the way to a sort of sitting room and closed the door behind us as if she owned the place.

For all I knew, she did.

"Lady Portia, I'd like to know what is going on."

"Ma'am?"

"You have been inattentive in your lessons. You're yawning frequently. There are dark circles under your eyes, and now I find you asleep in a public salon."

"I'm sorry, ma'am. I—well…concern for the princess has

been keeping me awake at night." All entirely true. "If I had managed to catch one of the assailants that day in the orangery, I could have ensured her safety. It's all my fault."

The glare she gave me was identical to that of the officer from the night before. It was cheering to know I created friends wherever I went. Turning her back on me, she went to a table and picked up a small bundle which I had tied with blue silk ribbon in the appropriate, time-honored style for love letters.

I swallowed hard.

She settled in a comfortable chair, leaving me standing. Then she placed the letters in her lap, resting a hand lightly on them. "Would you care to explain these?"

"No?" I didn't bother to feign outrage that she had searched my room. She wouldn't care. More importantly, she would have seen right through it. Searching people's things was, after all, an item of the curriculum.

"You've been sneaking out to see a young man, haven't you?"

"No, ma'am. I have not."

"You are trying my patience. Who is this young man? How did you meet?"

"I have not been sneaking out to meet him. But I will admit that I've met a young man. We've done nothing improper." Not in *that* way, at least.

"I assume he is not of the peerage?"

I nodded and looked at my shoes.

"Tell me about him."

This I had not expected. "What, ma'am?"

"Tell me about this beau of yours."

"He's not my beau."

She raised an eyebrow and tapped the letters in her lap twice.

I found myself describing Jack, but that was *only* because it would be easier to remember if I kept things simple. After describing his physical attributes, and his cleverness and wit, I stumbled to a halt.

Pinned like a bug to a specimen board by Dame Guinevere's gaze, I clasped my hands behind my back. "Ma'am, I swear to you I have not been sneaking out to see him at night."

"There is to be no further correspondence with this young man. Do you understand?"

I hung my head. "Yes, ma'am."

"Frankly, young lady, I am disappointed in you for a variety of reasons. Not the least of which is how obvious you have been. Have you learned nothing during your time at Saint Scholastica?" Ah, here was the lecture. This I had expected. "The other girls have been concerned about you."

That meant someone had expressed their "concerns" to Dame Guinevere. The rat. Which of my dear compatriots had it been?

Whoever it was, it was a fair bet they cleared it with Eleanor first, assuming she hadn't actually put them up to it. I thought about telling Dame Guinevere that Eleanor had been sneaking out at night but decided against it since I'd have to say how I knew. Instead, I made a mental note to settle scores.

Dame Guinevere carried on with her discourse on my shortcomings. I needed to look more to the future. I needed to remember my purpose and not be distracted.

That at least she was right about. I kept my expression somber, but inside I'd had an epiphany. The best vengeance I could wreak upon Eleanor and her cronies would be to turn them to my devices. Even an enemy can be used, if you know they're your enemy. I would make them pay, and they'd never even know it.

Dame Guinevere droned on as I plotted. After several

moments I gave a hint of trembling lower lip, before bravely staunching the waterworks.

I was afraid I had overplayed my hand, because Dame Guinevere paused and narrowed her eyes as she looked me over. "Do you understand what I have been telling you?"

"Yes, ma'am. I do. I'm sorry for my conduct, but since I cannot see Mr. Harding again, may I have his letters back?"

"Absolutely not. And do not use the pigeon carriers. There are too many ways for messages to be intercepted."

I let my shoulders slump.

"You may return for your fitting."

"Yes, ma'am."

As I left, she was untying the ribbon on the stack of letters. How long would it take her to realize the letters were in my poorly disguised handwriting and start digging deeper?

Chapter 19

I knew I should play it safe and not go out that night. My hubris would undoubtedly be my undoing, as Dame Guinevere had always made abundantly clear, but I had to take the risk. Time was not on my side. Another attempt could be made on the princess at any time. If I didn't figure this out, and the kidnappers succeeded, well, I didn't know if I could bear that. I would simply have to be extra careful not to get caught.

Colleen led me to her laboratory as soon as we had returned from the modiste. She was well aware of my plans and, while I had been spending a good deal of my free time running about the city accomplishing little, had split her time between research and inventing.

She wasted no time with preliminaries. "This is a bolas." From beneath her workbench, she pulled out a pair of interconnected long ribbons with a cluster of decorative baubles at three of the ends. "You'll want to practice with it a little."

"What is it?"

"It's a way to slow down or disable an opponent. You swing it like David's sling. Then you let it go. Aim for their legs. These endpieces are weighted. It will wrap around the limbs and trip them up."

"Interesting."

She handed me the device. "If it's thrown with enough force, it can even break bones."

My eyebrows went up. "Aah."

She smiled at my increased interest. "The ribbons are woven of spider line, so it won't break and will be harder for someone to untangle and remove." Then, using a dressmaker's mannequin, she demonstrated the proper technique for throwing the device.

I was impressed. "How did you come up with this?"

"It's an ancient weapon from South America. Simple, but effective and nearly silent. I designed it this way because it could also be used as a pretty sash."

"Ooh, it would go well with my green dress."

"Yes, I spoke with Marianne. She confirmed the best color combinations." Colleen grinned widely as we digressed for a moment. "That's why I chose this coppery material for the weighted pieces."

"Good thinking."

"There's another thing. Lord Bancroft's estate is downriver, outside of London proper. Since we don't have access to our own airship, the fastest way to get there will be by boat."

The thought of a river trip made me groan. "Can't we take the flying train?"

Given we both knew that if the estate was outside of London the trains wouldn't go far enough, Colleen ignored me, carrying on as if I hadn't even spoken. "I've made us these." Again, she reached below the workbench. This time she came up with a couple of fashionable riding bonnets similar to a man's top hat, except for broad ribbons that could be tied under the chin.

"You never cease to amaze me."

She cast me an exasperated glance and continued though

my compliment had been sincere. I knew as well as she that it must not be only a hat. Rather than debate my meaning, I listened attentively as she explained that the high crown concealed a flotation device. All we had to do if we were thrown into a body of water was untie the ribbons, remove the hat from our heads, and hang on.

Finally, based on my description and the example I had brought her, she had recreated Jack's distraction device. She gave me half a dozen that looked like sweets wrapped in paper twists. "Don't get them wet. If you do, they will be ineffective until they completely dry out again."

I nodded my understanding. "You know, I really do think your inventions are marvelous."

She tossed me a smile over her shoulder. "I know you do."

Glad we had that cleared up, I stowed away the paper twists. "And I'm glad you're going with me tonight."

At lights out, Colleen and I deployed her origami constructs in our beds in case Dame Guinevere or anyone else should decide to check on us. It was hardly a foolproof plan, but it was better than nothing. We then headed out the window. With Dame Guinevere on alert, it was simply too dangerous to attempt egress by other means. I was half hoping Jack would be outside in his guise as a cabman. I could have convinced him to drive us. It might take longer, but it would be so much more comfortable. Of course, since I wanted him, he was nowhere to be found. Now that we were ostensibly working together, maybe he no longer felt the need to watch my doings. I sighed and braced myself for the inevitable.

Colleen was leading the way. She looked back over her

shoulder and gave me an encouraging smile. "It'll be all right. I've already made arrangements. I sent a pigeon and rented a fast boat. We'll make the trip as quick as possible."

Thank the Lord for small mercies. I hastened my step and came abreast of her.

A rising fog made it easier to ensure that we weren't being followed as we neared the Thames. Still, just standing on the dock watching the incessant bobbing of the boats as Colleen paid the boatman and spun a story to explain our chaperone-less presence made nausea clamp around my throat. Couldn't the boats at least move in sync?

No. Instead, they moved at random, first one and then another lurching upwards.

"You are sure the water is not too choppy to be safe?" I asked the boatman.

He scratched the side of his neck, glancing between me and the river. "Uh, no, miss. River's as smooth as glass tonight."

Glass, my eye. This man was clearly not to be trusted.

Colleen pulled me away. "C'mon. We've rented his fastest steam sloop. It's the third down."

I climbed into the boat to which she directed me. Within a couple of moments, she had piloted us onto open water. My stomach surged forward with the boat. I focused on breathing through my nose. The horizon bobbed like a drunken seaman. I closed my eyes. Breathing in. Out.

In my mind, I ran over the limits of what we knew and had guessed so far, looking for holes. If Jack was right about Fennick and his motives, then that upstart claimant to the throne would have made sure to have compelling evidence of his right to the power he claimed. The Royal Marriages Act required that any descendant of George III obtain written consent from the monarch before a marriage could be contracted. I was willing to bet that any such document would be a forgery. But it would be a good quality forgery.

Colleen was already working on identifying an expert who could authenticate any documents we found.

Fennick would need other proof as well. The marriage license for Prince Edward and Julie de Saint Laurent, probably written affidavits from a clergyman who claimed to have married them, and other witnesses to the marriage. They'd probably all now be conveniently dead or unavailable. Perhaps a statement from the person who had delivered their children. What else could there be?

Our boat cut across a wave or something. My eyes flew open and my grip tightened on the bench upon which I sat. It felt like we'd been dropped off the edge of a cliff.

Colleen cast me a glance over her shoulder. "Sorry, we caught another boat's wake. You all right?"

"Lovely." Breathe. Breathe. My innards gurgled. I couldn't focus on the shore, but nor could I keep my eyes closed. My gaze found a spot of flaking paint on my bench and I stared at it as if my life depended upon it.

What else could there be?

What else?

There could be correspondence between Fennick and his parents or perhaps between his real parents and those who had actually reared him. They'd have to have come up with some reasonable explanation as to why, if the marriage and birth had been legitimate, his parents had allowed him to be reared by others and the honors due him denied.

The Marriages Act also required that the approval of the marriage be recorded in the Privy Council records. I would have wagered every penny of a year's allowance that they had appropriated the missing volume of the records from the council archives. Probably before the first assault had been made on the princess. No doubt, it had long since been reduced to a pile of ashes.

Truth was, it would be difficult to predict all the potential proofs they may have created. If we could find the documents they meant to use to validate Fennick's claims—and remove them—we could buy ourselves time. They'd have to have new fakes made. That ought to give us a couple of days when we knew they would not make another attack. We could focus and consider a plan to bring the fellows to justice instead of the harum-scarum chasing after clues we had been doing so far. I doubted anyone was likely to simply take my word for it.

Ooh. My stomach churned again. Breathe.

If the expert thought the documents were genuine…We'd cross that bridge when we came to it, but I thought it unlikely in the extreme. I was convinced that whatever documents they had were in large part forgeries. Otherwise, they would not have had to manufacture a succession crisis in order to make his claim. As the elder, his rights would have been primary. I couldn't imagine what excuse Mr. Fennick would give for why his royal father had never acknowledged him to the world.

My thoughts seesawed from point to point as topsy-turvy as the waves around us.

King William had always been fond of Victoria although he loathed her mother. If Victoria was not on the scene, could he be persuaded to support another's claim if it meant the duchess got her comeuppance?

A spray of river water struck my face. I flinched and shuddered. My throat was tightening and the back of my mouth was starting to water in the way that generally spelled disaster.

Breathe. Breathe.

Focus on something else.

Even if we excluded all other suspects, plenty of questions remained. Was Fennick the mastermind, or was it Bancroft? Maybe it was someone else entirely. If Bancroft was behind the conspiracy, it was an interesting departure in character or at least what was said of his character. Plotting a coup of this sort required nerves of iron and a willingness to gamble. Perhaps years of disdain and dismissal had turned his mind or made him cast aside fear in favor of revenge.

How much longer could this trip possibly—

"We're here." Colleen cut the boat's speed and did some other things at the helm. I had no idea what, I just wanted her to do them faster.

She thrust a rope at me. "When I come alongside the dock, hop out and tie us up."

I nodded.

Deftly, Colleen drew us close to the dock. I clambered over the side on wobbly legs, so grateful to be near solid ground that I risked falling in the drink.

The fog was thinner here than it had been in the heart of London. I caught a glimpse of the bulk of a manor house set on a rise overlooking the river. I was no expert on architecture, but it looked Elizabethan. The sort of place that boasted of its resident ghost and gloried in cold baths and lack of central heating under the—mistaken—conviction that such amenities built character. It was, in fact, a lot like home.

As we drew closer, I could see in the moonlight that it was indeed old and venerable with half-timbered walls above and brick below. Casement windows with tiny glass panes might or might not provide a means of entry, depending upon whether they had been made to open or not. Despite its age, the place looked well-tended. I saw no evidence of neglect in neatly laid out flowerbeds and well-trimmed hedges. In fact, I rather thought I might like the place in the daylight.

We moved carefully, each using a pair of the opera glasses. If skulduggery was afoot in this place, they'd be sure to have posted guards. We managed to find a way in through a laundry window. I was finding that laundries were frequently vulnerable. And no wonder. During the day they were steamy pits full of tubs of boiling linens, irons heating on the fire, and sweaty women laboring over backbreaking work. The only reason mechanicals had not been deployed to take over such a task was that no one had created one that didn't break down excessively due to rust.

Once inside, we paused before opening the laundry room door. Ears pressed to the door, we listened for any hint of movement. We had spotted a single pair of guards making a lazy circuit around the building. I anticipated more watchers, so it was best to be cautious.

It didn't take long to locate Bancroft's study. It was everything people generally think of when they hear the word study—wood-paneled walls adorned with hunting pictures and a large tapestry, a row of bookshelves which held richly bound volumes, a pair of comfortable dark leather armchairs, and, in pride of place, a massive wooden desk.

I took his desk while Colleen circled the room checking for a wall safe. On the blotter was a partially completed letter to Louisa Conroy. I read it carefully. From the effusive compliments, I had to conclude that this had either been written by Fennick or was being drafted for him to copy out later. Besides the florid language, the most noticeable thing about the letter was the litany of questions about the princess's upcoming birthday ball. They were woven in neatly. Not plopped on the page in a solid lump that would draw the attention of a casual observer, but persistent enough—and specific enough—that they gave me pause. What sort of man, writing to his sweetheart, would need to know the precise time of the princess's planned arrival at the ball or how many people would be accompanying her in her carriage?

If Louisa was a knowing party, I doubt he would have taken such care with the letter. He could have created a list of questions without trying to disguise the intent.

"Psst."

I glanced up.

"I've found a safe."

I nodded and joined Colleen.

Gingerly, she swung a painting away from the wall. It moved silently on hinges revealing the metallic face of a safe. We stared at the dial then looked at one another.

"Dame Guinevere *would* have saved the seminar on safe-cracking for next week."

Colleen rewarded my feeble attempt at humor with a little snort. "Any guesses?"

"I'm sure he'd want it to be something he could remember. Perhaps a date. Do you know his birth date?"

"Maybe. I believe it was listed in *Debrett's*." She looked at the ceiling for a moment then twisted the dial. I tugged on the door handle. No luck. Colleen shrugged. "Perhaps his wife's birth date or maybe the day she died?"

"What is it?" I asked.

She sighed and shook her head. "I haven't the foggiest."

"Maybe he wrote it somewhere."

"No one would be that silly."

I moved back to the desk and began a methodical search while Colleen continued to stare intently at the safe.

A hush fell over the study again except for the rustling of

paper as I searched. Most of the papers in the first drawer were either bills or receipts. The second held records of payments from his tenants and investments. Nothing suspicious here, although I noted briefly that he had significant holdings in Upper Canada, Quebec, and Nova Scotia. Perhaps one of these was what brought him into contact with Fennick.

"He had a son that died," Colleen said. "I'll try his date of birth."

"Good idea."

The third drawer held correspondence. It would take hours to go through it thoroughly. I didn't have hours.

"No joy," Colleen muttered.

"Hmm." It seemed unlikely that he would hide a combination in amidst his correspondence. I pulled out the top center drawer.

Just inside was a slip of paper with three numbers on it. I read them aloud. "5-12-22."

Colleen straightened. "December fifth was the day his son died."

I closed the drawer and stood. "Try it."

She nodded and spun the knob. "Wish us luck."

"Good luck." I could practically taste the victory of finding the documents we sought.

Before she could finish dialing in the numbers, a siren began blaring.

We both flinched and ducked low, covering our ears with our hands.

Still hunched over, I came out from behind the desk and grabbed her hand. "Run!"

Men pounded through the outer corridor.

That wasn't going to work. I veered away from the door but there were no other exits. Snatching up the fireplace poker,

I ran for the window. We'd have to make our own. Colleen snatched up the fireplace tongs and thrust them through the doors' handles. Perfect. That should hold them for a moment.

I drew back the poker and struck the window for all I was worth. One single tiny diamond-shaped pane shattered. I struck again, decimating three panes.

Voices pooled in the hall. Snatches of upraised conversation reached us.

"Lordship, we heard sounds from the study."

"Good work, lads. We've cornered them."

"—nowhere to go—"

The door behind me shook as someone tried to open it.

Colleen flung one of her distraction devices at the door. It gave a resounding crack like a rifle shot and the scurrying of feet echoed from the other side of the door. That would make them hesitate another moment or two.

I dropped the poker and cast about wildly for another option. There. The wooden desk chair ought to fit our requirements. I dragged it over to the window, hefted it above my shoulder and, with an exceedingly unladylike grunt, heaved it at the window. A splendidly loud crash split the night, provoking even greater exclamations from the hall beyond.

Colleen and I were already clambering through the window.

Gasogenes bobbed toward us from around the corner of the house.

We fled. I lost my bearings as to where we were in relation to the river and simply ran away from our pursuers.

Luckily, we had the advantage of Colleen's opera glasses and soon outpaced our pursuers. Unfortunately, there was little cover to be had. The wide lawn seemed to stretch endlessly on every hand except for the bulk of what appeared to be the stables and, beyond that, another larger shed. If those were the outbuildings, it meant we had come out somewhere on the backside of the house. It was a starting point anyway.

With a nod of agreement flying between us, we made for those buildings, hoping to put something solid between us and our hunters.

As we came abreast of the stables, we could hear grumbling voices inside. The grooms were awake. There'd be no sanctuary in there. We pressed on toward the larger structure.

No one lingered about this building. We crept inside noiselessly. Colleen went first then I backed in after her, making sure no one had spotted us. Closing the door, I turned to whisper to Colleen and ran smack into her. She was standing stock-still and staring upward.

I followed her gaze and found myself looking at a gleaming new airship.

The look on Colleen's face made me understand love at first sight.

I gazed around the hangar. A large panel of machinery occupied the portion of wall to our left. Tables containing various tools and parts stood against the other wall along with cabinets that no doubt held more of the same. A single door punctuated the wall on the far end of the structure. Thank the heavens no one stood guard. "We only have a minute or two. Let's decide on a plan."

No response.

"Colleen."

"Mmm?"

"Colleen!" I repeated more emphatically.

"I think this is the airship from the kidnapping attempt. There are rotors." She pointed.

"No doubt." My sarcasm was lost on her.

"This is information which should be turned over to Inspector Ogden."

"And we will at the proper time."

"Yes, the proper time."

I peeked outside. The gasogenes had fanned out in a long line and were headed our way. Worse, they were between us and our boat tied up at the river.

I ducked back inside. It wouldn't take them long to find us, but we needed to buy time and skirt them somehow if we were going to have a chance to get away. Inspiration struck. I grabbed Colleen's arm. "Can you start that machine?"

She finally looked at me. "Yes, I think so."

"Good. Do it."

I could tell how much she wanted to because she didn't argue with me.

In the meantime, I snatched up a hefty wrench from one of the worktables and repeated Colleen's earlier move, thrusting it through the door handles. Then I moved to the panel of levers and gears. I had learned enough about machines and gadgets from Colleen that I could tell this had been built into the hangar, not something that would be used to operate the airship. So, what did it operate?

I ran my gaze over the neatly labeled panels and smiled. If I was right...

Behind me the airship chugged into life.

A cry could be heard in the distance.

I opened the steam valve and heard the telltale hiss and rattle in the pipes. In a few seconds, the gauge showed that pressure had built into the green zone. Figuring that was a good thing, I pulled on the lever marked "Sky Bay Doors." A crack appeared in the ceiling high above my head. Slowly, the roof ratcheted apart.

Later, I would do a triumphant dance. For now, we had to get out of here.

Colleen grinned like a fiend at the bridge controls.

I waved for her to come down. She waved for me to come up.

I shook my head and ran aboard. "I opened the roof. Can you set it to go straight up?"

"Yes." She pulled on a couple of levers and the ship began to ascend.

"Good. Let's go."

"Aren't we going t—"

"No. Let's go." I dragged her from the bridge and out to the catwalk. We were already several feet off the ground and rising. "Jump!"

We leapt and rolled as we landed, just as the circus trapeze artist had taught us last year.

From outside came a racket of hollering and something heavy striking the doors.

"C'mon." I pointed toward the door at the far end of the hangar.

Colleen nodded, and we sprinted forward. We flung open the door and barreled through just as the barricaded door opposite began to splinter.

Chapter 20

We made a wide circle around the building then headed to the dock. They had found our boat. To my relief, however, the distraction had worked. A single man had been left behind to guard our vessel, and his attention was fixed upon the airship rising inexorably above the hangar. Shots rang out in the distance.

I bit my lip to keep from laughing. They were trying to shoot down their own airship. I caught Colleen's eye, tapped my chest, then pointed at the fellow. She nodded. I ducked low and moved toward the guard. The darkness and his distraction aided me. I was ten feet from him when he spotted me.

Before he could bring his weapon to bear, I darted in and pushed aside the gun then turned and slammed my elbow into his throat.

He crumpled, clutching at his windpipe.

Colleen and I hustled past him.

I crouched in the back of the boat, focused on making sure no one else was in range to shoot at us or otherwise impede our escape. When neither the lights of the estate nor even the sadly deflating airship could be seen any longer, I turned to Colleen with a chortle. "Did you hear them firing at their own airship because they thought we were on board?"

She laughed with me. "And the way that poor guard went down. He never knew what hit him."

"I can't believe we actually got away with that. I thought for a moment we were done for." The boat rocked beneath me, and I sat gingerly.

"I should apologize."

"Why?" I managed to choke out around my sudden nausea.

"I've read about new technology being developed for safes which alarms if there are a certain number of incorrect attempts at the combination."

"It's a dashed clever idea." I swallowed. "But I don't see why you should have thought it would have been installed here."

"I should have at least considered it."

"You hadn't even finished entering the last number. Even assuming this safe was wired in that way, I don't think you set it off."

Colleen shrugged. "Then what was it? I'm a big girl, I can admit it if my blunder kept us from learning anything really useful."

"First, I think someone else may have set off an alarm somewhere."

She turned her head to look at me. "Who?"

I waved for her to pay attention to her handling of the boat. "Jack, or I suppose it could have been Eleanor, maybe even someone from A Division. Second—" Briefly, and with pauses to allow myself to breathe through the rising nausea, I described the letter I had found.

Colleen sighed when I finished. "Even with the evidence of the airship, there's not enough to warrant any arrests. The rotor design was not as unique as the newsprints implied."

I wasn't sure if her disappointment was because of the lack of compelling proof or the fact that she had not seen some truly revolutionary new airship design. I cleared my throat. "No, but it could indicate that they are planning to snatch the princess from her birthday ball." Breathe. "They will know precisely where she will be. And amid the questions about ball gowns and ribbons—" Breathe. "—were all sorts of questions about the precise timing of events and other details."

"Don't worry. We're almost there."

I nodded, but it was too late. I let my head hang over the side as my dinner made a sudden reappearance. Colleen passed me a handkerchief when I was done, and we stayed quiet until we had at last docked and were back on dry land.

As soon as I was no longer green, Colleen picked up the thread of our conversation while we walked back to Cadogan Hall. "The question is, with the limited access we have, how do we keep the princess safe at all times?"

Interrupted in a longing for my toothbrush, I sighed. "Particularly since there could be other participants in the plot. If we only round up one or two, others could still decide to move forward."

"Not if we were able to get Fennick."

That was a good point, except… "I doubt he'll be personally involved in the actual kidnapping. It could scuttle his chances if he was ever recognized."

"We could tell Dame Guinevere what we've discovered."

I vetoed that notion. "Absolutely not."

"Our highest priority ought to be protecting the princess, not catching the plotters. That's the job of the police."

She sounded a bit like Jack.

"The police think they've got their man and have stopped looking," I pointed out. "And if we don't catch all the conspirators, we could just be pushing trouble down the road. This plot may not have worked, but they could come up with something else."

We paused for a moment, stepping into the shadow of a grimy alley as a bobby walked by on his beat. When we were sure he had gone, we resumed our journey.

"The problem," I said, "is that there are too many angles the danger could come from, and we're trying to protect the princess blindly." I groaned and rubbed my shoulder, which was aching from contact with the hangar floor. "If only we could tuck her safely away in a vault until the danger has passed."

"Yes." Colleen sounded far away all of a sudden. She wore the dreamy expression that usually accompanied the invention of some new gadget.

There was no use talking any further. She wouldn't even hear me. Instead, I stewed in silence. Perhaps I should try to make contact with Jack again. Maybe he would have some ideas. I'd also like to know if he was the one who had set off the alarm.

We had regained our room, put on our nightdresses, and removed the constructs from our beds before Colleen spoke again. "You think the draft of Fennick's letter asking all those questions about the ball was because that's where they're planning to strike next?"

I settled back against my pillows. "Yes. They'll want a foolproof plan because they've been foiled twice before. And when they strike again, it will throw doubt on the guilt of their current scapegoat." I rolled over and punched the pillow trying to force it into a comfortable shape. "Who knows what their plan will actually be. It's too hard to try to anticipate and block them. Like trying to guess Lord Bancroft's combination without knowing much about him."

"What if we preempted them?"

"What?"

"What if we kidnap the princess instead?"

I gaped at her.

"We take her some place safe and keep her there. They will be uncertain of what's happening, but based on what we've seen from them so far, I think they will seize the opportunity to move forward with their plan or risk losing the chance."

I sat up, my head buzzing with sudden possibilities. "Who knows what might come out of the woodwork if the princess were to actually disappear."

Colleen nodded looking smug but slightly scared.

"Do you really think they'd move forward with their plan if they didn't know they could control the outcome? They wouldn't want to risk her showing back up. It would ruin everything."

"How could we reassure them? Make them think they're safe."

I stood and began pacing, staring blankly at the floor as I walked. Colleen lay with the covers pulled up to her chin and her lips moving slightly. Quiet settled over the room.

We'd have to give them false information. But how could we get them to trust it?

I yawned. I was so tired, but sleep would elude me until I figured this out. We didn't have much time, we needed to act. I scrubbed at my face with both hands.

Maybe we *should* just turn over what we knew to Dame Guinevere. Would she believe us? Would she take our word and trust that the best thing for the princess would be to disappear for a while? How would she get the duchess and Sir John to agree?

Sir John.

That was it. "Louisa!"

"What?"

"We use Louisa." I plopped down on my bed. "If the princess is suddenly gone, and the conspirators don't know where she is or what is going on because it's not their plan, they will need intelligence from someone on the inside. Their inside source is Louisa. We have to figure out how their letters are exchanged. Then all we have to do is intercept their letter and substitute it with one of our own."

"All right. That shouldn't be too hard."

"This plan is daring though, how will we pull it off? Where would we hide her?"

Colleen nodded. "I've got an idea or two on that score."

I nibbled on my lower lip. "I don't know if the princess would agree. She is bound and determined to be independent due to Conroy's blasted overbearing rules. She won't be persuaded by arguments that it would be for her own safety."

"You'll have to convince her."

Dame Guinevere pulled me from class early to visit the princess. Apparently, with the ball scheduled for the next day, the princess would be busy later. Eleanor, Harriet, and Irene stared daggers at me as I rose and left the classroom. Poor Marianne just looked a bit wistful. As I passed, Eleanor muttered something and the others sniggered behind their hands. I made no response. They could choke on their spite. I had things to do.

Dame Guinevere, usually full of pithy advice and pungent observations, was silent on the ride to Kensington Palace. But once, when I turned my gaze from the ever-fascinating London streets, I caught her studying me intently. I would have liked to return stare for stare, but I found myself blushing under the scrutiny.

"Yes, ma'am?"

"Nothing, dear."

Either she had found layer two of our distraction and was wondering how the king and queen could possibly place any trust in me, or she was trying to devise some suitable punishment.

Our admission to the palace was becoming rote as we were recognized and shown into a sitting room immediately. Princess Victoria acted stiff and made no effort to escape her mother's overbearing presence.

Knowing our time was limited, I came as close as I dared without drawing attention. "Highness, I need to speak to you."

She sighed, but a moment later concocted an excuse about showing me her gown for the birthday ball that allowed us to leave, accompanied only by Baroness Lezhen.

On the way to her workroom, the princess made a further excuse that sent the baroness searching for ribbons and silk flowers to see which would best offset the dress.

"That ought to buy us a couple of minutes." She was growing more comfortable with finding ways of making space for herself.

"Yes, ma'am."

"I trust you don't have any plans to invite the dreadful Louisa to attend me?"

"No, ma'am. I'm sorry about that. If there had been any other w—"

"Have you made any progress at all?"

"I believe so."

Two spots of color burned in her cheeks, but her voice remained even. "I wish to be kept informed. I do not like remaining in the dark all the time."

I didn't try to protest that there had been no opportunity

to give her a report and that we had no other safe means of communication. I simply launched into a recitation of what we had learned on our most recent excursion. Gradually as I spoke, Victoria's demeanor began to soften. Only after providing my full report did I broach the plan that Colleen and I had begun to concoct. In the princess's current mood, I would only have one shot at getting her to agree. Fortunately, I knew her weakness.

"The reason I had to ask Louisa to join us was because she caught me in her room and I had to make up an excuse on the spot. Before that, I found letters to her from Mr. Fennick. I could not afford to allow her suspicions to be raised because it's not clear if Louisa is a co-conspirator or a pawn and, if the latter, who is moving her. Is it her father or Fennick?"

Victoria nodded. "I'd bet it's her father."

"Colleen and I have come up with an idea about how we might find out the extent of the conspiracy against you." I outlined our plan.

The princess frowned. "I want no part in hiding. That's not how I intend to reign, and I will not start my majority in the wrong spirit."

"No, ma'am. We wouldn't suggest that either. This would be a strategic move to force the villains to reveal themselves without them actually having you in their power."

"You think we could force their hands?" A slow smile spread across her face. The first I'd seen all day.

"That's the idea." I was sorely tempted to push harder but restrained myself.

"How?"

I explained the plan in more detail. Again, I didn't try any additional persuasion, I had a feeling that such an attempt would backfire.

At the moment, her fondest desire was independence. She didn't want to be pushed or manipulated into anything but allowed to decide for herself.

"I see." She was talking more to herself than to me. "I don't suppose the plan could work if Louisa and her father didn't think I'd disappeared. I do have to be out of view…but it's not hiding."

I literally bit my tongue to keep quiet.

"All right. We will attempt this plan. But I expect to be better informed than I have been so far."

"Yes, ma'am. What would be a secure way for us to communicate? Is your correspondence read by anyone else?"

"Yes." She sighed. "Mama reads all my letters, usually before I'm allowed to read them."

"I thought that might be the case."

We began to consider possible codes but were interrupted when Baroness Lezhen returned with her hands full of flowers, ribbons, and feathers.

As the talk turned to gown trims my thoughts were bounding ahead to the next night. Colleen and I had twenty-four hours to come up with a foolproof plan to kidnap a princess. We hadn't a moment to spare.

Chapter 21

All the young ladies of Saint Scholastica were fluttering and excited as we rode in fine style toward the birthday ball, including Colleen and me, though perhaps we had different reasons.

The other girls had all been visited by representatives from their fathers' banks bearing various jewels from the family vaults. I may have been biased, but I thought Eleanor's display looked like she was trying to blind someone with the quantity of her gems. What would happen if I gave her a little nudge? Would she tip over, borne down by the sheer weight? Any other night I would have been seriously tempted to try it.

I had no jewelry to speak of but, though I had no gems, even I had a new ball gown. And not just my old dress made over. A gift from Colleen who had commissioned it unbeknownst to me. The gown had been made of a beautiful periwinkle blue moiré with a wide border of gold filigree lace at the base. More of the gold lace decorated the sash and puffed sleeves. It even had a short train.

It was easily the loveliest gown I had ever owned, but Colleen had made it even better. She'd had slash pockets added, which allowed me to store useful tools. The gown concealed another secret as well which would help make our whole plan possible. In addition to this unorthodox uniform, I carried the fan blades she had made for me.

We had come prepared with everything we could reasonably carry. It was a wonder we didn't clank when we walked, but we faced so many variables. What if Fennick's team tried to grab the princess before we could put our plan in motion? What if something went wrong and a hue and cry was raised before we were clear of the palace?

Our carriage chugged past the main gate, and I peered out the window to see Saint James's great diamond-shaped clock-face set in the brick façade above the gate and flanked by the two crenellated towers. We had to wait our turn to enter the palace grounds via the Ambassador's Court and disembark. I looked around avidly as we waited, noting the location of the guards in their most festive dress uniforms.

The palace windows were aglow with brilliant light. The orchestra's strains could be heard from the courtyard where wigged footmen in brilliant livery greeted and assisted each of us out of the carriage in turn. Then, like streams joining a river, we flowed with other revelers toward the great doors which had been thrown open wide. Large torchieres lined the carpeted walk that led all the way from the disembarkation point to the door and inside.

The crowd we joined was jolly with a great deal of laughter. The ladies' gowns were brilliant swirls of color complemented by the flash and glitter of their best gems. Even the gentlemen had largely rejected the sobriety of plain black and white. Almost every fellow present had found some means of further decoration, from a decidedly daring colored waistcoat to the shoulder sashes of diplomatic office. The military men in coats of brilliant scarlet or sapphire stood out like peacocks spreading their feathers in aggressive display.

Princess Victoria was easily the shortest person in the receiving line, but she held herself regally. Every person received a warm, welcoming smile and her joy in the day was palpable, her smile infectious. Standing in that line awaiting our turn to greet the highest and mightiest, it occurred to me that she was going to make a magnificent queen. As long as she survived to take the throne.

I realized in that moment that the fear lurking in the unexamined corners of my mind all along had been that, once the question of succession was raised to their satisfaction, Fennick would have the princess killed. My resolve hardened to granite. We were going to catch the criminals targeting her and we were going to make them pay.

I bobbed my way down the line, curtsying before the royals. If Dame Guinevere's fixed smile was anything to go by, we looked less the picture of graceful charm and more like hens pecking after a worm. But I managed not to disgrace myself, or her, in spite of my gown's train.

Past the receiving line, the stream of people turned into a series of rapids as we whirled against groups that had stopped to chat, caught in the shoals for a moment before surging around. It seemed everyone in the country with any pretense at fashion had wrangled an invitation to this ball. Once we made it past the entry hall my overwhelming impression of the palace was of red. Red carpet. Red wall hangings. Red curtains. Red cushioned furnishings. This surplus of red was relieved by touches of white and gold, but the overall impression remained.

What I needed was a clock. We were on a precise schedule. I trailed behind my classmates peering around like a tourist. It wasn't hard to drift away from them as we entered the ballroom. In fact, the ball was so crowded it was practically inevitable. The atmosphere was uncomfortably stuffy with too many bodies with too many opinions crammed into a space meant to comfortably accommodate about half as many. I deployed the fan Colleen had given me for its original purpose. Which, in that crowded space, was just as much a lifesaver as the blades.

Eleanor already had some handsome fellow leading her onto the dance floor. I couldn't place the fellow, but they spoke to one another as if they were already well acquainted. Very well acquainted. Interesting.

I watched for another moment before reining my attention back in. To my right, a fellow was earnestly beseeching Colleen to dance but she was demurring. Several others were clustering around her, hoping to get a chance to speak to her too. This was hardly a surprise. Her hardest task of the evening would be breaking free of her admirers. As I passed, I gave her a little shove in the small of her back. She gave an involuntary step forward and this was all the encouragement her would-be suitor needed to sweep her out among the dancers.

Good. She was being too conspicuous by declining to dance with a handsome, presumably eligible, young man. I bit back a grin. It would do her good.

I soon had reason to regret my flippant attitude.

Inspector Ogden, togged out in evening kit, materialized smack in front of me, an odd, searching look on his face. I stopped short. He did not speak, but neither did he move out of my way as he studied my face.

What was he doing here? I scrambled for something to say. "Good evening, Inspector." I instantly wanted to bite my tongue off. Hoping he had missed my gaffe, I tried to look over his shoulder. It would have been easier if he wasn't so tall. "Would you exc—"

His hand snapped toward me palm up. I looked at it then

his face. He was grinning like the cat that stole the cream. "May I have this dance?"

The only excuse I could think of that wouldn't have been hopelessly rude was that we had not been introduced. But I had just called him by his title, and I didn't want to arouse his suspicions any more than they already were. There was only one reason for his presence here. Despite his arrest of Reese, he was concerned about a further attempt upon the princess. Either he realized Reese had been set up or he could not have been operating alone. The inspector meant to snare anyone who might still harbor dreams of capturing a princess. I would have found it admirable if I wasn't planning a kidnapping attempt of my own this evening.

I didn't have to try to manufacture a blush. "Certainly."

He led me onto the dance floor. Unfortunately, it wasn't a stately progress dance where we'd have minimal opportunities for discussion. A waltz was striking up. I sighed inwardly.

"Have you had any luck in finding your young man?" He was still smiling. Drat the man.

"I'm sorry?"

He clarified. "The young man you were supposed to marry."

"I'm afraid you're mistaken sir. I have never been engaged. Nor would I be so careless as to misplace the gentleman if I was." I smiled sweetly and met his gaze. "Perhaps you've mistaken me for someone else."

His own smile grew a bit flat. "Anything is possible."

Continuing to look as angelic as possible with freckles and red hair, I said no more.

He was a skilled dancer, maneuvering me through the crowd deftly. I found myself mildly surprised by this. How many opportunities did a policeman have to waltz?

"Do you happen to have a brother?" he asked.

"I'm afraid not." I bit my tongue to keep from elaborating. Dame Guinevere had drilled it into us that, in a situation such as this, less was more. "Why do you ask?"

"Hmm."

This fellow was entirely too observant. In future, I would have to give him a wide berth.

After a moment the inspector continued. "I cannot shake the feeling that we've met before."

I felt his gaze boring into the top of my head. It was really no fair that he was so much taller than I. I raised my eyes to meet his again. "I'm certain I would have remembered."

He shook his head. "We must have though, or how did you know I was an inspector?" Another wolfish sort of smile. He thought he had me.

I lowered my gaze and tried to muster a dainty flush. "I'm afraid you've found me out." I looked back up at him. "You visited my school recently. I'm afraid I inquired about who you might be."

Inspector Ogden actually laughed.

I had a hard time not joining him, but by biting the inside of my lip, I managed to keep looking abashed. I let my lashes flutter. "Do you think I'm forward?"

"Just tell me this," he said, holding me farther away so he could get a good look at my face as the last strains of music died away, "were you the one with the princess during the attempt on her in the orangery?"

I fluttered my fan. "Do excuse me. Another gentleman has claimed the next dance." I fled into the crowd.

I hadn't gone far when a fanfare erupted, and King William escorted Princess Victoria into the ballroom and onto the dance floor. A quadrille began and other couples joined them. Good. I knew where the princess would be for the next fifteen minutes. It was unlikely that any attempt would be made while she was with the king and in the midst of such a large horde.

I studied the throng. Which of these finely dressed revelers may mean her harm? In my line of sight stood at least two other stolid fellows in evening dress that had to have been borrowed. Police or someone more sinister? No way they were from one of the noble houses. Were they from A Division like Inspector Ogden, or were they here for a more nefarious purpose? Come to think of it, his suit hadn't been at all badly cut for him. Hmm. In any event, I needed to avoid them.

A rather sinister looking fellow with a long, wispy black beard and enormous eyebrows passed me speaking loudly and with a thick Russian accent. My fingers itched to tug on that beard and see if it would come off. He was too much the epitome of a fierce Cossack. Or what about that woman in the poisonous shade of green? Surely, that décolletage was too low for a girl's eighteenth birthday party. She had a hardened air about her, and I could tell from where I stood that her glittering jewels were glass. Clearly, that was suspicious.

My gaze caught on a tall figure, who although he was standing strictly upright, still conveyed the sense that he was lounging against a wall and looking on with amusement. He shifted and, sure enough, it was Jack. I wasn't particularly surprised to see him. He was surrounded by a bevy of young women, including Harriet and Marianne. How had *they* managed to latch onto him? He said something and his adoring…harem burst into titters.

He lifted his gaze and found mine across the crowd. I could have sworn he winked. Then someone walked in front of me and the moment was lost.

I rolled my eyes. I had a job to do. If I did it correctly, his evening was about to get more interesting. But first, I needed to go somewhere with a modicum of privacy. I estimated that I had about a half an hour.

Knowing that Jack, Inspector Ogden, and any number of others might be watching, I acted as nonchalant as possible as I made my way through the ballroom. For once, being small was an advantage. I simply let the crowd swallow me up.

It was time for a change of costume.

I snuck away to one of the upper rooms of the palace that weren't technically open to guests. It took only a moment to remove my bodice and turn it inside out, replacing the glories of pale blue and gold lace for staid black. I rolled the puffed sleeves out to their full length and buttoned them at my wrist, then looped the short train of my gown onto its hooks so that it would be tucked out of sight and reversed my skirt. A short white apron tied into a bow at the back. As a final touch, I affixed a white cap on my head, so it covered my lethal picks. They wouldn't be as accessible, but I would still have them in a pinch. On my way out of the room, I picked up a cloth-covered tray that sat upon an end table. The disguise was complete.

Rendered effectively invisible by maid's garb, I began searching the palace for any sign of nefarious activity in the offing. The costume worked admirably. No one gave me a second glance, but I was able to go everywhere I wanted. I interrupted two separate trysts, withdrawing with a ducked head and a quick curtsy each time, my cheeks aflame. People were incorrigible.

Then I found it. In one of the upper bedrooms, a fellow in a fine evening coat and flawless cravat bent over some sort of rig that stood before an open window. He jerked upright at my entry.

"Excuse me, sir." I bobbed a curtsy.

"What do you want?" he snapped.

"I…" I moved several paces into the room. "Sir, would you like me to fetch a footman to help you with that?"

"No." He moved to step in front of whatever he had been fiddling with. "Go away, you stupid girl."

"Yes, sir. If you're sure, sir?" It was a large basket. A gear system with ropes had been affixed to the window. I knew in a flash that they meant to stuff the princess into that basket and lower her out the window. No doubt, some sort of vehicle would be ready on the other side to receive her.

"Very sure." He stepped forward.

I bobbed another curtsy and turned as if I intended to go.

He grabbed me then. An unpleasantly moist hand clamped over my mouth. I bit him, and he grunted. He let go with that hand, but his other arm pinned my arms to my sides.

There is something to be said for having a low center of gravity. I sagged in his grip, pulling him off balance, and in the same movement hooked my foot around his leg and pulled his knee forward.

He staggered and fell, releasing me.

I pounced and secured his neck in the crook of my arm, locking it in with my other forearm behind his neck before he had any idea what was happening.

He flailed. But after a few moments his movements faded then stopped.

I grabbed the curtain ties and bound him hand and foot.

I took a closer look at the device and confirmed my original thought. The basket was large enough to hold a small person. This vessel had been attached to a rope whose length was looped securely around a shaft which would turn with the use of a crank at one end, which then operated a gear assembly that would allow the rope to feed out.

There was definitely going to be an attempt on the princess

tonight. I cut through the rope and left it dangling. Since I didn't have anything heavy enough to do real damage to the metal pieces, I dropped a few of the noisemakers into the gearing. If anyone tried to use it, that would give them serious pause.

The fellow I'd tied up was groaning himself awake. I left him be. He wouldn't be calling for guards. Not if he was part of a kidnap plot.

I closed the door behind me and hurried back to the ballroom. No time to waste.

I found Colleen, who, costumed like me, was standing in a hallway just outside the ballroom half-concealed behind an enormous potted fern. I hovered outside too, not wanting to risk being spotted by Dame Guinevere or anyone else who might recognize me if they chose to look. The princess, flushed and laughing, was escorted off the dance floor by a handsome young lordling wearing a waistcoat in a violent shade of yellow and side-whiskers that threatened to overwhelm a still boyishly rounded face.

The princess pulled out her fan and flicked it once, twice, in our direction, before fanning herself delicately. That was the signal that she was ready. She took leave of her escort then headed for the door. I moved before her but slowly, trying to anticipate which direction she would take.

Two ladies that the duchess used to enforce the Kensington System followed hard on Victoria's heels.

As she came abreast of me, I curtsied.

The princess spoke in a low voice to the women following her. "Madame, I assure you, I do not need company. I am merely going to take my ease in the Queen's Levée Room."

Thank you, Princess, for that. Now, I knew where she was going. The room that had been set aside for ladies of the princess's party to take their ease was the perfect place to put our plan into action. I couldn't have planned it better myself.

Colleen and I followed them at a distance. When we entered, the ladies were standing with their backs to us and their heads close together. The princess had disappeared behind a discreetly placed screen.

One of the ladies glanced toward us. "Oh, good. We want some pastilles and ices."

Colleen and I approached them together.

Barely casting a glance in our direction, the other woman spoke. "Why are you still here? Are you stupid or deaf?"

Suddenly, I didn't feel so bad about what we planned. I took two swift steps toward her.

She turned, her expression shifting from disdain to fear. I delivered a sharp jab to her neck and she collapsed into me, bearing me down with her. Grunting, I pushed the woman off and scrabbled to my feet as the victim of Colleen's headlock sagged to her knees. While Colleen made sure she had been incapacitated, I approached the princess who had stepped from behind the screens.

She looked at me wide-eyed. "I insist that you teach me how to do that."

"Another time."

Colleen handed the princess a package containing a third maid's uniform. "Your Highness, please put this on. It's your costume to help us get you out of here."

"All right." The princess took the bundle and headed back toward the screen.

"Hurry. They won't stay out for long," I called.

The look she cast put me in no doubt that I was treading on thin ice with my future monarch. "Perhaps you'd care to help me then."

"Yes, ma'am."

I assisted the princess to dress while Colleen bound and gagged her erstwhile guardians. We had her ready to go in a scant few minutes. Colleen checked to make sure no one was immediately outside the door as we exited. We scooted into the hall. Since I had already scouted the route, I led the way. Midway down the hall, I passed through the green baize door that separated the servants' domain from the rest of the palace.

There was almost as much bustle here as in the ballroom. Servants of all kinds and descriptions bustled this way and that. The princess gazed around at the hive of activity in the same touristy way I had goggled at the public rooms of the palace.

We hurried past other servants keeping our eyes averted to discourage conversation. Through one door, a few younger girls were trying to sneak peeks at the lords and ladies in their regalia. As we passed behind them, I heard their giggling whispers. "Did you see the princess? She looked so handsome."

"My nan says she's going to be queen before we knows it."

"Well, if your grandmother says so, it must be true. What do you reckon it'll be like having a queen?"

"It'll be like the days of Good Queen Bess. Won't be nowh— anywhere in the world like England."

The princess glowed at this prediction, and I guided her on.

Three footmen approached. One was quite short and wiry. His jacket hung on him a bit and his powdered wig sat slightly askew. Another's jacket was so tight it threatened to burst at the seams.

Colleen and I exchanged glances.

They were all wrong. One of the major functions of footmen was looking smart in their livery. This lot would never have been tasked with such a visible role. I ducked my head and moved to shield the princess from their view as we passed.

I don't know if I needed to have bothered. They didn't pay us any attention. Another glaring sign that these were no footmen. A real footman never missed an opportunity to flirt with a maid.

Eventually, we came to an enormous kitchen with a soaring arched ceiling and a sort of cupola with windows that let in light overhead. Heads low, we threaded our way through the rushing kitchen staff and toward the exit.

Not a soul challenged us, but as we exited, I realized a clutch of guards stood at the door. I threw them a saucy smile and giggled at Colleen who joined in with me which allowed us to cluster with our heads together, faces obscuring the princess's as we moved through them.

The soldiers leered after us, calling out something bawdy.

The princess stiffened and would have turned to give them the tongue lashing they deserved. Colleen and I each grabbed an arm and hustled her away.

Dozens of people milled about in the forecourt. Using them as cover, I flung a handful of noisemakers hard at the ground to my left. They sounded like someone had set off firecrackers or maybe even fired shots. There was a scattering of shrill cries and a scuffle as people instinctively shied away from the sound.

The guards began barking orders and running toward the noise.

We kept moving.

The streets outside the palace thronged with Londoners in celebratory mood—"Any excuse for a party" would have been an appropriate slogan for the capital's citizenry. The air was filled with the scent of sausages, sugared nuts, and tarts from a dozen vendors. Hawkers passed bearing baskets of strawberries and great jars of brandied cherries. My mouth was watering but there would be no supper for us tonight. We passed thousands of Londoners drinking to the princess's health and her red-faced indignation at the effrontery of the guardsman seemed to have been forgotten.

Once we reached the river's edge, Colleen took the lead. A small rowboat was waiting tied at the bank. Colleen tipped its minder handsomely. He tapped the brim of his hat with his knuckle and scurried away.

With the princess stowed safely between us, Colleen and I took the front and rear seats. Colleen stretched an odd spindly looking device between the oars, affixing it to the end of each, then folding down and lengthening three telescoping legs, which she rested in the bottom of the boat. She gave me the nod and I, against my better judgment, unleashed us from the shore. While I focused on my breathing, Colleen's device began to rotate, operating the oars, and making it so that all she had to do was steer.

Princess Victoria clapped her hands. "What a clever contraption!"

"Thank you, ma'am." Colleen sounded pleased, and I could imagine the smile on her face, though I couldn't actually see it in the dark.

Even as this thought flitted through my brain brilliant light illuminated the world, searing my eyes. An instant later, the light was followed by a tremendous bang. We all started and ducked low. Fireworks. They were being set off in the princess's honor. As we pulled farther away from the dazzling display, she watched them almost wistfully.

If they hadn't already figured out at the palace that the princess was gone, they soon would. Someone would have been sent to fetch her so she could see the fireworks.

I fought against my nausea and was intensely relieved to see the bulk of the Tower of London looming before us. We were taking the princess to the safest place in all England. And the Beefeaters had nothing to do with it.

It was a risk. During our recent classroom excursions throughout the city, we had been educated about a handful of secret hidey-holes that had been prepared by the Praetorienne as refuges should they be needed in a disaster. Unfortunately, we had only been told, not actually shown these places. I meant to approach Dame Guinevere about remedying this oversight in the curriculum, but that would have to wait. For now, we knew that the secret entrance was near the Traitor's Gate on the waterside. Thus, our approach by boat.

Colleen had pored over her notes from the lesson where Mrs. Dutton had gone over these locations which, like our organization itself, were some of the most closely held secrets in the land. This had been necessary because my scanty notes were illegible. As we approached, she turned off her rowing device and let us bob close to the walls.

The brilliant fireworks proved a boon as they enabled us to see far more than we otherwise would have been able to make out without a light. Colleen soon identified the keystone, pulled it out, and tugged on a lever inside. A muffled splash like an anchor being dropped came from somewhere nearby then a section of the wall swung up. Above us, I heard the voices of a couple of Beefeaters gossiping comfortably. We rowed inside and the door ratcheted closed. A tunnel stretched before us and, irrational as it was, I wondered if we had come to the wrong place.

Colleen lit a pyrogene suspended on the prow of our little craft. It swung with the movement of the boat casting shadows that shifted weirdly. I startled again and again, thinking something was looming out of the darkness at us.

After some hundred feet or maybe two hundred feet—my

sense of space had been completely distorted by the swaying lamplight and rocking boat—the tunnel opened out on one side. We tied up to a metal post with a rope. I clambered out, grateful to be on dry ground. I turned to offer the princess a hand but she was already standing on the landing at my side.

"What is this place?" Victoria looked around eagerly. "How did you know of it?"

"I suppose the best term for it is a refuge. The Praetorienne go back to the time of Queen Elizabeth. We take our role very seriously." Or potential role. We weren't *actually* Praetorienne yet, but it seemed a poor time to mention that technicality.

An arched door was set into the wall. I grabbed the pyrogene and held it aloft. Together, we moved to the door.

Colleen and I exchanged a glance. We didn't really know what might be on the other side. Mrs. Dutton hadn't specified, and there had been no time to inspect the place before the ball.

I handed the pyrogene to Colleen while I examined the door. Taking a chance, I tried the knob. It squealed in protest. To my mild surprise, it turned and, with a heave, I swung the door wide to reveal a stone staircase spiraling down into the darkness.

At the head of the stairs, a clutch of pyrogenes hung neatly on hooks. That meant someone had been here at least once in the last dozen years or so.

Victoria shared none of our trepidation. She clapped her hands. "I feel like I'm the heroine of one of my gothics."

"Well, Your Highness, let's just make sure there are no vampires or other monsters below, shall we?" I lit two more pyrogenes and gave one to the princess before leading the way down the stairs.

Down and down we went. The bare stone walls on either side gave nothing away, except that it could have used a good clean out. Spiders had spread their webs in happy profusion. The ground was thick with dust, and a musty dampness from the river water permeated the air.

I couldn't even guess how far down we had gone when we came abruptly to another door. This one was locked.

I rubbed my forehead. All this was taking too long, and we didn't have much time. Colleen and I needed to return to the ball. But worrying wasn't going to solve any problems. I bent my focus to my lockpicks.

The lock wasn't difficult to pick once I focused. I tugged on the handle and the door groaned open. We held our lamps aloft again, but it turned out to be unnecessary. As the door swung out, a series of clanking sounds came from within and first one light and then another clunked into dazzling life. As I stepped through, I realized these were no utilitarian light banks fit for a clerks' office, these were enormous crystal chandeliers.

The chamber revealed to us was spotless, not a spider web or hint of dust in sight and luxuriously appointed in modern style. The floor was covered in green and gold Turkish carpets. The walls were a deep aubergine, with white trim and a number of fine oil paintings. Comfortable sofas and a deep reading chair looked exceptionally inviting. Bookshelves enticed readers with all sorts of literature, histories, math theories, memoirs, Greek tragedies, even recent novels. A footman mechanical stood at attention near a cabinet which I presumed held the means of liquid refreshment. Radiant heat oozed gentle warmth into the space. A secretary desk stood against another wall fully stocked with writing paper and implements. In one corner, a pianoforte and violin were flanked by a cabinet holding musical scores. Another corner held an artist's easel complete with a supply of canvases and different paint mediums.

Two doors led away from this room, and I took one while

Colleen took the other. My door opened into a short hall. The first room I came to was the garderobe, which to my surprise was quite modern looking. Then I recollected that Queen Elizabeth's godson, Sir John Harrington had invented the first Ajax and had made one for himself and his godmother. She must have had more installed. Out of curiosity, I pulled the chain. It flushed perfectly. So too, the taps provided cold and hot water on command.

Farther down the hall were two small bedrooms and one large bedroom, which was presumably for the queen. As everywhere else, these were luxuriously appointed. A maid mechanical gently chuffed into life at my entrance to the largest chamber, tootled over to the bed, folded back the bedclothes then fluffed the pillows. As I watched, a nightdress, robe, and velvet, fur-lined slippers were retrieved from the wardrobe. Clearly, the princess would be in good hands.

I let the maid get on with her duties and walked to a set of hanging curtains at the far side of the room. Was it meant to provide the illusion of a window to make the underground refuge seem more open than it was?

I drew them aside and was confronted by a door. I opened it and was met with a stone wall.

I didn't believe in that wall for a second.

It was an escape route.

It had to be.

I gave it a push. Nothing happened.

I tried again, harder. Still nothing.

There was no knob to grasp to pull it inward.

I ran my fingers over the wall searching for a crevice or a piece that might fold out to make a handle. I ran my hands over the wall again, pushing experimentally at every nook and cranny in the masonry to check for a concealed button that would open the portal. I was at knee level and about to give up when I glanced down. A narrow metal plate jutted from the base of the wall. It had been painted to blend in with the carpet, but was nevertheless, ever so slightly raised. I stepped on it and heard a faint click. Pushing still yielded no results, so planting my slippered toe on the metal plate I tried pulling it toward me. The narrow section of the wall swung in easily and soundlessly. On the other side a staircase led up into darkness.

Colleen met me in the hall. "I've checked the kitchens and larders. There's plenty of food and four mechanicals went to work as soon as I stepped foot inside."

"This place is chock-full of all the modern conveniences," I said then reported my own findings.

"I showed the princess how to instruct the mechanicals. She had never worked one before."

"What? Never?"

Colleen shook her head.

The princess emerged from the garderobe looking immensely satisfied. "This is quite the snug little retreat, isn't it?"

"Will you be all right here alone, Highness?"

"I should say so. I've always wondered what it might be like to be alone." She gave a dreamy little sigh.

"We will be back to check on you when we can get away or have something to report." I attempted to offer comfort, though she didn't seem to need it. "If you feel you cannot stand another moment here, or if you feel at any point that you could be in danger, there is an escape route." I showed her the exit I had discovered and how to open it.

Colleen and I swapped our dresses right side out again, rolled the long sleeves back up into their poufs and removed our caps. In a trice, we were ladies once more.

Now that we had reached the moment for departure, I was

reluctant to go. Could we really leave the princess here alone when she had never done anything for herself before, including operating a mechanical?

Victoria sensed my concern and scowled. "I am quite intelligent enough to manage on my own for a day or two. And if I am not, then I have no business presuming to stand in line to the throne of the greatest nation on earth and will cede the position to my uncle Ernest." She flapped her hands at us. "Now go and find out who has been behind all this. I want this threat resolved once and for all."

With Victoria's admonition ringing in our ears, Colleen and I rushed back to the ball. As we approached, the noise of the party could still be heard from inside, but the jolly guards at the gate to the Ambassador's Court were long gone. Now, they were grave-faced and grumpy. They refused us admittance, but we had anticipated something of this sort and were ready for them. With a great deal of blushing and stammering we explained about sneaking away from the ball. We did not explicitly state why we had left, but the flavor of indiscreet romantic trysts definitely hung in the air.

At last, tired of our pleading, a stocky fellow hurried off to procure Dame Guinevere. The look she gave us when she arrived made the grown men nearby take a step back.

"I should have known." She spun on her heels and marched back inside leaving Colleen and me to hurry after her.

The guards didn't utter a peep. They certainly made no other move to prevent our entering the building. I could feel their pitying gazes following us as we rejoined the throng inside.

Stalking ahead, Dame Guinevere led the way to a small parlor. Within a few seconds she had evicted the occupants, ordered us to sit, and taken a seat opposite. "Tell me."

Chapter 22

"**M**a'am." I came just shy of saluting. "We saw two persons dressed as maids hustling the princess out of the castle. She was dressed as a maid too. We followed, but they took the servants' stairs. We would have been horribly conspicuous going through the servants' quarters, so we looped around, because we thought they might bring her out by the kitchens."

Dame Guinevere's scowl was deafening.

Colleen picked up the thread of the story. "We were a bit behind, but we followed them to the river. They boarded a steam launch. We kept following, but, ma'am, we had to steal a rowboat to do so." She hastened on. "Don't worry. We did return it."

The headmistress's cocked eyebrow was eloquent. "Yes, that was the portion of your tale that had me riveted."

Unfair. That was like kicking a puppy. Colleen blushed and looked at her shoes.

I rushed to draw the fire. "We continued the chase despite the odds against us. Although we did lag behind, we were able to keep them in sight long enough to see them pull up to one of the mid-river jetties. Several people got out and immediately climbed aboard a waiting airship. They took off before we could draw close. But we followed it long enough to know it was heading southeast." I briefly considered describing the insignia on Bancroft's airship but decided against it. We wanted the conspirators to think they were in the clear, take the gamble, and put their plan into action. "Then we hurried back as quickly as we could to tell you."

To her credit, Dame Guinevere did not waste time on recriminations, though I could see them practically burning her tongue. Instead, she drew her already ramrod straight posture even taller, resettling her hands daintily in her lap. "Why did you not alert the guards?"

"The princess didn't cry out. If it was a kidnapping, they had obviously employed some threat to keep her quiet. Since we didn't know what the threat was…"

"What do you mean 'if' it was a kidnapping?"

"Well, ma'am, it was possible a threat had been detected and she was being rushed away for her own safety." *No one could say I didn't give her a sporting chance.*

"Yes, ma'am," Colleen put in. "You do always say that discretion is the better part of valor."

Point to Colleen. It took everything in me not to break into a grin.

Dame Guinevere's jaw tightened. "The kidnappers were female. Describe them."

Colleen was on a roll now. "I'm not sure we can say they were female. They were certainly dressed as females, but we never got close enough to see their faces well."

I nodded agreement.

"Then how did you know it was the princess with them?"

My turn to return the volley. "She kept looking over her shoulder."

"How many people were on board the airship?"

Colleen and I exchanged a glance. "Perhaps half a dozen?" she ventured.

"We can't be sure. There may have been people on board waiting. It took off immediately after the people from the boat joined them."

Dame Guinevere grew silent. One hand raised so that her finger rested against her lips. For the first time since entering this room, her gaze left us as she stared into the middle distance. The silence stretched for a moment.

I've never been very patient. "Ma'am, when was the princess found to be missing?"

No response.

"Ma'am?"

"Hmm?" She refocused on me, and I repeated my question. "It was after the fireworks. I went in search of her when I discovered she did not come out to enjoy them with the king and queen. I found her 'guardians'—useless creatures—bound and gagged. Incidentally, they also said the perpetrators were maids."

I was very glad we had decided to keep our story as close as possible to what had actually happened.

She had several more questions, pinning us down on timing and other details.

"Well," she smoothed her skirt, "A Division is officially tasked with investigating crimes against the royal family, and they must be told what has happened. Recovering the princess is our highest priority at the moment and if the police can help with that, then so be it. I need not tell you that it will have to be redacted. The investigator must not know anything of the Praetorienne or our mission. It is a sacred trust."

Colleen and I both nodded.

"Very well." She stood, and we made to follow. "You will stay here, and I will find the inspector and bring him here."

Inspector Ogden.

My stomach sank. This I had not anticipated. It made sense in retrospect, but I had not expected Dame Guinevere would be so willing to involve the police.

Chapter 23

D ame Guinevere returned with Inspector Ogden in tow. He looked grave indeed. His brow furrowed, lips turned down, hands clenched at his side.

When he caught sight of me, his eyes flashed. He perked up like a pointer finding a kill. "We meet again, miss."

I smiled politely and explained to Dame Guinevere. "Inspector Ogden was kind enough to ask me to dance earlier."

"Indeed, and without a prior introduction." She bestowed an arctic smile upon him. "Inspector Ogden, may I present my charge, *Lady* Portia Blithe, the only child of the Marquess of Bridgely, and this is the Honorable Colleen Tinewall, daughter of Sir Martin Tinewall."

I wouldn't have thought it possible, but she had actually managed to make him blush. It was faint and blotchy, but it was definitely a blush.

He attempted to act as if he was not blushing. "I understand you ladies claim you saw the princess being abducted."

"We did." As Dame Guinevere had instructed, I launched into a redacted version of the redacted version we had told her.

Dame Guinevere listened for a moment, then excused herself.

I was a little surprised that she left us with him unchaperoned, but I suspected that with the princess missing she had a great deal to do and could not afford the time to listen to a story she already had heard.

Inspector Ogden conjured a small notebook from somewhere and began jotting things down as I spoke. When I came to the part about us following the supposed kidnappers, his eyebrows rose. When we described continuing to follow them as they left the ball, I thought his eyebrows might actually take flight. We omitted the part about stealing a rowboat and implied that we followed along the shore long enough to see them get on the airship.

When we finished, he asked some of the same questions as Dame Guinevere. We gave him the same answers.

He tapped his notebook with the end of his pencil. "You ladies were remarkably...proactive."

"Our families and our school have taught us the value of patriotism and loyalty." I smiled sweetly.

He smiled back, although I don't think it could have been described as sweet. Predatory possibly. "Lady Portia, I feel as if you are often at the center of events."

"I? I can't imagine what would give you that impression."

"No? Well, perhaps it is just a hunch." He stood abruptly and strode close to where I sat. He reached toward me.

I pulled back. I thought for an instant that he was going for my hair picks. Instead, he plucked something from my sleeve and held it up. It was a bit of cobweb caught among the lace.

It must have come from the stairs outside the Tower keep.

"Thank you." I gave a little shiver. "I loathe spiders."

"Don't mention it."

Colleen interrupted. "You must have picked that up somewhere along the riverside when we were trying to follow the kidnappers."

I nodded. "That's probably true."

Inspector Ogden closed his notebook. "A search of the palace is being made for the princess. If she is indeed missing, I may have more questions for you."

I desperately wanted to ask if the fellow I'd left tied up upstairs had been found. But I couldn't figure out a reasonable explanation for how I would have known about that. At least, not one that wouldn't give the game away.

"Certainly, Inspector." Colleen tried on the sweet smile.

Dame Guinevere returned and stood in the doorway. Her timing was uncanny.

The inspector gave us a brief nod and departed, murmuring thanks to Dame Guinevere as he did so.

Dame Guinevere did not sit, so we stood. "The guards placed near the kitchen exit have been interviewed and they recall the departure of three maids together, shortly before the fireworks began. We have not been able to verify your story of following the maids through the gate. At that moment a disturbance occurred in the crowd." She paused, but despite the unspoken invitation to add more to our story, we kept still. "We have, however, confirmed that the rowboat you described was missing briefly, but then returned." She rubbed her forehead, and for a moment I felt sorry for her. Her job could not be an easy one. "The king and queen have been informed of events as have the duchess and Sir John. You are to tell no one else what has happened."

"Yes, ma'am," we chorused in unison.

"You will rejoin the ball and act normally. A story will soon be circulating that the princess has taken ill. We will then be leaving."

"Yes, ma'am."

She gave us each a hard look in turn, then opened the door and ushered us out.

We returned to the ball and took up a position against the wall, as far away from the dancing and matrimonial dealmaking as we could. Although that wasn't very far in such a crush.

I deployed my fan for its original purpose. The crush of people had made the ballroom hot and stuffy. I was anxious to go. Like Dame Guinevere, I had a lot to do.

Eleanor pressed through the crowd flanked by Harriet and Irene. She stopped in front of me. "Where have you two been?"

I was in no mood for Eleanor. I stared at her. "I cannot imagine why you think you have a right to know."

"Don't play holier-than-thou with me. Dame Guinevere was looking everywhere for you. And I know you've been sneaking out at night. I told her."

"Why would I do that?"

"Probably to consort with some disgusting dockhand or something. That's about as high as you could hope to marry."

My patience for her was nonexistent at the moment. "Go away, Eleanor."

She only smirked. "There's a rumor floating about that the princess has been kidnapped. She hasn't been seen for hours."

Colleen and I exchanged a glance, trying to look as if this was news to us.

"I'd bet anything that you flubbed something and let the princess get kidnapped."

I'd have liked very much to smack her face, but this wasn't the time or place. Besides, the game Colleen and I were playing had much higher stakes than schoolgirl squabbling.

"Eleanor, I do believe that, if you had a looking glass, you would find your jealousy is showing."

Her face had gone crimson, and it clashed terribly with the lavender of her gown. "I? Jealous of you?" She stepped so close I could feel tiny droplets of her spittle on my cheeks as she spoke, but there was no way I was going to be the one to back away. "I'd rather die than be a wretched, penniless, red-haired, charity case with no prospects."

Glancing around, Irene placed a restraining hand on her friend's arm though her words were for me. "We're going to be watching you—"

"Lady Portia." A dashingly tall figure stepped to my side. "Mr.—?"

"Harding," Jack supplied. "May I have this dance?"

A gentleman showed up on Colleen's other side and asked her to dance.

My eyes met Jack's. "Delighted." And I really was. He offered the perfect escape.

"You look lovely this evening," he said as he escorted me out to the floor. "That color suits you."

"You look dashing as well. Much more the thing than a cabman."

His grin was roguish. "I guess I'm just Jack of all trades."

I kept my expression flat at this sally. "How did you wrangle an invitation to the ball?"

"I am here as a representative of the colonial government of Upper Canada."

"Impressive."

"What is going on with the princess? People are saying she's disappeared."

"Dame Guinevere said she has taken ill."

The skepticism on his face was rich. "Has she taken ill?"

Drat it. He refused to let me get away with verbal jousting. Truth be told, I was growing weary and it had lost much of its appeal for me as well. "All right, the princess is gone."

His lips tightened into a thin line. "That's what I was afraid of."

"Is that why you came tonight?"

"Of course. What else do you know?"

"Don't ask me." I shook my head. "Please. I can't tell you more. I'm sworn to secrecy."

He was silent for a long moment. "I understand." He dipped his head, drawing my gaze upward. "You still look lovely."

I resolutely ignored the fluttering in my middle. "I can tell you that you're on the right trail investigating Fennick, but I'm still not sure who else is backing him."

His next words caught me like a blow to the solar plexus. "Fennick's gone to ground. He's disappeared from Bancroft's mansion."

Chapter 24

D ame Guinevere and the four other instructors who had accompanied us to London worked through the night. Their coming and going never ceased. There was no way to sneak out with them all up and moving about. Thoroughly foiled, I finally went to sleep at about half past four.

In the morning, we assembled for breakfast as usual, but none of the teachers were present. Dame Guinevere popped in briefly when we were nearly finished and told us the palace had confirmed that the princess had taken ill the night before. Also, all classes and activities for the day were canceled. She endeavored to make it sound like these two events were unrelated. The reason she gave for the cancellation of our classes was simply that we'd returned home so late after the ball. She made it sound as if it was for our benefit, not because the teachers were too busy.

Marianne raised her hand. "Is the princess going to be all right?"

Dame Guinevere's eyes were underscored by dark half-moons, and her response was more snappish than usual. "Don't be melodramatic."

Eleanor glared at me across the table then turned to the headmistress. "I would be happy to arrange for a gift of flowers to be sent on behalf of the school."

"She's sick, Eleanor. Not dead." Dame Guinevere was just as short with her.

Thus snubbed, Eleanor again looked at me, sneered, and gazed out the window with her arms crossed and her lips pursed in discontentment. If she wasn't careful, as my mother had warned me repeatedly, her face could stick that way.

Dame Guinevere departed, leaving us to finish our breakfasts. As soon as she was gone, Irene tossed down her napkin. "A likely story. The princess is hardly ever allowed out anyway. Why bother with this drivel that she's taken ill?"

Marianne glanced up from cutting into a sausage. "You don't think she was?"

"Of course not, you twit." Eleanor was looking for someone to vent her spleen on. "Sir John is very careful with the princess's reputation. He wouldn't want people to think of the princess as sickly unless he had no choice."

"They might not have ordinarily made such an announcement, but since she had to leave her own ball, it was bound to be noticed. He'd have had no choice," Colleen said reasonably.

"Oh, the silent one speaks." Eleanor ripped a bun apart. "Go back to your test tubes. You wouldn't know a suspicious circumstance if it kicked you in the bum."

I seriously considered giving Eleanor the kick she described as nervous titters went around the table at the shocking language. Pink spots appeared in Colleen's cheeks and probably my own as well.

"I'm going to send a pigeon to my aunt. She's one of Queen Adelaide's ladies-in-waiting," Irene announced. "She's bound to know something."

"Good idea." Eleanor chewed thoughtfully. "Harriet, why don't you write to that German fellow who kept asking you to dance last night? What was his name? He is one of the duchess's nephews."

"Helmut."

"Yes. Him. He's staying at Kensington. Write to him. Tell him what a wonderful time you had and ask after his little cousin's condition."

"I don't know if I can, Eleanor. That would be so forward."

Eleanor narrowed her eyes at Harriet who seemed to shrivel a little and quickly added, "If you think it's really important."

"I do."

"All right."

"Good." Eleanor was suddenly all smiles. "Then I will determine if her physician has actually been to Kensington to see her."

"Oh, that's clever," Marianne said.

"Is there something I can do?" I asked humbly.

"Yes. Tell us what happened last night."

I shrugged and ate a bite of toast.

She stared at me a long moment. "I still don't believe you. Just stay out of our way and keep your mouth shut. We're going to get to the bottom of this. Dame Guinevere and A Division have thoroughly botched things. I will have to find the princess myself." Eleanor dropped the remainder of her bun onto her plate. "Irene, Harriet, Marianne, come with me. We have some planning to do."

The three obediently rose and followed her from the room, though Marianne looked longingly back at her half-empty plate.

Colleen and I were alone. She gave me a sideways glance. "You don't do humble very well."

"It's hard with Eleanor."

"If she was smart, she would have taken you up on your

offer and given you all sorts of meaningless tasks to keep you occupied."

"I certainly never claimed she was smart."

We raised our juice glasses in a mock toast.

"So, what is your plan for the day?" Colleen asked.

"I thought I'd start with Kensington Palace to see how the Conroys are reacting. The princess still thinks they're involved and that's the kind of intelligence that can be gathered during the day. You?"

She gave a small sigh. "I suppose I'll be in my laboratory."

We finished our breakfasts then parted ways.

If there was going to be skulduggery afoot, I was determined to do my share of skulling and duggery.

Chapter 25

An hour later, I turned up in Colleen's laboratory. I cast myself into the only comfortable chair and huffed. She looked up from whatever it was she was doing.

"I'm being stymied," I announced.

"Who would dare?"

"There's no call for sarcasm. I don't know what I'm going to do."

She sighed. Removed the weird-looking goggles she wore and set aside the bit of tubing she held. "What seems to be the trouble?"

"Eleanor, of course. She's set her pack to watch me. It's the only explanation."

"For what?"

"I've tried three times to sneak away from the building and every time I've been thwarted by one of her blasted minions. They're lurking about wherever I go. I know she set them on me. And I can't leave through our room, because I can hardly scale the side of the building during the day without drawing attention." I got up and went to stand beside her. "What are you working on?"

Of her many strange-looking contraptions it was perhaps the strangest. A bowl-shaped object about a foot in diameter was connected to some sort of tubing which was in turn connected to a box that had a number of dials and switches. From this housing another tube ran, ending in a cone-shaped opening.

"It's a listening device." She drew my attention to the inside of the bowl-like ending. "This works like the outer ear capturing and funneling sound waves. The reaction is sort of distilled and passed into the tube. There's a thin membrane inside here, which is like the eardrum. And then three small pieces inside mimic the three bones in the ear. The trick was finding a material lightweight enough. Well, that and the mechanism to enlarge the sound." She was using small words so I could understand, but I still had only the barest notion what she was talking about as she continued. "The sound is multiplied and emitted through the other side. The box controls the sensitivity of the listening cup and volume of the output." She waxed on at length about how she had been inspired by a medical invention called a stethoscope.

"Colleen," I interrupted, looking from the device to her and back again. "This is remarkable!"

"I am quite pleased with it so far."

"Does it work?"

Her smile dimmed a bit. "To an extent. There's still work to be done."

At my urging, she showed me how to operate it.

When she had finished, she cast me a sidelong glance. "Have you figured out a way to sneak out without one of the girls spotting you?"

"No. Not until I have the cover of night. It's not just them. The teachers are coming and going like fiends too."

"Maybe it's time to let someone else do something for a change."

I groaned.

"And you're going to have to stay here and provide the distraction as needed."

Had she no compassion?

"All right." I wanted to shout that it was unfair. But, of course, it was fair. I just wanted to go do something. I was no good at waiting. Dame Guinevere's frequent admonitions about dawdling had apparently taken root somewhere in me.

Colleen smiled brilliantly. "Good. Then I have come up with a plan to keep everyone guessing and allow me to escape unnoticed." She set about gathering everything we'd need as she explained her scheme.

A few moments later, a tremendous boom rattled the windows and set half the clocks chiming. Yells and some very unladylike cursing echoed along the corridor and then, predictably, the drumming of feet. The latter stopped short.

And under the mask Colleen had devised, I smiled. They must have encountered the smoke.

The smoke had been the real point of the exercise. It was thick and colored a dramatic green. Most importantly, it smelled incredibly foul.

The masks allowed us to breathe normally. They also covered the entire face. Each armed with four more of these masks we hurried out of the laboratory.

"I'm so sorry," Colleen called, her voice distorted by the mask. "I had a little accident while mixing some chemicals. It wasn't an explosion. Nothing's damaged. The gas isn't poisonous. It just smells bad."

Bad? It was noxious.

"Put these masks on. It won't take long for the smell to dissipate."

"How long is not long?" Lady Pomeroy demanded. She had a hand to her mouth and was looking green around the gills.

I handed her a mask.

"Perhaps a couple of hours," Colleen admitted. "Close up all the doors to any room the gas hasn't reached and open all the windows. And wear these masks. They will help you to breathe."

Dame Guinevere did not appear, which could only mean that she was out. Interesting.

In fact, it seemed Lady Pomeroy was the only teacher still in the building. No one could have resisted coming to find out what had happened. The other notable absence was Eleanor. The sneak.

When Lady Pomeroy donned her mask, she nodded. "Yes, this helps considerably. Come along, girls. Put them on." She then gave the household's human staff the afternoon off and instructed Colleen and me to see what we could do about getting rid of the smell.

"Yes, ma'am," we chorused as we headed back into her laboratory.

Once inside, Colleen quickly changed into a maid's garb and headed out again, leaving me to emerge at intervals to assure Eleanor's lackeys I had been safely corralled. It was even sort of fun for a time. I imagined it was something like the satisfaction the princess had felt the previous evening. She may have been confined, but it was on her terms. Periodically, I wandered the halls like I was looking for an unguarded way out. Then I would dramatically spot whichever of my classmates was following me at the moment and retreat to Colleen's lab.

A couple of hours passed in this fashion before I grew bored. I descended to plotting an escape from the hall dressed as Colleen. After all, if she was able to get out without being seen, then if they thought I was she, I should be able to get out too.

With the mask, all I would need was an auburn wig, the voluminous wrapper she wore over her clothes when she was working in the lab, and some sort of footwear that would make me about six inches taller. Understandably, it was this last that had me stymied. I was pacing near the first floor landing, pondering possible solutions to the problem when I happened to spot Dame Guinevere returning from wherever she had been. The look on her face at the smell when she entered was a picture. I lurked along the upper gallery.

Lady Pomeroy was waiting and handed her one of the masks. I only caught a few words of what she said, but it was clear she was explaining Colleen's "accident" in the lab.

Dame Guinevere shook her head. "Call a meeting of the teachers in my office. There is much to discuss." Her voice was clear and carrying. I would have given my eyeteeth to know what she had to say.

Then it struck me. Colleen's listening device.

I all but ran for the lab. I bundled the device into a canvas sack, trying to be careful. If I broke it, I'd never hear the end of it. Then I barreled toward the library.

I passed Irene and Harriet on the way. They looked at the sack in my hands and shook their heads. "If you try to get out without leave, we'll report you," one of them called after me.

I kept going.

I shut the door to the library behind me and wedged a chair under the handle. With no new assignments issued for the day I could normally have counted on being alone. However, I had no sooner stepped away than the doorknob rattled. I had been right to hedge my bets against meddlesome classmates.

"Let us in," demanded Harriet. The door shook again.

"Go away."

"We're all entitled to use the library, Portia," said Irene. "If you don't let us in, we'll go and get one of the instructors to make you."

"I wish you luck with that."

They tried the doorknob a few more times but I ignored them. Dame Guinevere's office was just on the other side of the far wall. I approached and knelt down, setting my burden down carefully.

I positioned the bowl flat against the wall. Then turned it on as Colleen had shown me. A squeal the likes of which I had never heard before impaled my ear, I jerked away the listening tube and twiddled the dials madly. After a moment, I could hear murmuring, but nothing distinct.

Then there came the squeal of a door opening. It wasn't slammed but the sound of it shutting made me jump again because it was so loud compared to everything else. Footsteps. Then Dame Guinevere spoke. Her voice at least was clear, if not particularly loud. "I've just returned from an emergency meeting of the Privy Council. Victoria's disappearance was reported. The inspector from A Division gave a report on the status of their investigation. Then Lord B—"

"But where are they with the investigation?" I couldn't tell who had spoken.

"Effectively nowhere. May I continue?" Today, Dame Guinevere's waspishness wasn't reserved solely for her students.

"Of course."

"As I was saying, after the report from Inspector Ogden there was a great deal of useless whittering about what should be done. Then someone mentioned the question of succession which sparked an even bigger uproar."

I strained forward, my forehead practically touching the wall, wishing I could hear better but glad I could hear at all.

Dame Guinevere continued. "The king finally brought the

meeting to order by pounding on the floor with his cane. When things had settled down, Lord Bancroft stood."

"Rabbit Bancroft? The fellow who always ran from the French?"

"The same. He presented the Privy Council a solution to its problem. And I will say his speech was well prepared. First, he stated that he has had the honor of hosting a guest sent to him from Upper Canada. The 'unimpeachable'—" I could hear the parenthetical quotes she placed around the word—"gentlefolk who had sent him to Bancroft had asserted that the fellow was the Duke of Kent's legitimate offspring through a marriage to Julie de Saint Laurent that took place in Nova Scotia in 1798 with the full knowledge and consent of King George III and his Privy Council."

If the uproar in the other room was any indication, I could easily imagine the result of this announcement in the Privy Chambers.

Dame Guinevere hushed everyone. "Bancroft asserted that he had investigated the claim thoroughly and had been presented a number of proofs. He had the gall to say that it had been his intention to present Mr. Fennick's claims at the next meeting of the Privy Council and to credit Providence with having prepared a solution in advance of the princess's loss."

Outraged murmuring grumbled through the wall. Then Lady Pomeroy spoke up. "What proofs could he have possibly offered?"

"Bancroft claims to have a marriage license for Prince Edward and Julie de Saint Laurent, a notarized affidavit from the priest who officiated at the ceremony, and a royal decree from King George approving the marriage. And before you ask," I could just imagine her imperious gesture, "the Privy Council records were sought. The relevant volume was missing from the archives."

"With King George's bouts of madness, if the records are missing, who can say for sure that the decree is not genuine?" It was Miss Yancy this time.

"And therein lies our problem."

"Ah, but did they produce any proofs that Mr. Fennick is the issue of that marriage?"

"The same rector who officiated at the alleged wedding claims to have baptized Fennick as a babe and to have evidence in the form of church registries of both the marriage and the subsequent birth. And who knows what else they may have concocted."

"If this was all legitimate then why was it kept secret? How has no one heard of this fellow?" Mrs. Dutton was belligerent, and I knew she was itching to wallop someone's nose for them.

"They claim that the marriage was not secret and indeed there are many in the colonies who knew Prince Edward and Julie de Saint Laurent as husband and wife. That is how he presented her while serving there."

A low rumble broke out among the teachers. I couldn't tell if it was shock or something else.

Dame Guinevere carried on as if no one had said anything. "Bancroft claims that subsequent to the marriage, King George learned that their relationship…erm…predated the marriage and wrote to Prince Edward during one of their petty squabbles trying to revoke the decree. Bancroft asserts that such a revocation would be invalid since the marriage had already transpired, but Edward, not wanting to provoke his father further during his mental decline, let the matter drop and also kept the news of his son quiet. This same son was adopted by the

Commissary General, who put around a story that his niece had died in childbirth."

"I heard a rumor to that effect when I was on assignment in America during the War of 1812." Mrs. Dutton sounded dazed.

"But why the subsequent scramble for a legitimate royal heir? Why didn't Edward simply announce his son to the world?"

"Bancroft claimed not to know for sure. However, he put it about that by that time Prince Edward had broken with Julie de Saint Laurent and they were no longer living together. It was convenient to him to allow the relationship to wilt away in obscurity. Well, that and the political capital which could be gained by exchanging her for a wife of suitable lineage and contracting a marriage that would be welcomed by King George. That move restored him to the king's good graces and allowed him to return home to England."

More murmuring.

Dame Guinevere sighed so heavily even the listening device picked it up. "Then King William suffered some sort of fit and had to be helped from the meeting. That catapulted the frenzy to a level near hysteria. The Earl of Munster waded into the fray."

My thoughts started to whirl. The First Earl of Munster was George FitzClarence. King William had created the title for his eldest, albeit illegitimate, son. Despite this honor, FitzClarence's antipathy toward his father was well-known.

Someone on the other side of the wall sounded as incredulous as I felt. "FitzClarence? He hasn't been able to hold a conversation with his father without an argument in ages. He hasn't attended a Privy Council meeting since his appointment and that had to be at least four years ago."

My spinning thoughts were starting to churn out a web of ideas. Fragile still, but maybe some research would give them more substance. I was willing to bet the deterioration of the relationship between father and son had begun about the time William had left his longtime paramour, FitzClarence's mother, and married Queen Adelaide.

He must have always known that because he had been born on the wrong side of the blanket he could never claim the throne, but having it so bluntly borne in upon him could not have been easy. His father had tried to make amends, buying him a commission, granting him a title and an allowance, making him a member of the Privy Council. But by an accident of birth he'd never have the throne. It would pass to his little cousin. A young girl who had no experience of the world and who wasn't even allowed to climb stairs on her own. Oh, yes. That cut would sting.

I had a feeling I had finally identified the daring gambler who had been driving the kidnapping scheme.

I snapped my attention back to what Dame Guinevere was saying. "He regretfully felt it was necessary to support the claimant, what with Victoria gone, and potentially defiled in some way that would make her unfit to possibly bear a future monarch,"

I ground my teeth.

"He felt it essential that the question of succession be settled immediately in order to avoid civil disorder or even war if something should happen to the king." There was another heavy sigh and she continued. "Particularly since the next option is Ernest."

"Who was present at the council meeting?" someone asked.

"What was the response to this ridiculous proposal?" questioned another voice.

Dame Guinevere was quick to answer. "Two factions emerged. Queen Adelaide, Lord Liverpool, myself, and several others were adamantly opposed to the idea of legitimizing Mr. Fennick's claim as it could set a dangerous precedent for all sorts of would-be claimants to the throne. Not to mention dispossessing the princess. It is not as if we have reason to suspect that she is dead."

"Hear, hear."

"I'm sorry to say that more than a few are considering the idea. The council is to convene again, at which time Fennick is to present himself. In the meantime, a more exhaustive search is being made of the archives, and an urgent summons from the king is being sent for all the members of the council across the country to present themselves."

"When?"

"Tomorrow evening."

A silence drew out taut until finally someone snapped it. "Then what?"

Dame Guinevere sounded exceptionally tired. "If the princess is still missing and the consensus is to support the claim, then a report regarding both the princess's disappearance and Fennick's claims will be forwarded to Parliament."

"Then we must find Victoria and return her to the palace before the council meets again. It is only her absence that makes anyone at all consider his claims." Lady Pomeroy was resolute.

I couldn't have agreed more. But my thoughts were far away as the other teachers reported on what they had done that day. None of them had turned up any evidence of interest. Which was good news for Colleen and me. While they were all haring after the princess, I needed to attack from a different angle. There had to be a way to expose FitzClarence and pull the fangs from the conspiracy.

I packed away the listening device and left the library. Harriet and Irene were leaning against the wall as I emerged. "The library is all yours, ladies."

Irene planted her hands on her hips. "What are you up to?"

I did not respond, simply returned to the lab.

I had just succeeded in putting the listening devise in its place on the workbench when Colleen arrived. She sighed and flopped into the one comfortable chair. It was the first time I had ever seen her flop anywhere.

"Long day?" I asked.

"I don't think either the duchess or Conroy had anything to do with the kidnapping. They were both distraught. The duchess has taken to her bed and was sobbing and wailing for her daughter. You could hear her from halfway across the palace."

I nodded. I hadn't really expected anything else of the duchess.

Colleen reached over and ignited a Bunsen burner which sat below a tea kettle. "Baroness Lezhen and a few other ladies were trying to comfort her. Conroy was equally gloomy. He's practically wearing a track from Kensington Palace to A Division as often as he is going over to ask for updates."

Colleen rubbed her forehead then gave a little shake of her head. "I even found Louisa crying in her room. She did eventually leave her room, and I searched it. The letters are still there, but I also discovered her diary. She's horrified at the princess's disappearance. She believes she has good reason still to resent Victoria, but she would never wish her to come to actual harm. And she finds her father's anguish heart-wrenching."

I couldn't say I was surprised. I hadn't really thought anyone at Kensington was knowingly helping the conspirators. I reported the conversation I had overheard using her listening device.

Then I shared some of the niggling thoughts that had wormed their way into my deliberations during my long wait that afternoon. "Neither Dame Guinevere nor any of the other teachers have mentioned the man I left tied up at the palace or that big basket. They couldn't have just disappeared."

"Someone set him free before the hue and cry was raised?"

"That's what I'm thinking." I fiddled with a bit of metal until Colleen took it away. "They could have simply pushed the basket out the window and into whatever cart they had originally planned to take the princess away in. I don't think anyone is investigating that angle at all. They don't even know about it."

We stared at one another for a long moment.

"So, we have twenty-four hours," Colleen said.

"Approximately."

Colleen untied her maid's apron and reached for her duster. "We have to play out the hand. Either we confirm the conspiracy and find out what we need to know, or we produce the princess to thwart their plans."

I didn't say anything because I didn't want to worry my friend, but a dreadful fear had begun to gnaw at me as I had listened to Dame Guinevere's account of the Privy Council meeting. Maybe we had miscalculated. It might not be enough simply to make the princess reappear. If we weren't able to completely disprove Fennick's claims, he might gain enough support from others who were nervous about a teenaged girl being the heir apparent, that his plan to dispossess her could still gain traction.

Chapter 26

Colleen and I spent the evening in the library engaged in research about George FitzClarence. One or another of our classmates kept coming in as if they wanted to browse the shelves. I'm pretty sure they couldn't have even positively said where the library was prior to that afternoon. I finally put a stop to their prying by shoving back in my seat and marching up to Harriet. "You are going to leave now, Harriet. And the next person who comes in is going to get beaten with the largest book I can find."

Her mouth dropped open. "How dare you! You can't speak to me like that."

"I don't want to speak to you at all. Yet here we are."

"I—I—" Her mouth screwed up in a knot. "You—"

"Will be sorry? No doubt. Now, scat."

"Dame Guinevere shall hear of this."

I smiled as nastily as I knew how. "By all means. Do go and tell Dame Guinevere that I have been unkind to you. She is in exactly the mood to listen to petty squabbling."

Harriet huffed then flounced out.

Colleen watched her go, shaking her head. "That's the difference between you and most of the girls."

"What?" I resumed my seat and picked up the street map I had been perusing.

"You don't expect anyone else to fight your battles. If another student threatened to toss you out of the library, you'd have stood your ground and made them try it."

"What would you have done?"

She shrugged. "Gone. But then I would smoke them out with a noxious chemical reaction."

I laughed.

As night fell, we pulled dozens of random research volumes, scattering them among the books we had actually used. Each of our classmates would have been trying to take note of what volumes we had been looking at, and they would have compared notes. The easiest way to conceal our real intent was to confound them with too much information rather than trying to tidy away the books we had been using. They would spend valuable time sifting through a great mass of information that had no relevance and trying to synthesize it into a theory. I sincerely wondered what they would come up with.

Now that it was dark, it was an easy enough proposition to escape Cadogan Hall via our window. In the sanctity of our room, we agreed to split our forces. Colleen went to check on the princess and report the day's findings, such as they were. Meanwhile, I headed for George FitzClarence's rented home in Mayfair.

Jack had indicated that Fennick was in the wind, but I didn't think that Rabbit Bancroft would have stood before the Privy Council and pled his case without knowing where the fellow was. So even though he was no longer enjoying His Lordship's hospitality, he had to be somewhere nearby. Possibly he was now in FitzClarence's charge.

When I found it, the house looked much like its neighbors. Painted white, with a black door and black shutters and tidy flower boxes full of geraniums, it stood stolid and phlegmatic, shoulder to shoulder with its brothers along the street. The very essence of England. It was hard to believe that such a place could ever house a conspiracy to seize the throne. Which, of course, made it perfect.

I didn't waste time trying to figure out a way to climb in the front. I skirted down the street and back around to the mews. The laundry window wasn't actually open, but it was unlocked and getting inside was so easy, even Harriet could have done it. Having been inside many similar houses, finding my way upstairs was no challenge either.

Patrols of liveried footmen moved through the house at regular intervals. That alone made me know I was on the right trail. The footmen carried miniature pyrogenes held high, but these left plenty of shadow for a creative girl to get lost in. The servants' common areas required only a cursory search. I didn't seriously think that anything incriminating would be located in such a place, but this was too important not to be thorough.

Similarly, I was able to whisk through the dining, morning, and sitting rooms. The opera glasses gave me a distinct advantage over the footmen, and I had no trouble avoiding them. The library needed more attention, but in truth the place was pitiful, two easy chairs with a single bookshelf scarcely populated and a very large drinks cabinet. The place smelled strongly of cigar smoke. Anyone withdrawing to this room wasn't there to read. The books were mere decoration. But there wasn't even a hint of a safe.

I came next to a study. This was more like it. This room looked lived in. A large secretary overflowed with papers and the books here looked as if they were used. At one side, a settee and two chairs were grouped together behind which a large window stood shrouded by drawn damask curtains. A deal table had been pushed to the side but still contained a set of playing cards. FitzClarence was indeed a gambler just as we had thought. A gambler with nerves of iron.

The desk seemed the logical place to start. Sectioning the desk into mental grids I went through the papers, careful to put them back as I found them. I had made my way through most of the mountain when my gaze found a note on the blotter. *Brown's Hotel, Charles II Suite.*

My thoughts were jerked away by a click at the window. I moved into the shadows, tucking away the opera glasses to have my hands free.

In the sudden gloom, the curtains bulged into the room, and I realized the window was actually a set of French doors. After a moment, the lump moved again and the curtains slid aside slightly. I was no longer alone.

I crept within striking distance. A match flared, and I pulled back the blow just in time. "Jack!" I whisper-shouted.

He yelped, whirled, burnt his fingers on the match, and dropped it.

A sound at the door sent us scrambling for hiding places. One of the patrolling footmen stuck his head inside the study and held his pyrogene high. The light lapped at my toes where I hunched in the shadow of a chair, and I pressed back into the darkness.

"Huh. Thought I heard…" The light ebbed then winked out as the door closed.

I peeked around the edge of the chair then stood.

"What do you think you're doing?"

The furious whisper by my ear made me jump almost high enough to touch the ceiling. I had to restrain myself from striking him. "Me? What are you doing here?"

He huffed air through his nose like a frustrated bull. He

looked like he wanted to paw the ground with his soft-soled boot. "You know why I'm here."

"Then perhaps we ought to stop asking idiotic questions."

He rubbed the back of his neck. "You're right. I think worry is getting the best of me."

I couldn't help myself, I put a hand on his arm. "She'll be all right. We just need to focus on determining who's behind the plot so we can end it."

As reward for my kindly impulse Jack tilted his head as if he could really make out my expression in the darkness. "What's going on? What are you hiding?"

There was no shaking his suspicious nature. "I was simply trying to reassure you."

"You're too kind."

Really, he was beastly. "I'm not going to stand around bickering, I have work to do." I moved to the desk.

"Have you searched for a safe?" Again, he was right at my ear, but this time I was ready for him and only flinched a little at the tickle of warm breath on my neck.

"Not in here yet."

While he circuited the room, I pulled the opera glasses back out and finished my search of the remaining piles of papers. I found nothing incriminating. Most of them were bills, invitations, and the sort of obligatory correspondence a child sends to their parents from school—I ought to know, having written hundreds of such letters myself. The conventional secret compartment held only a torrid letter from FitzClarence's mistress.

Jack had found no safe and had turned his attention to rifling through the books. I searched the drinks cabinet and the games chest, then examined the deal table for secret compartments, to no avail.

Out in the hall a footman clomped by. The light of his lamp

probed under the door, but he did not stop and stick his head in again.

I sighed. I had really hoped to find something definitive. I paced back to the desk and looked at the blotter.

Jack came and stood at my shoulder. "Did you find something?"

"It's the only anomaly." I pointed to the note about Brown's Hotel.

He stepped forward then moved to strike another match, but I stopped him and handed him the opera glasses. He peered through them recoiled. Raised them to his face again. "These are amazing."

In spite of my overall frustration, I grinned. "I know." I pointed again to the note.

"You know what these really need is a strap so they can remain affixed in place on the head, while leaving the hands free."

"Focus, please."

"Oh. Certainly." He dutifully bent to read the scrawled address. "Brown's Hotel. That's the new establishment started by a former manservant and maid to Lord and La—"

"Lady Byron. Yes, I know. The question is why would Fitz-Clarence have made this note?"

"Perhaps he is housing a...friend there?" He kept the opera glasses raised to his eyes as he looked up from the blotter.

I held out my hand, and he reluctantly handed them over. "I don't think so. I found a letter from his mistress. The direction is a house in Marylebone."

"You think that's where they've stashed Fennick?"

I nodded. "I think it's a possibility. Lord Bancroft's estate was invaded a few nights ago, so they may have decided to move Fennick for safekeeping." I didn't mention who had been behind that caper. "And you told me that Fennick had disappeared before the princess did. Brown's would be a discreet but comfortable place for him to be got out of the way for a couple of days. It's ideal as a location that is not tied either to the Baron or FitzClarence but which would allow them to produce him to the Privy Council tomorrow."

"Hmm. Have you searched the rest of the house?" He glanced around as if he could see through the walls.

"All of the rooms on this floor and the servants' rooms below. That's as far as I've gotten. I wouldn't recognize Fennick if I tripped over him. But you would, wouldn't you?"

"Yes. But I don't think we'll find Fennick here. I think you're right about that note." He put a hand on my elbow. "The night is still young. How about we take a peek at the Charles II suite at Brown's Hotel?"

"Now that is an excellent idea."

He led the way to the French doors and swung them open. He dug something from the latch, and I realized that he had kept the door from automatically latching shut behind him, by the simple expedient of a ball of wax shoved into the strike plate. He saw the trend of my gaze and pointed upward with a waggle of his eyebrows. The door had an alarm. He had managed to stuff a ball of wax between the clapper and the bell before it sounded. To have been able to do that he had to have known it was there in advance. He had very good sources of intelligence.

Come to think of it, how had he become suspicious of Fitz-Clarence? Did he have a source on the Privy Council as well?

I was trying to think of a withering *bon mot* to wipe off the cocksure grin he wore as he ushered me through the door. We'd no sooner made it through than the door from the hall opened.

I flung myself to the side of the door and pressed myself against the wall. Jack did the same on the other side. Contrary to my expectation, no light flared in the room beyond. Jack and I shared a glance, and I shrugged. Perhaps the intruder had left again?

I raised the opera glasses to my eyes and braved a look into the study. In our haste, we had not pulled the curtains entirely closed.

It was Dame Guinevere. For a dreadful instant, I thought she was on the side of the would-be coup. Then reason reasserted itself. If she had been invited here as a member of the conspiracy she wouldn't be snooping about in the dark.

Jack scuttled over to me and took the opera glasses from my unresisting hand. He raised them then uttered a strangled sound. "We've been spotted."

I took to my heels, but as fast as I am, Jack soon caught me up. All I can say is that his limbs are significantly longer than mine. We ran for several blocks, cutting through alleys and side streets. Once we were sure we hadn't been followed, we slowed to a walk. I was happy about that, which is not to say that I was winded at all.

"That was your schoolmistress."

I'll say this for him, he didn't beat about the bush. "What?"

"Don't start. What kind of school do you attend, anyway?"

"A patriotic one."

"That's all I'm going to get, isn't it?"

I offered a bland smile.

He sighed. "That's what I figured."

Brown's Hotel when we spied it was a handsome building that didn't look all that different from the house we'd just left. The main things that set it apart were a discreetly labeled portico and a uniformed footman standing at attention outside the door, despite the late hour. The beauty of a public building though is that it is, well, open to the public. We ought to be able to just walk inside.

While we were still down the street, Jack stopped me with a hand on my arm. "You, uh, look like you've climbed through a window and run a long way."

I glanced at my sagging hem and felt the wisps of loose hair settle against my cheeks as we stopped.

He was right. For Brown's, we needed to be the right kind of public.

"Can you do anything about it?" he asked.

"I can manage something." I gave him a pointed look, and he gave himself a once over as I had just done.

"I could spruce myself up a bit too, huh?" He drew me toward the nearest shop, a small tobacconist's with its display window full of banded cigar boxes stoically guarded by the obligatory carved Indian figure.

It took him scarcely longer to enter than if he'd had the key.

"You're pretty handy with those lockpicks."

"As are you. I seem to recall that you broke into someone's home the night we first met." He held the door for me, and I sailed past him. He entered hard on my heels and closed the door softly behind him. He lowered his voice. "If I hadn't already known there was more to you than meets the eye, I would have been convinced of it then. You'd given me that address, so you brazened it out when I didn't leave right away. I was pretty impressed."

I shrugged. "No daughter of the house would have let herself in. She would have rung the bell and woken a servant."

"Most people wouldn't have given it a second thought."

Cheeks warmed by the praise and suddenly acutely conscious of my empty hands, I peered around the tiny shop. It contained no back room. Nowhere that offered privacy.

Jack planted his hands on his hips as he too looked around. "Well—"

"I shall go behind the counter." It was the only place with even a modicum of cover. I didn't warn him of the dire consequences peeking would have upon his health and future. He understood and raised both hands slightly, almost like he was surrendering.

I moved behind the counter and ducked down. Providence willing, Dame Guinevere would never find out about this, or I was done for. For that matter, this side foray was the least of it. I was about to enter a hotel with a man. My cheeks flamed.

Crouching and trying not to fall over, I wriggled out of my bodice and then flipped it inside out, replacing the dark gray, preferable for a spot of unauthorized entry, with a lovely salmon pink moiré. No one could possibly think someone wearing salmon pink moiré was a threat. I released the tucks in the sleeves and puffed them out. I then slid off the skirt and flipped it around and put it back on. The brim of my bonnet had gotten a bit squashed. Regretfully, I removed it and left it on the counter. Then I straightened up my hair. It would have been easier with a mirror. When I was done, I thought I would pass muster.

Upon emerging, I found Jack now wearing a frock coat and messing with his hat. As if by magic, the bowler he had been wearing transformed into a top hat in his hands.

A neat trick. Colleen and I would be stealing that idea just as we had his little poppers. All was fair in love and technology.

We slipped back out onto the street. Jack offered me his arm, and we swept down the street like we were on a royal progress and surrounded by an adoring populace. Jack favored the doorman with a polite incline of the head as we approached.

That good fellow hastened to open the door for us. "Evening sir, ma'am." He raised a knuckle to his forehead as we passed him.

Smoothly, Jack dropped a coin into a discreetly extended palm as we passed.

Not for the first time I wondered about his background.

Inside, a fine Louis the Something-or-other desk was tucked to one side in the foyer with a chair behind. Presumably, this was where a concierge was stationed during the day. Happily, it was unoccupied. A marble floor was shrouded in thick, vibrant carpets. Potted plants and oriental screens gave a feeling of luxurious abundance and also created a sense of privacy for a couple of tastefully arranged seating areas. It was no wonder this establishment had been immediately embraced by society. It practically screamed discretion, if such a thing can be said.

Without missing a step, Jack led the way to a broad staircase and up to the first floor.

"Do you know where the Charles II= suite is?"

"No idea, but if the doorman is watching, I don't want to give him cause for concern."

"Good point." We were concocting a plan for searching the hotel when, to our delight, we found that the doors to each suite were labeled with their names on small brass plaques. Finding the Charles II suite from there was the work of a moment.

I stooped and picked the lock before Jack could. It was my turn to show off my skill. When I looked up at him triumphantly, he grinned and tipped his hat. Infuriating.

Creeping inside, we listened intently for any sign of movement but detected none. The room beyond the door wasn't a bedchamber, it was a well-appointed sitting room with a handsome couch and a couple of chairs clustered in front of the fireplace and tea tables placed to hand. Our instruction on fine art had lasted only a couple of years, but to my eye the land-scapes on the hotel walls were finer than those in the house we had just come from. Interesting. Perhaps George FitzClarence was broke and had sold off the good paintings to keep creditors at bay. I'd heard that also happened to gamblers. Maybe it had even lent more impetus to his scheming.

Jack circuited the room, inspecting first one and then the other of the doors that led off either side of the sitting room. A secretary in one corner was the obvious place to start a search. With a curious sense of *déjà vu*, I began a careful perusal of the contents. Tucked in the top drawer was an object wrapped in a handkerchief. When I unrolled it, a heavy ruby ring plopped into my palm. I held up the opera glasses and studied it. It was the ring Xavier Mahlenbeau had described to me several eons ago. A thrill shot through me and I wanted to crow. I had been right! Fennick was involved and he was here.

Jack joined me. "Bedrooms," he whispered and gave a side-ways nod to indicate the doors.

I held up the ring. "The man who commissioned the modi-fied perfumer from the first kidnapping attempt had this ring. The craftsman described it exactly."

"Should we take it?"

I itched to claim the evidence, to have something tangible to show I was not simply having a flight of fancy, but I shook my head. "If we do, there's nothing to tie it back to Fennick."

"Good point." He jerked a thumb at a painting to the side of the fireplace. "I think there's a safe behind that painting. I'm going to check it out."

I rewrapped the ring in the handkerchief and put it back in the drawer. I found the letters that Louisa Conroy had writ-ten to Fennick. They were what one could have expected. Ap-proximately one-third sappy attempts at poetry, one-third silly flirtations achieved mostly by extravagant compliments, and one-third complaints about the princess's ungrateful mistreatment of Sir John mixed with pride that they were living in a palace. Despite her grumbling, nothing in them indicated she was knowingly connected to the plot.

"Psst."

I looked up to find Jack waving me over.

I joined him, and he opened the safe with a flourish then offered me a bow. I shook my head but patted my hands together in silent applause.

A portfolio stuffed with documents sat inside. He had found the goods. Reverently, he pulled them out. Several loose documents sat on top, probably the sworn statements Dame Guinevere had described. Two letters signed by King George III. And the lynchpin of the entire fraud—the permission from King George, complete with royal seal. Beneath these documents was a bound parish register—no doubt containing the record of Fennick's birth and the alleged marriage. I didn't take the time to sort through it. The last item in the stack was the gold-embossed missing volume of the Privy Council records.

I stared at it. I had been certain they would have destroyed the record.

Jack was looking at in confusion. "Why would they have risked keeping this?"

I shook my head, as much at a loss as he was.

A scuffling sound in the hallway sent us diving for cover. We'd barely ducked behind a sofa when the hall door burst inward. Toughs poured into the room and the lights blazed into life.

My thoughts teemed with half-formed curses. What had happened?

Jack and I were spotted immediately and ordered to come out of hiding.

Hands raised, Jack and I stood slowly. The ruffians filled the room. They were all in shirtsleeves, a couple looking like they'd just woken up. We let them herd us into the center of the room.

"Well, well, well." The shortest of the bunch, a fellow with thinning hair strode forward and put his hands on his hips. He had been at Saint James's Palace last night wearing an ill-fitting footman's uniform. I mentally dubbed him Shorty. "What have we here?"

I couldn't refrain from rolling my eyes. Who was writing this fellow's dialogue? He sounded like a villain from a penny dreadful. And that was when the penny dropped for me. "The safe was alarmed, wasn't it?"

He grinned, and I felt slightly cheated that his teeth weren't yellowed or uneven like a proper villain's, but rather nice. "Wired it myself. It's a very simple concept really. As soon as the ends of the wires are parted from one another it flips a sign in the servants' quarters."

"Neatly done," I said.

One of the others tapped Shorty on the shoulder and lowered his head to whisper in his ear. As he did, I recognized him as one of the men who had originally attempted to kidnap the princess so long ago. My masquerade as a helpless female was about to come to a screeching halt.

I should strike first.

I gave Jack a nod and kicked out with my heel at the fellow who stood nearest me. I caught the side of his knee. He toppled with a cry and clutched at his injured joint. The confused gazes of his comrades snapped from him up to me.

"She broke my knee!"

I was already in motion. I reached back and snatched the picks from my hair, then with one in each fist I jabbed up at the first fellow who came at me. I felt the metal tip score along a rib, before he twisted away.

Jack was tearing into the fellows who were trying to bring him down as if he was a one-man hurricane. Two men already lay at his feet. Beyond him a blond, slightly overweight man in an elaborate brocade dressing gown stepped from the bedroom.

The next man caught my wrist in a tight grip before I could get close enough to him. He squeezed until he shook the pick from my hand. I swung at him with the other pick and struck his arm. He howled and pulled away, unfortunately, taking the pick with him.

The man with the wounded rib rushed me again from the side. I thrust my elbow up into his windpipe. He fell to his knees clutching his throat. I grabbed my fan from my pocket and deployed the blades. They spun, catching the light and causing the other men who surrounded us to step back.

Another heavy thud sounded and I glanced to my left to find Jack sprawled on the ground.

Now what? I couldn't carry him out and hold off the rest of these ruffians.

A brief buzzing sounded near my right ear, and then all went dark.

Chapter 27

My first sensation upon waking was pain. I ached everywhere. It felt like someone had seized the opportunity to kick me while I was blacked out since they hadn't been able to do so when I was awake. Cowards.

Allowing my head to hang forward was straining my back, so I gingerly lifted my head to ease the tightness. I tried to rub my aching temples but found that my hands were tied securely behind me. My tongue felt thick in my mouth, and I could taste blood. I hoped blearily that I had bitten someone but didn't think so.

Gradually, I became conscious of voices chatting in a desultory manner somewhere behind me and to my left.

"It is neat little device, isn't it? An army chap I knew back in Nova Scotia designed it. It's said to be able to drop a full-grown moose."

Moose? I blinked trying to clear my vision.

"How does it work?" Another male voice, politely interested.

"The motor builds up an electric charge, and all one has to do is to touch an opponent with the prongs and they will fall like they've been struck by lightning."

"Like Zeus's thunderbolt, sir?"

"Essentially."

A third voice joined the discussion. "I could use something like that when my old lady gets to nagging."

This witticism landed awkwardly, and was followed by a silence.

My scattered senses were slowly coalescing into actual thoughts. I was sitting upright, tied to a chair in the luxurious sitting room of the Charles II suite. The device they were discussing must have been what had defeated us.

I turned my head carefully because of the pain and found that Jack was tied back-to-back with me. He groaned and lifted his head.

Beyond Jack, the blond man, who had been in his dressing gown earlier, was now wearing a finely cut suit of dark serge. With a teacup and saucer in hand he stood from the couch where he had been chatting with Shorty. "Ah, our guests are rejoining us." He surveyed us with his head cocked to one side. Taking his time, he raised the cup to his lips and took a sip. "Who sent you?"

"No one." I tried for a sugary smile, but imagined that the result was marred by the fat lip someone had given me.

Despite my entirely honest answer, he scowled with a sort of malevolence I had never seen before. Not even from Eleanor. He set his cup back into the saucer with an audible clink. Then he held up a ring on a chain. It was Victoria's ring that she had bestowed on me when she commissioned me to act on her behalf. I had taken to wearing it on a chain around my neck because the only way to ensure it remained secret had been to keep it on my person. I swallowed but said nothing.

His lip curled up at one end. As he resumed his seat he jerked his chin at someone who stood on the other side of me. A ringing blow struck my ear and knocked my head back into Jack's.

I hadn't even realized someone was standing there. I found myself blinking again and working my jaw.

"There's no call to strike a lady!" Jack sounded outraged on my behalf.

The man snorted. "She's a menace."

"Still a lady. Which means you're no gentleman." Jack's retort almost made me smile.

"I am your next king." Fennick's voice caressed the words. Rolled them around in his mouth as if savoring something unutterably sweet. Then with a savage movement he flung the ring on its chain into the fireplace.

"Royalty, eh? I had no idea." Jack's voice meanwhile turned light almost nonchalant. "I thought we were due for a queen?"

This time, Jack caught the blow, but I shared in it when his head cracked into mine. I winced. His head was remarkably hard.

"Now, I will ask you again. Who sent you? Are you agents of the Privy Council or the king?"

"No one sent us," Jack insisted. "Look, we were trying to rob the hotel. We heard a lot of posh swells stayed here and figured it would be like knocking over a dozen houses at once."

Impressed, I watched Fennick to see what the response to this whopper would be. The would-be king's eyes were heavy-lidded. He wasn't bad looking. A tad on the short side and with a slight paunch, but his jaw was well-defined and he stood erect. The scowl he wore did him no favors. "Very well. We'll leave that for the moment. What are your names?"

"If we're all claiming royal titles, you can call me Your Grace the Duchess of the Old Bailey." My response earned me another blow. This one caught me on the cheekbone and sent fireworks off behind my eyes. For a moment, I sat dazed. Then I turned my gaze from Fennick to the burly man delivering the blows. He had a hooked nose, a missing front tooth, and hair cut almost as short as a convict's. As soon as I got free, I meant to settle scores with him.

"Roderick, don't knock them out, they need to be able to answer questions." Fennick's protest wasn't at the abuse, just the idea that his agenda might be disrupted. Then to me. "Where is Victoria?"

I said nothing and neither did Jack.

The next blow was to my midriff. I gasped and coughed, but the corset I wore offered some protection. I was glad it wasn't another blow to the head. I needed to think.

Jack absorbed another punch. Then another and another.

No matter how I twisted my wrists I could gain no slack in my bonds. And even if I worked my hands free, I'd never have time to untie my feet before they retied my hands. I needed to think of something. Anything.

A lump lodged in my throat as Jack grunted again.

"Hold a moment." Fennick set aside his teacup as Shorty spoke to him in a low voice I couldn't quite make out. Then he nodded. "An excellent point. We ought to focus our efforts on the weaker vessel." He turned to me as if we were having a polite conversation. "Where is Victoria?"

"Kensington Palace?" The next punch caught my sternum, and I retched.

Jack bucked, straining at his bonds. "Leave her alone."

I cast about wildly for a way out, but my usually fertile imagination had not a single solution to offer. I said nothing. Where was a good idea when I really needed one?

One thing I was sure of. I had been right to preempt Fennick's plan. He was ruthless. Once he'd made the princess disappear, he would have eliminated her to make sure no stumbling block remained in his path to the throne. He would have taken no chances and he would have offered no quarter.

The blows continued for a time interrupted only by Fennick's questions. I had stopped listening. I wasn't going to tell him anything. Ever.

Behind me, Jack grumbled, breathed threats, and fought ineffectually against the bonds.

I'm not sure how much time actually passed, before Fennick pursed his lips. "Put the poker in the fire and get it good and hot." A frisson of fear skittered along my spine and settled like a cold weight in the pit of my stomach. "We will get answers from them if it takes all night, but I don't think it's going to take long."

"No!" Jack's hoarse shout made everyone start. "That's enough. I'll take you to the princess. But don't hurt her anymore."

Hot outrage flashed through me, scalding away my numb cocoon and bringing me back sharply to the moment. I struggled against my ropes, trying to find a way to silence him. "Shut your mouth, Jack. You can't tell them anything." Even as I said it my befuddled thoughts caught up. He couldn't take them to the princess. He didn't know where she was.

"I knew one of you would come around." Fennick nodded, satisfied.

"He doesn't even know where she is. Don't listen to him."

Fennick raised an eyebrow. "If she says another word, kill her."

"That would be a bad idea, sir," Jack spoke quickly, probably trying to keep me from saying anything else. "We'll need her to get to the princess. She's hidden away in a secret room. I know the location, but not how to access the secret room."

I could hardly believe it. He was spilling his guts. How did he know where we'd hidden the princess? Burning tears of frustration at being unable to control the situation sprang to my eyes. "Jack?"

No one was paying me any attention, so the small plea didn't end with my death.

"Where is she then?" Fennick demanded.

"Where is the best place to hide something?"

Fennick crossed his arms and glared.

Jack sighed. "This is more amusing if you play along. The best place to hide something is with things of like kind."

Fennick still said nothing.

"They've stashed her at a school for young ladies."

Fennick started to laugh.

I almost did too as I finally understood.

If I'd been free, I might've kissed Jack's poor battered face. I covered my delight by shrieking and thrashing as if trying to break loose. "How could you? I'm going to scratch your eyes out."

Fennick stepped forward and grabbed hold of my hair. He shook me savagely. "Shut up. I do not want to attract attention from anyone else in the hotel." When he released me, I let my head fall in thorough defeat as I pretended to weep.

Fennick turned his attention back to Jack. "If I have to, I will simply break into this school and tear it apart brick by brick."

Jack shrugged. "I suppose that's an option if you don't mind antagonizing some of the noblest families in the nation by taking their daughters hostage and destroying their school. Despite the fact that you will need their support in the House of Lords. Or you could get in and out without any of them even knowing you were there."

"Who are you?" Fennick's voice was more thoughtful now.

"Private agents hired by Sir John Conroy on behalf of the Duchess of Kent to protect the princess." Jack's glib response was almost enough to convince even me.

"Ah, Conroy, hedging the bets he's placed on the princess. That makes sense." Fennick gave a thin-lipped smile. "I too have a patron who knows I am his path to influence."

A tap at the door made everyone in the room jump. Fennick pointed at each of us in turn. "Utter a single word and you both die."

He gave Shorty a nod, and the fellow hastily buttoned up his jacket as he moved to the door. He stuck his head out. "Yes? Oh, it's you."

He opened the door to reveal a wizened little fellow with a halo of white hair crowning an otherwise bald head. This apparition wore knee breeches and a coat of somewhat rusty black velvet which smelled distractingly of mothballs. He carried a black bag that looked like a doctor's kit.

"At last," Fennick said.

"My apologies, lordship." The old fellow's voice was little more than a wheeze. He cast furtive glances at Jack and me every few words. "I had a touch of the pleurisy and was staying with my daughter. I just got word—"

"Yes, the important thing is you are here now."

"Yes, sir."

"Pay no mind to these villains." He waved a negligent hand at Jack and me. "We caught them robbing the place and will be taking them to the magistrate shortly. Now, I believe you know what is wanted? You've done good work already and if you do well with this final project there will be an extra guinea in it for you."

"Yes, sir." The bald head bobbed eagerly.

"Then here is the volume." Fennick extended to him the Privy Council records.

Somewhere in my fuzzy brain I finally understood. He was their forger. This was why the Privy Council volume hadn't been destroyed. He was going to alter the record by adding a line or two recording the notice to the council of the intended marriage between Edward and Julie de Saint Laurent. Then they would put the volume back in the archives. It would be their *coup de grâce*. In the morning, the records would be miraculously found by the council archivist. It would be believed that the volume had simply been misfiled on another shelf or something.

They had thought of everything.

Everything but me, Colleen, and Jack. We had to stop them.

The forger skirted Jack and me, his eyes resolutely refusing to land upon us as he moved to the desk and began laying out his implements.

Fennick stood. "Do excuse us. We have important business to attend to."

"Certainly. Certainly." Once more the forger's head bobbed.

"Marshall, stay with Mr. Barnaby and see he has everything he needs."

I was hauled to my feet and my hands unbound. I was planning my attack, but they rebound them in front of me before loosing the ropes around my ankles. From somewhere, a voluminous shawl was produced and wrapped around my shoulders so that my bound hands weren't visible. I was then gagged. Finally, a poke bonnet was placed on my head, the long brim casting my face in deep shadow. Only then were my feet untied.

We had been trained in the French art of savate, which was like boxing, but with the feet. I laid out a plan of attack, but having my hands tied was a distinct disadvantage. Not to mention the fact that I couldn't abandon Jack. Though I had not been blessed with an abundance of patience I'd have to remain vigilant and choose my moment carefully.

Fennick looked me over then nodded his approval. "She'll do." Fennick turned his attention back to Jack. "The address?"

Jack shook his head. "I'll take you there, sir, but it's as much as my life is worth to give you the address now."

To my surprise, Fennick laughed again. "Fair enough."

If Jack ever needed a new line of employment, he'd make a dandy snake charmer. He was released as I had been. To hide his bonds, they enclosed him in a great coat and tucked the empty arms in the pockets. The coat was too heavy for June, but anyone we encountered in the city at this time of night would have seen far stranger things. It was cleverly done, and I wondered if they had used the ruse before.

Fennick gave another satisfied nod then took hold of my elbow, and we led a very odd procession indeed. As we crossed the threshold, Fennick leaned close to my ear. "One wrong move and you will die." He punctuated his threat by the press of a gun barrel against my bruised side.

I could do nothing but nod.

Chapter 28

Cadogan Hall sat dark and wreathed in silence as we approached. Not a single light shone from any of the windows visible from the street. Odd. It was excessively late, but I would have expected someone to be up. The princess was still missing after all. At least, as far as any of the school staff knew.

Along the route to the Hall, our little procession had been met by another delegation. Fennick and Shorty now had a dozen compatriots. My view was obscured by the bonnet they had stuffed me into and the constant forward pressure of Fennick's grip on my arm, but my initial impression of these men was of hardened thugs whose muscle went to the highest bidder.

Too bad I had exhausted my pin money for the quarter.

Despite what could be seen as their easy virtue, I wasn't going to make the mistake of underestimating them as fighters. If, as I suspected, they had come from the slums and rookeries of London then they had learned to fight in order to survive, and if they'd lasted into adulthood then they had learned their lessons well.

My stomach began to roil. Our one saving grace could be the element of surprise. I hoped it would be enough.

"How do we get in?" Fennick demanded.

I shook my head.

Jack had somehow managed to turn up next to me and he leaned forward as if trying to look me in the face. I thought I caught a furtive wink. "You must be reasonable, P—oh. You'll have to remove the gag if you want her to respond to your questions."

Fennick huffed but made a gesture, and Shorty removed the odious bonnet and the gag. I have never been so tempted in my life as I was at that moment. I wanted to bite the fellow's hand off.

I restrained myself.

Barely.

I made a show of working my jaw though I wasn't sure they could see my face clearly. At Fennick's second impatient huff, I finally spoke. "I get in and out through a small window to the laundry at the back of the building. But I don't think you will be able to do the same."

At his insistence, I described the location of the window, and he sent a man to check. The fellow returned a few moments later breathing rather heavily for the short jog. "She's right, sir. I don't think most of us would fit through it. It can't be more than seven or eight inches deep."

"Perhaps you could wait for me here," I ventured.

"I think not." Sarcasm oozed from Fennick's tone.

"I snuck out, I can hardly go through the front door," I retorted.

"Oh, but that's exactly what you're going to do."

"I can't do that. I'll get kicked out of school."

"It's no concern of mine." His smile was downright nasty. If I hadn't already loathed him, I would have worked for his downfall from that very moment.

Gripping my arm far more tightly than necessary, he propelled me the rest of the way along the sidewalk and up the front steps. His henchmen were right behind us hauling Jack with them. He gave an almighty tug on the bellpull while his men took up positions on either side of the door out of sight of whomever might open the door.

He yanked on the cord again hard enough this time that I could hear the ringing inside.

A moment of silence measured in about two lifetimes was at last punctuated by a light flickering into life in the hall. Then another wait. The iron of the bolt scraping back set my teeth on edge, and from the wince that passed over Fennick's features, it struck him the same way.

The door swung inward revealing Dame Guinevere clad in a dressing gown and with her hair down around her shoulders.

I gaped.

I had never in my life seen her less than completely dressed. Ever. And what was she doing answering the door?

Even in her deshabille she managed to look haughty. When she saw me, she pulled her shoulders back into an even more rigidly erect posture. "Lady Portia. What is the meaning of this?" She made an imperious gesture for me to come to her side, but a hand on my shoulder kept me where I was.

Her attention shifted as did her manner. She clasped her hands in front of her chest. "Sir, I cannot thank you enough for escorting my wayward student home. When I think of her being on the London streets alone at night, it quite makes me tremble."

Fennick's grip loosened on my shoulder and he guided me before him into the room. "Madam, do be silent."

Behind us his men poured into the room and fanned out. One of them shoved Jack forward.

Dame Guinevere gave way before the onslaught, backing

farther and farther into the hall. Her gasp sounded shocked and terrified.

Fennick gestured at my headmistress. "Shut her up before she screams."

Dame Guinevere continued to draw them deeper into the room. It was fascinating watching a master at work.

If they'd had any idea what she could do, they would have been running for the door. While Dame Guinevere drew several of the men away from Jack and me, Fennick gave a tug on my arm so that I turned to face him. "Show me to the princess," he ordered.

One of the fellows lunged for Dame Guinevere, and she called out, "Now."

Fennick was pulling me closer, his spittle hitting my cheek as he repeated his demand.

I headbutted him. As he roared, I flung aside the shawl and let the ropes that had bound my hands fall to the ground. I had long since been free. Seriously, a double bowline knot? Amateurs.

I spared a glance for Jack and found he too had freed himself during the trip to Cadogan Hall. His grin as he administered a bit of payback was ferocious.

The fellow who had been holding him fell so hard I winced in sympathy.

Shorty moved toward me cautiously, hands raised in a classic boxer's pose. Brass knuckles gleamed on his right fist. He'd learned. There would be no wild haymakers or unchecked rushes from him.

I let him circle but wasn't about to let him back me into Fennick and his wicked little lightning bolt device. I didn't fancy another jolt. He wasn't the only one learning.

Roderick rushed at me. I hadn't forgotten that I owed him.

I sidestepped then whirled. Using his momentum, I grabbed him by the scruff of the neck with one arm and turned him with me, sending him staggering into Shorty. They both went down, and I was there in an instant delivering a kick to the side of Shorty's head that made his eyes flutter shut. A blow to Roderick's neck produced similar results.

I looked up in time to see another fellow charging at me. Reflexively, I raised my hands in front of me, but then he was on the ground at my feet, swearing.

"Got him!" Colleen was at my side and in the next instant I realized she'd brought him down with one of her bolas. As she finished him off, feet pounded on the stairs as the other girls and teachers rushed to join the fray.

At the head of the pack, Irene looked positively gleeful as she launched herself down the last few stairs at a ruffian who was running away from Dame Guinevere. Right behind her, Eleanor sword in hand, looked fierce. Marianne was screaming like a banshee, and Harriet's chosen weapon was a parasol.

I almost felt sorry for the poor men who had dared to invade the temporary, rented precincts of Saint Scholastica.

I looked around for Fennick.

He was right behind me and closing in fast. He raised his hand.

I thought he had pulled out the shocking device. I dropped and performed a spin kick to knock his legs from under him.

There was a thunderclap and a flash. The acrid stench of smoke.

He fell hard, and I realized as the weapon clattered from his hand that it had been a gun.

I delivered an elbow to his solar plexus that left him stunned and snatched up the gun before anyone else could get any ideas. Then I turned to explain who he was to Colleen.

She lay on the ground. Her eyes, glassy and wide, stared at me. Her mouth moved but she made no sound. Blood pooled beneath her.

A screech tore out of me as my heart hit the floor. I dropped to my knees beside her.

There was practically a stampede around me as teachers and students incapacitated the remaining attackers. Within a few moments the remaining combatants had fled or been taken captive.

I crouched next to Colleen, clutching her hand and trying frantically to find the source of the bleeding through my tears.

Chapter 29

Jack dropped to his knees next to me. "What's happened?"

"She was shot."

Colleen's face was deathly pale, her breathing shallow.

I found the wound at last. The shot had penetrated her left thigh. Blood soaked everything. I had learned enough field medicine to know that a wound to the femoral artery could prove deadly in just a few minutes.

"I need a tourniquet," I managed to say.

Jack ripped off his tie while I moved her skirts out of the way and held pressure on the wound. The content of our emergency aid classes sped through my mind.

While I maintained the pressure, I directed him in tying off the tourniquet.

"No, bind them all." Dame Guinevere's voice came snappishly. "Miss Yancy you will fetch Inspector Ogden from A Division." She knelt beside me, and her voice turned gentle, which scared me more than anything I had yet heard or seen. "Well done, Portia. Let me see."

Jack stood. "I can fetch a doctor."

"Dr. Klaus Nordman." Dame Guinevere rapped out an address not far away, and Jack took to his heels. She moved my hands away from the wound. Without taking her gaze away from her assessment of Colleen's injury, she snapped. "Eleanor, Harriet, Irene, Marianne. You will please move the prisoners into the dining room and stand guard over them."

Lady Pomeroy came to kneel alongside us. She handed Dame Guinevere a wad of bandages that she had made up into a poultice with some sort of herb. "Yarrow and blackberry root, they are antiseptics and astringents to restrain the bleeding," she said by way of explanation. Ever the teacher.

Dame Guinevere applied the bundle to the wound and pressed down.

I patted around until I found the smelling salts stowed in one of Colleen's secret pockets and waved them under her nose. She didn't move, but she groaned, and I choked back a sob.

She wasn't dead. Not yet. I could still hope.

"Report, Portia," Dame Guinevere commanded.

I gaped at her stupidly, my thoughts slow to catch up.

She lifted her gaze from her ministrations to Colleen and raised her eyebrows expectantly.

I began gathering the frayed ends of my thoughts. "Mr. Fennick, the blond fellow, is the would-be-king. The plan to kidnap the princess was hatched in order to create a succession crisis. The forged proofs he intended to offer to establish his claim and the forger too are in the Charles II suite at Brown's Hotel."

"The princess?"

"Safe. She's always been safe." I was suddenly so tired I at last understood how heroines in gothic novels could swoon.

"Mrs. Dutton."

The maths and ciphers teacher was at our sides in an instant.

"Would you and Eleanor be so kind as to go to Brown's Hotel and retrieve any and all documents you can find. They may be in a safe. I also will require the production of a certain forger that you may yet find on the premises."

"Name's Barnaby," I murmured.

Dame Guinevere made me describe everything I could recall about the suite, the location of the documents, and the forger. I did so as calmly as I could though it felt completely wrong to do anything besides attend to Colleen, and I had some difficulty focusing.

As soon as I had concluded, Mrs. Dutton and Eleanor rushed off.

Dame Guinevere again bent her attention to me. "Portia, we need to allow Mr. Carstairs to move Colleen into a bedroom so that the doctor can examine her when he arrives."

I looked up at the school's head footman blankly but didn't release my grip on Colleen's hand.

"You can help us make her more comfortable when we get upstairs."

I nodded and stood clumsily. It felt like an eternity had passed since Mr. Fennick had invaded the school, but in reality, it had been less than a quarter of an hour. I trailed after Dame Guinevere, my head low examining my bloody hands.

We got Colleen out of her blood-soaked garments and into a clean white night dress. Lady Pomeroy cleaned and redressed the wound with a fresh poultice to help staunch the bleeding. She then managed to rouse Colleen and gave her something for the pain.

When Doctor Nordman arrived, I was ejected from the room despite my protests.

We'll see about that.

I stomped straight to Colleen's laboratory and retrieved the listening device. I maneuvered it into place in time to hear his assessment.

My brain had trouble translating what he said into understandable words. She had lost a great deal of blood and it would be touch and go for a while. Her thigh bone had been shattered by the ball. He intended to take her to Guy's Hospital for an emergency surgery. He very much feared she would have to have her leg removed as the bone was so damaged and would otherwise continue to bleed.

Dame Guinevere found me a few moments later still sitting on the floor with the listening device cradled in my lap and tears running down my cheeks.

I didn't bother with any excuses. "I want to go to the hospital with her."

She didn't bother with recriminations. "You cannot."

"Please. He was aiming for me."

"Lady Pomeroy is going with her. We will not leave her to languish in the filth of Guy's. The procedure is to be performed by Dr. John Lister, a young surgeon who is a personal friend of Dr. Nordman. He has the best outcomes in all London. She will be returned to the Hall as soon as she is stable following the procedure. Dr. Nordman has also provided us with the name of a very reliable attendant who we will hire to nurse her." Dame Guinevere met my gaze and put a hand on my shoulder. "Everything that can be done will be done for her."

I nodded. Knowing I had no choice really. By the time I stood and we left the room, the school's steam carriage had been brought around and Colleen was being transported out on a stretcher. Her eyes were open, but I couldn't really call her awake.

I watched her departure in a daze, but then Dame Guinevere's voice at my side snapped me back to myself. "Do you require Dr. Nordman's attentions?"

I shook my head.

"Then you will bathe and change into clean clothing. Do what you can to cover the bruises. I must have your full report, preferably before we speak with Inspector Ogden."

"Yes, ma'am." She was right. There was still work to be done. I could do nothing more for Colleen now but pray.

I presented myself to Dame Guinevere five-and-one-half minutes later, freshly scrubbed, dressed neatly in a dark blue dress, and with my hair braided and twisted into a knot at the nape of my neck. My hands were shaking ever so slightly, so I kept them folded before me.

"Good." She gave me a nod of approval. "Now, where is the princess?"

Before I could say a thing, she continued. "Don't bother trying to deny it. I know you've been investigating, and I know you and Colleen were the ones who took her."

"How?"

"My dear girl, how inept do you really believe me to be?"

I opened my mouth, but that was as far as I got. There was simply no good response to that question.

Dame Guinevere sighed and folded her hands on the desk in front of her. "You were able to go about your investigations because I allowed it. Although, I will admit that I did not anticipate your stunt with the kidnapping. Now, where is she?"

"The Tower. The Praetorienne safe house."

She actually gaped at me for once, and I experienced a twinge of satisfaction. At last, she spoke. "Well, that was brazen."

"Yes, ma'am."

"How did Mr. Harding become involved?"

It took me a second to realize that she meant Jack. Under her careful questioning, I confessed all that I had been up to for the last several weeks. Well, almost all. I kept back a few minor details, such as changing my costume while Jack was in the room and other things which were irrelevant to the story. I watched her closely, and I think I managed to surprise her a couple of times, but overall, I wasn't telling her anything she didn't already know. Confound the woman.

"Inspector Ogden is going to have to be told of your interference. Without reference to the Praetorienne."

"Yes, ma'am."

"You will keep as close to the truth as possible but reveal only your own involvement. Your interest was prompted by your concern for the princess after the attempted kidnapping in the orangery which was foiled by providence and the fact that the rest of us were close on your heels. You had the idea to investigate the perfumer and followed where the information led you. You will make the retelling as mundane as possible. I do not want to hear a single word about scaling a building or laying low an assailant by means of bartitsu."

"Yes, ma'am."

As if on cue a tap sounded at the door, and the lady's maid Annie, cap askew, stuck her head in. "Inspector Ogden is here, ma'am."

The household was indeed in an uproar if Annie was answering doors instead of a footman.

"Thank you, Annie. Please straighten your cap, then you may show him in."

A moment later, Inspector Ogden was ushered into the office. He had removed his hat and held it loosely before him. "Ma'am. I understand that you asked for me because there has been an attack of some sort upon your school?" He spotted me sitting in the chair before her desk and his words tapered away. "It is always you, isn't it?"

Dame Guinevere was being a gracious hostess and chose

to ignore this last. "Thank you for coming, Inspector Ogden. Before we begin, I believe it will expedite matters if you know that I am a member of the Privy Council and quite aware of the princess's disappearance."

He managed to tear his gaze away from me at that. "Ma'am?"

She gestured at me. "My pupil, Lady Portia, was with the princess at the time of the first attack upon her person. The one I reported to you when I first invited you here."

His gaze swiveled to me, and I offered a meek smile.

"I'm sure you may understand, though perhaps not condone, how that experience sparked within her a patriotic zeal to determine who would be so depraved as to plot against the heir apparent and an intense desire to thwart any such future designs."

A flame sparked within his eyes, and I now had his full attention once more. It was not a friendly gaze.

"Perhaps it would be best if she explained things to you."

Mindful of Dame Guinevere's prohibitions I launched into a version of events that glossed over all the best bits but managed to convey that I had been sneaking about investigating and had learned that the culprits behind the kidnapping attempt had been Mr. William Fennick, aided and abetted by Lord Bancroft and, even more shockingly, George FitzClarence, the king's eldest son.

My interventions had so enraged Mr. Fennick that he had attacked the school that evening. At least two-thirds of Inspector Ogden was in wholehearted agreement with Mr. Fennick's sentiments at this point in the story. As I told the tale I could all but see the gears in his mind sifting through the pieces of information he knew and slotting them together.

He had reserved his comments and questions thus far, but

at last he burst out. "Why? Why should these gentlemen undertake such a foolhardy and dangerous scheme?"

"This is speculation on my part, but I believe their plot was driven mainly by longstanding resentment at being overlooked for the power and prestige that would have been theirs but for an accident of their birth. They felt it unfair and together decided to right what they thought was an injustice."

Dame Guinevere broke in. "There is proof of all this, Inspector. Not the least of which are Mr. Fennick and several of his men who were apprehended by my staff in the act of breaking into this house tonight. We have also taken the liberty of securing the fraudulent documents which the trio had intended to use to establish Mr. Fennick's claims, as well as the forger who was responsible for creating them."

He blinked twice. "Dame Gui—"

She raised a hand. "Please. There is no need to thank us. We were only doing our patriotic duty."

From the red tide washing up his cheeks, I highly doubted that thanks had been on the tip of his tongue.

"There is more, sir," I said, giving my very best schoolgirl impression. "The princess was never truly kidnapped. I helped her hide in a safe location in the hopes of thwarting the villains and smoking them out."

This was apparently too much for his nerves. He jumped to his feet. Cherry red patches burned in his cheeks and he wagged a finger in my face. "I ought to arrest you here and now."

Dame Guinevere offered a thin smile. "Don't be foolish, Inspector. What would the charge be?"

"Kidnapping."

"What kidnapping? The princess was party to the design. I will grant you it was foolhardy and the young ladies would have done better to bring their elders and the authorities into their plans, but I don't think you will find that a crime has been committed."

"If not kidnapping, then—then interference with an official investigation."

Dame Guinevere rose from her chair, palms planted on her desk. "In what way did she interfere? The police had already arrested some hapless and entirely innocent young Gibraltarian. If she is to be arrested for doing your job better than you, then perhaps all of A Division should be fired for failing in their duty."

I was very glad in that moment that those coldly furious eyes weren't trained on me.

Inspector Ogden was pacing now, his hands clenching and unclenching at his sides. "Where is the princess?" His volume was just short of a bellow.

"Inspector." For once, mine was the most modulated tone in the room. "We all know that you cannot charge Mr. Fennick or his henchmen with kidnapping the princess or sedition without attracting the attention of the press which neither the crown nor any of us wants. But he can be put away on charges of kidnapping—me."

He had stopped pacing and was looking at me with mere loathing instead of the prior incandescent rage.

I pressed on. "And of breaking and entering this establishment. There's also the matter of theft of the Privy Council records and attempted fraud, but those charges will have to be carefully crafted to avoid unwanted attention. By the time you sort all that out and decide on the charges with your superiors, you will be able to call upon the princess at Kensington Palace to satisfy yourself as to her well-being and receive her grateful thanks for your stalwart service in this matter." I was gambling a bit with this last promise, but I suspected that the princess would want to be gracious.

Dame Guinevere granted me a smile then straightened away from her desk, her face once more a blandly pleasant mask. "Let me show you to your prisoners." Much against his will, she led the inspector away.

Having received no other orders, I stayed where I was. When she returned, she motioned for me to stand. Then she held out her hand palm up. On it rested the signet ring.

"I suppose this should be returned to you?"

"Yes, ma'am."

She shook her head. "When Mrs. Dutton returned with it, I was terribly afraid for a few moments that Fennick did indeed have her." She turned terse. "Get your wrap. We're going to fetch the princess and return her to her doting mother. For your sake, I hope she's still there."

Chapter 30

It had never before occurred to me that the princess could be anywhere but where I'd left her. In retrospect, I still don't know if Dame Guinevere was genuinely concerned or simply trying to worry me. If it was the latter, it certainly worked. My heart felt as if it was lodged in my throat the entire time it took to reach the Tower.

What if the princess had gotten bored or scared and decided to leave? What if we had been spotted and followed to the Tower and someone had simply gone in and removed her?

We had made it so easy. She had been all alone, and it was my fault.

The trip to the Tower seemed to take an inordinate amount of time. When I would have gone to the river to find a boat, Dame Guinevere shook her head and sighed. "Did you girls really go around the long way?"

Apparently we had. She brushed past the beefeaters and led the way into the Chapel of Saint John the Evangelist, within the White Tower. I'd never been in the chapel before. It put me in mind of pictures I had seen of the Roman Coliseum. It was horseshoe shaped and rimmed by great arches with another layer of arches above. Through these upper arches light from an outer layer of windows streamed in shafts that illuminated the space from the front and one side. On the third side, solid stone filled the arches.

A handful of tourists drifted along pointing at things. Dame Guinevere took a seat in a pew and lowered her head as if in prayer. I glanced around wondering if I had missed something, then did the same.

After several moments and a couple of pointed throat clearings from Dame Guinevere, the tourists finally departed. As soon as they were gone, she rose. "Hurry before any more pests come in."

I hastened after her, and she led the way to the first of the recessed stone arches. She stooped and pushed in one of the stones and the entire recessed panel shuddered. A little shower of stone dust sifted to the ground. She stood and pushed on the wall, and the whole thing swung in easily. Glancing about to make sure we were still alone, she gestured me to go before her.

I all but dove into the space that had been revealed.

Dame Guinevere pulled the stone panel closed behind us, leaving us in darkness. I was tempted to pull out the opera glasses, because, of course, I'd brought them, but I didn't need to. Dame Guinevere produced a pyrogene and held it high. She led the way as we descended down and down into the depths below London.

When we at last came to a door, she held it open and ushered me through. I found that this entrance had put us in a kitchen. Three mechanicals were at work, and I could smell coffee and baking bread.

That had to be a good sign, didn't it?

Colleen had taught the princess how to operate the mechanicals.

I still didn't draw a full breath until I entered the sitting room and clapped eyes on the princess.

She was there, sitting before an easel and humming to herself. My appearance didn't seem to startle her. She dropped her paintbrush and jumped up, rushing to me as we entered. "You will never guess, I have—" She stopped when she saw my companion. "Dame Guinevere." Her voice was suddenly restrained, wary.

My headmistress gave a gracious incline of her head. "Highness."

I bobbed a curtsy. "Princess, I am very pleased to report that William Fennick and his thugs have been apprehended. A Division will be pursuing the other conspirators, but without him, their teeth have been pulled. They'd have no reason to want you harmed and every reason to know that if any harm were to come to you, they will be the first in the dock."

She clasped her hands together. "That is good news." Her relief set her at ease again and she began to chatter. "I have been enjoying this time of solitude, and look, I have become quite domestic. I've dressed myself with only a mechanical to assist me and operated all of the other mechanicals. I even managed a light luncheon yesterday, by watching the kitchen mechanicals and learning what they did at breakfast." She grinned and in a moment of candor leaned forward. "But to be honest, I haven't been raised for solitude. I will be happy to go home now. I'm quite looking forward to telling my mother all about my daring and I can't wait to see dear Lezhen." Her flow of words suddenly stalled, and she took a step toward me peering closely. "Have you been injured in our defense?"

My cheeks burned. "It's nothing of significance, ma'am. But Colleen—" I swallowed. "Colleen may lose her leg."

The princess went pale. "What? The beautiful girl? I…" She appeared to be at a loss. "What hap—"

Dame Guinevere stepped in. "Your mother is making herself ill with worry over you, Your Highness. Why don't we get you home now?"

Dame Guinevere led us out of the secret refuge by yet another passage, and we escorted the princess home to Kensington Palace. We had the pleasure of seeing her reunion with her mother which was as tender as anyone could wish. I also had the pleasure of leaving before the princess explained to her mother that her disappearance had been my suggestion. I had a feeling that when the duchess found out she was going to try to have me drawn and quartered.

I wanted to go back to the school to see if Colleen had been returned, but Dame Guinevere had other errands. The foremost of which was breaking the news to King William.

He and Queen Adelaide left their breakfasts to receive us in a private sitting room at Clarence House. It was a beautifully proportioned room with great windows that allowed the early morning light to stream in. The walls were covered in ivory silk and pale blue curtains framed the windows. A carpet of blue and ivory covered the ground and a great white fireplace had a cheerful blaze going though it was a trifle warm for a fire.

After offering our courtesies, we were invited to sit. I found myself very conscious that my gown was not one I would have chosen had I known that this particular errand was on our task list.

From her manner, Dame Guinevere was enjoying herself and paying me back for the heartburn I had caused her in the past few days. She smiled broadly. "Your Majesty, I am pleased to report that Princess Victoria has been returned to her mother. She is entirely unharmed."

"Thank God!" King William seemed to sag in his seat from

the relief. "Who was behind this? I want to know all the details."

Dame Guinevere cast a significant glance at the footmen flanking the doors to the sitting room.

Queen Adelaide caught the glance and raised an eyebrow, but dismissed them. "Close the doors on your way out."

The men withdrew as bidden then Dame Guinevere leaned forward in her chair. "I'm afraid that what we have to tell you may be painful, Your Majesty."

His lips tightened, his chin set, but he nodded. "Go on."

Dame Guinevere nodded to me, and I launched into the story she had approved, describing first William Fennick's motive and Lord Bancroft's sponsorship. Having allowed me my moment in the sun, Dame Guinevere took over the telling at that point. She revealed that we had found the Privy Council records and the forger who had created or doctored the other documents that Fennick had intended to use to prove his claim. Then she hesitated.

I didn't envy her this part of the tale at all, and hoped she didn't look to me again.

King William held up a hand. He looked as if he had shrunk in the few minutes it took to go through the report. "It was my George, wasn't it?"

Queen Adelaide put a hand on his arm.

I'm not entirely sure what I had been expecting, but it wasn't this.

Dame Guinevere chose her words carefully. "There appears to be a link, although I do not know if there would be enough evidence to put before a jury."

"At the Privy Council meeting, I began to wonder." He stared straight ahead for a moment.

Dame Guinevere at last spoke again, her voice low. "Fennick and his men will be tried for other crimes and incarcerated. I do not expect him to be discreet. However, perhaps with the assistance of A Division we can prevent some of this from coming to the press."

The king grunted. "We must think of what is best for Victoria now." He sighed. "I am not long for this world." He waved aside our murmured protests. "I've held on so far mostly to spite the duchess." He gave a derisive little snort, and I couldn't tell if the derision was meant for the duchess or himself, possibly both. "The princess should not start her reign with any hint of uproar about whether she will be strong enough or capable enough for the task. She is already handicapped by her youth and gender. She cannot afford to seem weak in any way. George will be advised to take a long visit to the Continent to clear his debts. He shall be given two hours to pack and leave. That wife of his may follow within twenty-four hours. They will not be welcomed back to these shores."

Dame Guinevere nodded. "That seems like it would be a reasonable solution."

"I don't know where I went wrong, you know. I gave him every honor and privilege I could under the circumstances." The king seemed to have retreated into himself now. He was more musing than carrying on a conversation. "Something in him curdled. I don't know if it was thwarted ambition or pride. It has made him miserable since the day I took the throne."

For a moment, he wasn't the king, just a tired old man weighed down by regret. I bit my lip to keep from blurting out some bit of sentimentality that could only offend.

Queen Adelaide came to the rescue by standing, prompting the rest of us to do the same. "Thank you, ladies, for bringing the report. I understand that the news could not have been easy to deliver. We are relieved that the princess is well and will see her soon."

It was an unmistakable and, frankly, welcome dismissal.

All I could think about was Colleen.

Chapter 31

We did not arrive back at Cadogan Hall until after breakfast.

"Do you think Colleen is back yet from the hospital?" I asked Dame Guinevere as I climbed stiffly from the steam carriage.

"I think it will take at least a day before she will be able to withstand the trip home from the hospital."

I had been afraid of that. "May I take the steam carriage to go see her?"

"Absolutely not."

My headache was suddenly at the fore, probably because of the tight clenching of my jaw. I would climb out my window in the middle of the day if I had to.

Dame Guinevere took notice of the brewing mutiny. "My dear girl, you are about to fall over you are so tired. You would be no good to her in your current state. You need to sleep a few hours."

I opened my mouth to deny it but a yawn started and I had to bite my bottom lip to keep it from leaking out, which in turn started the bleeding from my split lip again.

Dame Guinevere shook her head at me. "I will make you a bargain. If you will promise me to go up and try to sleep, I will allow you to take the steam carriage to the hospital when you awaken as soon as you have dressed and eaten."

"I don't know if I will be able to sleep."

"A good faith effort is all I ask."

"All right. I suppose that's fair."

"Then it is a deal."

We climbed out of the carriage, and I headed for my room. Tired as I was, I was too anxious to sleep. I would rest for a few moments to satisfy the terms of our bargain, then I would get up, wash, and head to the hospital.

I hauled myself up the stairs totally ignoring the other girls who clustered in the hall. Something in my face must have warned them not to say a thing, for though I could see their questions piled up and threatening to spill out in their looks, no one spoke as I marched past.

I dropped onto my bed and lay back, resolutely ignoring the empty berth across the room. My eyes felt hot and gritty. It wouldn't hurt to rest them for a moment.

The next thing I knew, a watery, late afternoon light was streaming in, I lay on my stomach with a touch of drool at the corner of my mouth, and I was excessively stiff. I groaned.

Dame Guinevere had tricked me. I was sure of it. Maybe she'd drugged me. Although I hadn't eaten or drank anything.

I gathered my sluggish limbs and sat up. At least the burning behind my eyes was less. My muscles would loosen up with some movement though my various injuries were making themselves known.

A covered tray sat on the side table. When I removed the lid, I found a sandwich of thinly sliced roast beef and sharp white cheddar, a glass of milk, and an apple. I gave it a good sniff and picked up the edge of the bread to inspect the contents more closely. No hint of white powder.

My stomach gave a gurgle. Deciding it probably wasn't drugged and it would be a shame to waste a meal that had already been prepared, I dug in.

By the time I finished eating, washed, and changed, I felt almost fully human again. In another twenty minutes, I entered the hospital ward housing my best friend. A dozen identical beds lined the walls on either side of the room. Lights strung overhead provided an inhumanly bright glow. A scent hung heavy in the air. I won't describe it except to say that it was nauseating.

Colleen was propped up in bed and being fed soup from a bowl. I offered to take over, an offer immediately accepted by the harried-looking attendant, who practically bounded away after thrusting the bowl at me.

I watched the attendant's hurried departure then took the vacated seat and looked at the bowl. It wasn't soup after all, but a sort of thin gruel.

Before I could lift the spoon, Colleen snatched it from my hand. "I'm not entirely helpless."

That made me look at her, I mean really look, for the first time.

She was horribly pale, her eyes rimmed by dark shadows. Nose wrinkled, she shoveled a bite into her mouth and swallowed. "What happened to your face? What's been going on? No one here either knows or will tell me a thing."

"Colleen, I'm so sorry. It's all my fault you got hurt." Without me actually wanting to, I had taken in the fact that where her left leg should have been there was only emptiness beneath the covers. Tears welled in my eyes. "I'm so sorry."

Colleen threw her spoon at me. It struck my chest and gruel spattered everywhere. "Shut up," she snapped. "It's not your fault. The world doesn't always revolve around you, Portia.

I made my own choice to become involved, thank you very much."

I wiped gruel off my face and narrowed my eyes. "You are very lucky that you are in a sickbed."

She mustered an unrepentant grin. "And if you think you are going to make yourself the star of my drama, you are going to be very surprised." She reached out and took my hand. "Seriously, Portia. You think you are responsible for the world, but you're not. I will get over this. People have survived worse. The loss of a leg is just my next challenge."

I swallowed against a rising lump in my throat.

She carried on. "I don't need someone who is full of negativity and despair. I need someone right now who can remind me this isn't the end of the world."

I nodded.

"Good. I've already had some ideas on how to construct a mechanical leg that will move like a real one. The trickiest bit will be the joints. I think the key will be ball joints and sprockets."

"What alloy are you envisioning? Iron will surely be too heavy."

She smiled at me for real this time. Gave my hand a squeeze and then released it. "Be assured that I will be pressing you into service as my research assistant on this project. But first, I demand to know where matters stand."

I glanced around at the occupants of the other beds and scooted closer to fill her in on events. She listened attentively, but as I drew to a close her eyes were drooping and I could see the way she blanched from pain. I removed the bowl from her lap and helped her lie down comfortably.

A woman in a long gray dress and white apron began snuffing out the lights on the ward. It was time to go.

Colleen just nodded when I promised to return in the morning.

I stopped the ward attendant on my way out and asked them to give her something for the pain.

When I arrived back at Cadogan Hall, Annie greeted me in the entry. "Dame Guinevere asked to see you when you returned."

"All right." I sighed. "Her office?"

"Yes, miss."

My rap on the office door a moment later was met with a brisk. "Enter."

I did so. The usually immaculately ordered office was in an uproar. Papers littered every flat surface. "You wished to see me, ma'am?"

"Ah, Lady Portia. I trust Colleen is doing well at Guy's?"

"Yes, ma'am. I think she would do better here though, ma'am. As soon as possible. She'll recover faster with access to the library and her laboratory."

"I shall take that under advisement." She removed the pince-nez perched upon her nose and rubbed at the marks left behind. "Her parents have been notified of her accident and are on their way to see her."

"I'm sure she'll be happy to see them."

"You may be seated, Portia."

I picked up the stack of papers currently occupying one of the chairs. Expense ledgers from three years ago. Odd.

"Give those here."

I handed them over, and she piled them on the floor beside her. "You will be happy to know that Mrs. Dutton and Eleanor were successful in apprehending the forger as well as the forged documents. That artistic gentleman was at work altering the Privy Council record when they arrived. He has since admitted both to the Privy Council and to Inspector Ogden that he crafted the decree from King George approving the union between Edward and Julie de Saint Laurent and one or two of the other documents, but that was the crucial piece. Without it, any marriage between them, if it actually occurred, was void, and Fennick's house of cards tumbles to the ground. The forger claims he thought it was all a bit of innocent playacting and that he had no idea there could possibly be skulduggery afoot. He is cooling his heels in the lockup at A Division until it is decided what to do with him."

I was mildly surprised, but grateful that she was updating me as if I was a colleague rather than a pupil.

She carried on with what I could only think of as her report. "Neither the Earl of Munster nor Lord Bancroft presented themselves at the Privy Council meeting. When he was sought, Lord Bancroft was found to have committed suicide at his home in the early morning hours."

I lowered my gaze to my neatly folded hands. I had not admired the man, but neither had I wished him dead. He had been a bitter pawn, a weak man wishing to punish the society that had made him an object of scorn for the last twenty years.

"The Earl of Munster was not found at home either. It seems some urgent business arose on the Continent that demanded his immediate attention."

"I'm sorry that he has escaped a reckoning, ma'am. I think he was the mastermind behind it all."

"Ah. Well." Dame Guinevere gave a slight shrug, sounding surprisingly philosophical. "We know what he is now. He is unlikely to be able to return to England, and will remain an exile for the rest of his life." She sighed. "I do not think King William is likely to last very much longer. His health is failing quickly. His son's betrayal struck a deep blow. Once Victoria is queen, it would be very difficult for anyone to challenge her right to rule."

"Yes, ma'am." It was true. Once Victoria took the throne, it would take far more than a pretender with some forged documents to wrest it from her grasp.

Dame Guinevere picked up a pen. Put it down. Picked it up again and tapped the end on her desk.

I waited, allowing the silence between us to lengthen. I had never seen her unsure before.

"To my regret, Portia, you are in deep disgrace with the board of regents."

The mysterious board of regents. It was the group who supported and oversaw the school and assigned the Praetorienne when they graduated. I only knew the identity of one member, the reigning queen.

Dame Guinevere continued. "They feel that the Praetorienne are meant to be a unit, not individuals with individual aims and means. And there is a very strict reporting hierarchy. The board has made their views very plain. They feel that a student acting as you have, alone and without authority, jeopardizes not only the organization but the security of the ones we have all pledged to protect, and that cannot be tolerated."

My throat felt constricted, my whole chest tight and all of me hot. I wanted to scream and demand to know where they had been and what they had done about the kidnapping attempts.

"You are being expelled."

A buzzing started in the space between my ears and I stared at Dame Guinevere blankly, not quite believing what I was hearing. The pigeons had come home to roost right enough.

"I have also tendered my resignation as headmistress of Saint Scholastica, though I will be finishing out the year."

My mouth dropped open. "You can't do that, ma'am. You *are* the school. I knew that I was running afoul of the rules, but y—"

Dame Guinevere held up an imperious hand. "My dear girl. It is my choice, as it was my choice to allow you to investigate. There are others capable of running the school. I am simply sorry that you won't be graduating with your cohort this month and will be ineligible for service with the order afterward. I feel you deserved that much and more."

My mouth was dry, but I licked my lips anyway. "Shall I go pack then?"

"Tomorrow will do. The official story will be that you have become ill and are being sent home to recover in the country."

Resigned to my fate, I nodded, but then I paused. "What about Colleen?"

"I felt no need to inform the board of any unsubstantiated tittle-tattle that Colleen played any role in the affair. Aside, of course, from her heroic defense of the school when it was attacked."

The twinkle in her eye gave my heart a squeeze. I couldn't imagine the school without her. The backs of my eyes grew hot again.

"Ma'am, are you sure? I'm certain your resignation could be undone if you chose."

She shook her head and offered me a smile. "I could not in good conscience stay on. Not when I could have stopped you if I had chosen."

We would have to agree to disagree on that score.

"I quite admired the way you deployed that decoy at the British Museum lecture. Had I not been looking for something of the sort I would have been easily taken in. The only thing I haven't entirely worked out was why the colonial boy chose to involve himself to such an extent?"

The colonial boy.

My heart gave another squeeze. I'd have liked to have told Jack good-bye and to thank him for his assistance, even though he would probably insist that I was the one who had assisted him.

"Well, ma'am, that was pure luck."

Chapter 32

I sat in the window seat with my arms wrapped around my knees, staring out at the wind-whipped hills of the Blithe estate. Ominous gray clouds were piling up to the east. We owned everything as far as the eye could see. It was lovely. And dull. Behind me, my mother droned on in her habitual complaint about servants' wages and the outrageous costs of things nowadays.

She sighed heavily. "If only you hadn't gotten sick and ruined all your prospects." It was a refrain which had quickly been incorporated to her standard litany.

"I'm sorry, Mother," I murmured. My rote response.

She continued on as if she hadn't really heard me. As indeed she probably hadn't. She wasn't really conversing with me. More *at* me. "And you've always been so disgustingly healthy, too." She raised her quizzing glass from the needlework in her hand to peer at me. "At least all those nasty bruises are fading at last. Trust you to have fainted at the top of a set of stairs. You're lucky you didn't break a leg. Or your neck."

"Yes, Mother."

The weather exactly matched my mood. Two days ago, the

country had been plunged into mourning by news of King William's passing. The church bells had been tolling mournfully since then. He had been a grand old man. Even gallant in his own way. I had liked and pitied him. Aside from the sorrow, I was slowly going mad wondering what was happening in London.

How was the princess, or rather, Queen Victoria, coping? Had she sent Sir John packing yet?

I was certain it would have been one of the first things she did. That and tossing all vestiges of the hated Kensington System out the window.

A maid wheeled in the tea cart followed by the butler. "Mail, madam. The boy said it was delayed because of the rain." He extended a tray to my mother who picked up the small stack of letters.

In a moment, she held one out to me. "This one is for you."

Even from where I was sitting I recognized Colleen's handwriting. I jumped up and took the missive. "Excuse me, Mother."

Clutching my prize, I ran to the stables and borrowed the kitchen boy's velocipede. It was the closest I could come to excitement in these wilds. Heedless of the rising wind, I rode the machine to the top of the highest hill and devoured Colleen's words in peace.

Bless her. She knew me well enough to include the bits that mattered. Conroy had indeed been sent packing, or rather to be more precise, Victoria had moved herself to Buckingham Palace and left Conroy and her mother both behind. The new queen was wildly popular among the people at the moment. She was a refreshing change from the crotchety old men who had ruled our island for the last several decades. She was behaving just as she ought and endearing herself to one and all.

The person who had not been behaving at all as she ought was Eleanor. She had eloped with an artist. According to Marianne, she believed that once the deed was done, she would be able to bend her father to her will, and he would have to accept what had already been accomplished. But her father had well and truly balked. Eleanor had been cut off without a cent, and she and her new husband had reportedly fled to Paris.

I laughed aloud at the news. Eleanor had never been investigating, she'd just been philandering. And I had been so worried. In a way, I almost pitied her. She didn't have the first idea of how to exist without a great deal of cash at hand. No doubt, her current education was far more challenging than Saint Scholastica had been for her. Shaking my head, I read on.

As for Colleen, she had added a motor to her wheelchair to help her move around more quickly and had nearly completed the first prototype on her mechanical leg. The key difficulty at the moment was finding a secure means of attaching it that could be quickly and easily undone. The next challenge would be finding the proper material. Something light, but not too light, and sturdy. It needed to be sturdy.

I sighed and raised my face to the wind. Letting it blow away some of the stuffiness that came from being cooped up too long in the house.

As the first raindrops started to patter around me, I tucked the letter into my pocket and released the brake. I let out a huge whoop as I hurtled down the hill.

Almost at the bottom, I spotted a steam carriage coming down the lane. I threw the brake and turned hard. The velocipede slewed and skidded, but I managed to rein it in without crashing.

The carriage stopped abreast of me. Dame Guinevere stuck her head out the window. She glanced at me then back up the hill. "This must be what *déjà vu* feels like. Do you never do anything else when you are home?"

"Dame Guinevere?"

"Would you care to join me in the carriage? I'm sure that contraption can be tied to the back."

"Yes, ma'am."

Mind awhirl, I walked the velocipede behind the carriage. I started to wrestle it onto the hitch when the tall groom came around the other side. "I can take care of that, miss."

Relieved, I simply nodded and hurried back to the door and climbed inside. "Ma'am, what are you doing here?"

She smiled. "I've brought a message." She pulled out a thick ivory-colored envelope with a hefty red seal embossed on the back.

My hands were only shaking a tiny bit as I opened it.

> *My dear Lady Portia,*
>
> *I am sure you will have heard that I have now assumed the role of Queen of our great nation. A role preserved for me by the loyalty and faithful friendship of those whose deeds have proven that they desire not only my well-being, but also understand that I have a mind and will of my own. I now find myself seeking the same qualities in those who would continue to serve me. I desire that you would attend me at Buckingham Palace at your earliest convenience.*
>
> *Queen Victoria*

I looked up from the letter to Dame Guinevere.

She wore the widest smile I had ever seen on her face. "Victoria will accept no substitutes from the other Saint Scholastica girls. She wants her closest ladies-in-waiting to have proven their loyalty. She has asked for you and Colleen by name."

My heart was beating so hard I was sure the groom outside could hear it as he started up the carriage and we lurched toward the house.

"Victoria has also ordered that you must be given all honors due you and restored to good standing among the Praetorienne. She argued that if the school's intent is to churn out young ladies who can and will protect their monarch, then you must have passed with flying colors."

I couldn't believe it.

The rain was drumming steadily against the roof of the carriage now. How quickly could we make it back to London?

Mother would probably insist that we wait until tomorrow to set out.

Dame Guinevere seemed to understand that I was trying to process all she had said. She paused before proceeding. "Colleen, meanwhile, has been granted her own workspace at Buckingham Palace where she can invent to her heart's content."

"And you, ma'am? Have you decided to stay with the school after all?"

"No. I have accepted a permanent position with the queen as well. I shall be her most senior lady-in-waiting next to Baroness Lezhen. Do you think you will be accepting the position?"

I looked up at her and my grin made her give a satisfied nod and settle back against her seat.

We pulled up smartly in front of the house and the groom opened the door, lowered the step, and handed Dame Guinevere out.

Excitement was fizzing through me so hard it was threatening to come out as a shout of laughter. I wanted to dance or sing or spin. Instead, I accepted the hand extended to me and climbed sedately from the carriage.

The groom touched the brim of his hat with his free hand. "Welcome back, miss."

I finally turned my attention to the groom who still held my hand. It was Jack, and the laugh I had been holding in burst out.

Author's Note

To my knowledge there was no secret order of royal guardians nor any actual plot to kidnap Princess Victoria before she could take the throne, nor even a pigeon corps, but despite my flights of fancy, I did try to weave in as many real details as I could to anchor the story.

Prince Edward, Duke of Kent and Strathearn did in fact inspire a mutiny in Gibraltar while he served there and he did have a relationship with Julie de Saint Laurent, both before and after her first husband died. When the prince was sent in disgrace to Canada, de Saint Laurent accompanied him and indeed many in Halifax society thought they were married. Rumors of a morganatic marriage persisted for years as did the belief that the couple had a child.

Sir William Fenwick Williams was believed by many to be the issue of this marriage. Although Williams seems not to have tried to set the record right with respect to his parentage, and may have even encouraged the rumors, far from being a scheming pretender to the throne, Sir William had a long and honorable career in the army and politics, serving as both commander in chief of British forces in North America and later as lieutenant governor of Nova Scotia.

The Kensington System that Victoria hated so much was instituted by Sir John Conroy and was, in fact, as restrictive as I've depicted, down to having to share a bedroom with her mother. It was one of the major factors that made her loathe him.

For the sake of this story, I renamed Conroy's daughter. Her real name was Victoire, but given the similarity to the princess's name, I used one of her middle names, Louisa, to avoid any confusion. Although on that note, Victoria didn't go by Victoria either until she assumed the throne. Her first name was actually Alexandrina and she was often called "Drina" by friends and family. Once again, I shifted the truth a touch to keep the characterization clear.

There was a real, albeit short-lived rebellion in both Upper and Lower Canada which began in December of 1837 and lasted a year. This uprising was led by William Lyon Mackenzie in Upper Canada and Louis-Joseph Papineau in the southern colony. Both leaders sought and received aid from a number of American volunteers, but neither movement was particularly successful.

A Division was and still is responsible for security for the royal family. By modern standards their procedures where there were any were woefully inadequate. Victoria survived five assassination attempts during the first several years of her reign. She owed her continued existence more to dumb luck and the ineptness of her attackers than to any skill on the part of her guards. Which got me thinking…What if instead…?

If you have questions about the real vs. the imaginary in this story, feel free to contact me via the contact page on my website www.lisakaronrichardson.com. I may not have all the answers, but I love making things up!

Acknowledgments

Ingenious would never have seen the light of day without the encouragement and skill of my very first writing friend, Jennifer AlLee Farey. I also need to offer my sincerest thanks to Roseanna White, Janelle Leonard, and Hannah Currie from WhiteSpark. You guys are incredibly talented, all-around awesome creativity ninjas, and I so appreciate your investment in my writing. You made the process of publication as much fun as the writing and far more enjoyable than it has any right to be.